Bill,
I am so glad we are buddies!
Congrats on the new baby.
Best regards
John Ber[...]

The Cheater:

A Novel of Love, Hate, Murder and Lies

by

John R. and Joseph J. Berardino

DORRANCE
PUBLISHING CO
EST. 1920
PITTSBURGH, PENNSYLVANIA 15238

Dorrance Publishing Co.
585 Alpha Drive
Pittsburgh, Pa 15238
Visit our website at *www.dorrancebookstore.com*

-

ISBN: 978-1-4809-9127-9
eISBN: 978-1-4809-9103-3

Acknowledgments

Dr. Howard Streigold acted as medical advisor to this book. A fine doctor and friend, his dedication and persistence to this book is deeply appreciated.

We had the benefit of working with great manuscript editors – Jeanne Kraus and Linda Rosen. Thank you for your incredible efforts.

Our writer's critique groups were very helpful in correcting errors and improving the writing. The Pembroke Pines Inkbloods and the Boynton writers performed admirably in that regard.

Dedications

John R. Berardino

To my wife Melissa- From the first time we met on the school bus as kids, I knew you were my one true love.

To my children – Chloe, Claire and Jack- I love you and am proud of you. You can do anything you put your mind to.

To my mom- I miss you more every day. Thank you for a lifetime of love and laughs.

To my dad – This book has been an incredible journey. A once-in-a-lifetime-project, I could not have completed it with anyone else.

Joseph J. Berardino

This book is dedicated to my family- Lucy, Cindy, John and Tiffany; to Scott and Melissa; to Tracy and Jeff; and our nine and a half grandchildren –I love you.

Especially to my co-author John- a driving force and incredible partner. Your dedication has made this the greatest honor of my life.

CHAPTER 1

BE BETTER THAN ME, 14 FEB. 1975

By the age of forty, I had listened to over two billion words, but the ones that transformed my life were the last ones my father uttered as he lay on the blood-smeared hospital sheets—"Be faithful to your family, Lawrence. Don't cheat on them. Be better than me."

I thought back. On my eighth birthday, I felt like I was probably the luckiest kid around. My family was everything to me.

On my birthday, my eyes popped open in my sun-lit bedroom. I sat up, wide-awake, my puppy Buddy sleeping next to me. I rubbed his deformed ear—he woke and crooked his head towards me, egging my petting on. I didn't have time for a long pet so I jumped off the bed, and ran into the living room, hoping Dad would be there for my birthday. I stopped short. My parents were both there, but once again, bickering.

Mom was speaking. "We've been together ten years, and I've never met your friends from work. Are you embarrassed by me?"

"Look, honey, I'm not close to anyone I work with. You know how much I have to travel."

My parents noticed me and stopped arguing. I loved them so much. They seemed to argue more and more. Did this mean they were splitting up?

My father glanced over his reading glasses. He smiled at me. "Happy Birthday, Lawrence." He played it cool. "Sleep well?" I ran over to him.

Dad grabbed me in a big bear hug. "We're having a special day." He squeezed me tight, making me laugh. Even now, years later, I can still smell his rich oaken Ralph Lauren aftershave. "Your mother and I have some family treasures for you."

Mom entered from the kitchen, came over and hugged me tightly. She pushed me away from her to get a good look. "Happy Birthday, Lawrence." She kissed my forehead.

She picked up three wrapped boxes and handed me the first.

Eagerly, I opened the box and found a silver crucifix on a chain. I had seen that crucifix before and knew how she cherished it. "This was my mother's." She held it up and watched it twist and gleam in the sunlight. "She gave it to me on my eighth birthday; she wanted me to give it to you on your eighth. She said to tell you it would protect you always. I miss Grammy so much."

She looked about to cry. Her words put a damper on the mood, but she flashed a quick smile. "And one day, many years from now, you will give it to your firstborn on their eighth birthday."

I slid the chain over my head and swore I would never lose it. I dreamed of having a son, and maybe even a daughter one day.

I grabbed the smaller package and ripped off the colorful wrapping. It was a silver set of wings. Dad explained, "These were your grandfather's pilot wings he wore during World War II. He wanted you to have them. They saw him through some very tough times in his life, and he hoped they would do the same for you."

"Love you, Dad." I looked over. "You, too, Mom."

He handed me another little package. It had a red box inside, and the word, Victorinox printed on it. Opening the box, I saw a shiny red penknife. "This is from your mom and me. A real Swiss Army knife. It has all the basic tools to get you out of a tight spot. It's a great survival tool with scissors to cut bandages and a sharp blade to perform surgeries."

I loved that knife. I wrapped my arms around Dad's neck. "It's the greatest knife ever. It will help me to be a doctor."

"And, you will be a great doctor. Last, but not least, we are taking Buddy to the beach for the day." Dad announced. "It's Friday and you are skipping school."

That was the best news I had heard in a long time. I ran to my bedroom to put on my jeans. I opened my wallet, pinning the pilot wings inside. There was the picture of Mom, Dad and me in front of our Christmas tree from last year. I remember how Mom said I looked like a perfect mash-up of different family members. Mom's golden hair and brown eyes. Dad's square jaw and Roman nose. All these years later, I still have that picture, and it stirs my soul.

In my other back pocket, I deposited my Swiss Army knife. For good luck, I touched the cross around my neck, put on my tennis shoes, and ran out of my room, with Buddy on my heels.

Mom and I hurried out the door to the driveway, Buddy beating us to the van. Dad was already out in the van. Mom stopped and glared down at the front wheel with pursed lips.

"I thought you bought new tires."

Dad responded, "I've been too busy traveling for work. I'll get them done next week."

Mom sighed.

Dad must have been as enthusiastic as I, because he backed the van out of the driveway so fast, it threw me hard against the back of Mom's seat. Gravel flew up and ricocheted off the bottom of the van, sounding like hail in a thunderstorm.

He glanced at me in the mirror. "Today is your day. Hold on to Buddy."

I tucked my golden retriever pup under my arm and we were off.

Dad drove east while Buddy curled up asleep with his head in my lap and his legs sprawled wide in total doggy relaxation. His sleeping habits made me laugh. He kicked his legs like he was running, and he let out a little dream yelp and a stinky fart.

I could see other cars speeding by on the right, and when I noticed a Volkswagen, I shouted, "Punch Buggy," and lightly hit Dad in the shoulder.

Dad grinned at me in the mirror. We had done the punch buggy routine ever since I was a little kid. I felt complete.

Someday I would be just like my father, wearing his white lab coat, graduating from medical school. In my vision of the future, Buddy was sitting beside me on the podium wearing a black mortarboard. I looked down and beamed at Buddy as I stroked his belly.

A black car passed us on the right. A dog hung his head out of the window, and the wind ruffled his fur. Dad turned to look at the dog, and I heard a loud pop at the front of our van. My father over-corrected and we swung back left.

I clutched my best friend, Buddy. Our van flipped over and seemed to spin from side to side. I lost my grip on Buddy. My world went dark.

I don't know how long I was out. When I came to, I was upside down, cars were stopped around us, and people were hurrying over. I looked for Buddy but couldn't see him. The seatbelt strangled my waist, and my head pounded. I shivered.

Mom groaned. Then she scared me. "Lawrence, I promise." She coughed three times. "I promise I…I will love you forever," she whispered.

I could see her in the mirror. Blood covered her face. She bit her lip, and her whole body convulsed.

My heart hurt. My thoughts were racing. *Mom is hurt bad.* I reached out to touch her but the belt restrained me. Blood was splattered on the spider-webbed windshield in front of her.

"I will love you forever…I will be with you always…"Her words trailed off in a whisper.

"Mom! Mom!" I shouted. She didn't answer me. Through my tears, I saw red flashing lights all around us. I could see a taxi cab, the back door was crumpled and open. The side was caved in where our car had hit.

My father was spread across the ceiling of our overturned car. Dad came to, wobbly and shaken, and asked me if I was all right. I nodded yes, in shock more than anything. I saw him unstrap my mother and stagger as he pulled her out of the van. He laid her on the pavement between our car and the center barrier and collapsed, coughing. He rolled up a beach towel and made a pillow under her head. Before he collapsed again, he leaned down, brushed her hair, and kissed her tenderly, almost falling on top of her as he did.

He looked over at me. "Hold on, Lawrence." He wiped his palm across his forehead and struggled to sit up. "I'll have you out in a minute."

He turned back to my mother, grabbed another beach towel, balled it up and compressed it over her stomach. With his left hand, he picked up her wrist and held it, staring at his watch. His lips were tight. A young paramedic raced over, placed his hand on my father's shoulder and knelt.

"I'm a doctor. Get my son out of the van." My father wrapped his hand over his mouth and coughed. Blood seeped between his fingers.

"Sir, are you injured?"

"Help my son, I'm fine."

The paramedic tried to open the back door, but it was stuck. "Hold on, I'm coming in through the front."

The paramedic struggled with my seatbelt. I pulled out my Swiss Army knife and dropped it. He snatched it up, pulled the blade out, and sliced through the belt. I held onto his neck while he lowered me down and helped me out of the van. Buddy followed us out of the van looking dazed. The paramedic placed me on a gurney.

"Get my puppy. Don't let him run in traffic," I pleaded.

The medic reached down and picked up Buddy. "Officer, will you put this dog in your car and call animal control for me? We are headed to the hospital."

"No, Mister, Buddy stays with me. He's my dog."

"No, kid. We can't take him to the hospital, give him a big hug, you will see him later." The young tech half handed Buddy to me so I could give him a hug but not hold him.

"Let him ride to hospital, Mon," a Jamaican voice interrupted. "Bwoy needs his puppy dog."

Years later, I still remember that first vision of Slim with the red ambulance light sweeping across his lean features. His face was thinly gaunt, carved out of rich hardwood teak with a square jaw. His calm kind demeanor complemented his deep rich caramel complexion. His eyes were large and moist, about-to-cry-eyes, the color of molasses.

He turned his head to the right to watch for traffic. Around his left eye, God's paintbrush had left a large white birthmark the shape of a heart. He looked back at me and I glanced away, embarrassed to be staring.

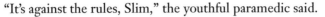

"It's against the rules, Slim," the youthful paramedic said.

"Come on, Mon. We can let the bwoy have his puppy. We worry about it at the hospital."

"I'm the senior med tech here," he pointed to his chest, "and I say no."

Slim grabbed Buddy from the other man and stared him straight in the eyes. "Gimme the dog. If boss say anything, I say it was me."

The medic pushed my pocketknife into Slim's hand. "Here, this belongs to the kid." He sounded annoyed and walked away muttering.

Slim smiled and placed Buddy under the sheet next to me. It made me feel great. "Your name is Lawrence and this here is Buddy?" He rubbed Buddy's head.

"Yes, he's my dog. How are my mom and dad?"

"Don't know, Mon. We find out. First you go to hospital. I'm coming with you."

As my stretcher slid into the ambulance, I embraced Buddy tightly to my chest, clutched my crucifix and prayed.

At the hospital, my eyes blinked in the bright light. I had never been away from my mom and dad, and I felt alone in the emergency room. The scene was surreal; the entire place was white. I heard medical equipment beeping and tiny colored lights flashing. Shiny metal stands were everywhere.

Someone shouted, "Help me. I need meds." The place smelled of iodine and bleach, making my nose crinkle. We flashed by room after room, people wandering all over. Some hurried by in hospital scrubs—some were dressed as though they were going to church. Others stumbled along in ripped jeans and muscle shirts.

My left eye and ribs hurt. My head pounded. I reached down and held my left side. Somewhere an insistent beep shouted for attention.

I couldn't see Mom and Dad. "Where are my parents?"

I was pushed through two metal doors into a brightly lit room. It was reassuring to see Slim still with me next to the stretcher. He looked at me and said, "We gonna find out."

When the stretcher stopped, Buddy became restless and tried to crawl out from under the sheets.

"Keep Buddy still."

I clutched him. He knew something was wrong.

"Keep Buddy quiet, or *the mon*," he made air quotes as he rolled his eyes, "will find out and take him away. I get cage for him and we hide him." Slim grinned at Buddy. "You got to be quiet, Mr. Pup."

I remember a young doctor came in. He rushed through my examination. In less than two minutes he felt my head, looked into my eyes, and listened to my heart. "You're okay for now, but we'll run some tests to make sure." He nodded to Slim and hurried away, never noticing the dog-shaped lump sniffing and trembling under my sheet.

When Slim transferred me into the regular bed, he removed the gurney from the room. His last act was to hand me my Swiss Army knife. "This your lucky charm."

Slim returned in a jiffy with a small cage, barely large enough for Buddy. He took my pup from me and put him in the hidden corner of the room, behind a large recliner chair. He slid a blanket over the cage, and Buddy was quiet. Slim came over and sat beside my bed. "I got a Dr. Pepper™ and a Hershey Bar™ for you." He handed them to me.

"Thank you for helping me and Buddy."

"I will help you all I can, bwoy." He grinned. "You look like Tom Sawyer in the book. I like that story. I get book from library when I get off work."

"Thanks. I would like to read it." But mostly, I was worried about Mom and Dad.

"I have to go back to work. I check on you tonight." Slim clasped my hand briefly and left. The room seemed empty without him.

Shortly after he'd departed, a young nurse came in carrying a plastic cup of water and some pudding. She fluffed my pillow. "Hi, I'm Nurse Cindy. How are you?" She tucked in my sheets.

"Where's Mom and Dad?"

Nurse Cindy looked flustered. "Your dad is being operated on. When he gets into recovery, you can see him." She brushed my hair back gently and handed me the water and pudding cup. She turned on cartoons.

"Where's my mom?"

"I am not sure sweetheart, your dad will be out of surgery soon, and I will get you to him as quickly as I can." She hurried out. I watched the TV for a while, but all I could think about was my mom. I didn't know how long it had been, but Nurse Cindy hurried back in. "Your dad is in recovery and asking for you. I have a wheelchair, put on these slippers and robe."

"I can walk. I feel…"

"Get in the chair, it's quicker. I will run you there." She sounded tense, and her eyes filled with tears. "Your dad is awake and your mom is with him."

I was confused. "My mom? Is she okay?"

"She seems fine to me. Was she in the car with you?"

Tears welled in my eyes. I thought my mom was dead. My prayers had been answered. Nurse Cindy wheeled me down corridors, around four or five turns and hurried me to a bank of elevators. She pushed the button, and a door opened. The elevator dropped two floors and the door opened into another pristine hallway. My pulse raced as we passed numerous staff members. Some hustled around and carried trays of medicine, while others adjusted IV stands.

Finally, we entered a quiet well-lit recovery room. The nurse wheeled me to a bed twenty feet from the door. I saw a patient; ashen covered with tubes and bandages, surrounded by machines. It was my dad.

Mom faced away from me and wore a doctor's smock. She bent over to say something to my father. She seemed perfectly fine. "Dad! Mom!" I called them. I was so glad to see them.

Dad looked at me. The lady turned to look at me. I realized this was not my mom. She wore think black-rimmed glasses. I didn't recognize her and blurted out, "She's not my mom. Where's Mom?"

My father craned his neck, pushed himself halfway onto his elbow, and forced a smile. "Come over here so I can give you a hug."

His eyes were misty. His arm reached out, and I stood up and walked over to him. When I got close, Dad wrapped his weak arm around me and drew me near. Now I felt safe. I was with my dad. He pulled my head to him, sniffled, coughed, and held me tighter than he ever had done before. "Son, I love you." He had tears in his eyes and he sounded weak as he coughed again. My heart fluttered and my stomach lurched.

"Elizabeth, this is my son Lawrence," he whispered.

The lady turned her head down to look directly into my eyes. She burst into tears, put her hands over the sides of my head, and said, "He looks just like you."

She turned back toward him and said, "You are a cheating bastard."

She faced me and spoke through angry tears. "I never knew you existed. He never told me he had a son." She quickly headed for the door and ran out, crying.

Dad called after her, "Elizabeth, I always loved you, and I'm so sorry."

I felt lost. Who was she? Why was she talking to my dad like that? Why did my dad tell her he loved her? I didn't know what to say.

"Where is Mom?"

Dad held me back and stared into my eyes. He blinked quickly. A brief smile flitted across his lips, then disappeared. "There's not much time. I have to tell you—tell you some things." He coughed again, making it hard for him to continue.

"Where's Mom?"

"Lawrence," he swallowed before going on. "I am sorry, but your mom died. Remember," he coughed, "her last words were that she would always love you and she would always be with you."

My chest was tight. I couldn't breathe. "Dad, Dad, I want—"

"Son, I need you to listen, there is no time. I will give Elizabeth instructions about my will. She will make sure you are cared for. She will find someone for you to live with."

"Dad, I'm scared. Are you dying?"

'Listen, there is no one left in our family. You—you have to be the man, you have to man up." This was the first time my father talked to me like an adult.

"Dad!" I cried.

"Study hard." He coughed. Blood seeped out of the corner of his mouth and down his chin. "Become a doctor—a good doctor." He hugged me closer. "Promise me nothing will stop you, promise."

"Dad, I'm scared." My voice shook.

"Promise me you will be a good husband and father."

He placed his long arms around my shoulders and pulled me tight to his chest. "More important than that, Lawrence, be faithful to your family. Don't cheat on them like I did. Be better than me."

I remembered all the arguments I overheard between my parents over the years. They came flooding back into my mind. My father had told many lies. The man I idolized, admired and loved was a liar and a cheater.

"Son, I have not always been honest. No matter what you hear, I loved your mother and I loved you the most. "

I broke down in tears. Unable to speak, I sobbed uncontrollably.

"I was not fair to your mother, I could not marry her, I was already married," he said, looking up toward the door, sad and defeated.

"That lady who was in here, the lady doctor, she...she's my wife. She couldn't have children, and I fell in love with your mother. I wanted a boy like you so badly. I never told your mom. I'm sorry." He coughed. "The greatest mistake of my life." He breathed out his last words, "Be faithful to your family, Lawrence. Your wife and your kids. Be better than me."

Buzzers went off and a doctor ran in with Nurse Cindy. The doctor ripped two paddles off the wall. "Get him out of here."

Nurse Cindy guided me into the wheelchair and wheeled me out. The door closed and I heard a man yell, "Clear!"

CHAPTER 2

SLIM

When I reminisce about those confused and lonely days, I can't imagine how much worse my life would have been without Slim. He comforted me at the accident and continued to be my friend at the hospital.

Though the word orphan echoed through my mind, Slim had ways to help remove my loneliness. With his jubilant attitude and smiling face, he lit up my room.

Slim spoke of growing up as an orphan himself. "I never know my parents, my mom dropped me off as a baby and I never saw her again. Sometime life is tough, but you be fine, I promise." His favorite quote was, "It's not where you startin' from, it's where you finish."

"You know, Ray Charles is an orphan. Imagine growing up, no parents and blind. Now he is famous musician. And Babe Ruth? He was orphan. He fought to become the greatest baseball player of all time. On top of that, even an American president had no parents. Yes, bwoy, Herbert Hoover was orphan."

The next day, Nurse Cindy said, "Lawrence, Slim and I have worked out our schedules so we can help take care of Buddy's needs." She opened the cage, picked up Buddy, and he welcomed her with a sloppy hello kiss.

Slim entered carrying a book. His smile radiated from his soul and made me feel safe. He eased his lanky body into the chair beside my bed.

"I got *Tom Sawyer* from the library." He pointed to the cover picture of a blond headed boy about my age and grinned. Maybe he did look like me.

Slim opened the book and began to read. I loved hearing the story in Slim's musical voice.

Slim seemed genuinely interested in me. I wondered if it was part of his job or if just liked me.

"Why are you so nice to me?"

He looked at me. "Because you need me, and I needed someone when I was your age. I got no family. You and Buddy all I got, too," he said. "We family."

CHAPTER 3

CARVING OUT A NEW LIFE

Reflecting, these many years later, I realize how confused and alone I felt. Up until this point, no one had explained what was happening. I had spent hours wondering if I would go home with a stepmother, I didn't know. Perhaps, I would go to an orphanage. The best choice of all would be for Slim to adopt Buddy and me and make us a real family.

"We have a privately-run children's home that is state sponsored. The staff will welcome you as their newest resident. It is a safe and enriching environment where you'll be cared for and educated. It's called God's Home and has almost 200 kids living there," Mrs. Mayor said.

"What about my dog, Buddy? Can I bring him? What about Slim?"

"I am sorry but they do not allow pets at the home. Your friend Slim can visit you as often as he likes, and he can bring Buddy."

Nurse Cindy wheeled me out of the hospital and into a van. My mom warned me to never get in a car with strangers and I didn't know any of these people.

"Where is Mr. Slim, does he know they are taking me?"

"No honey, they just showed up and told us they were taking you today. But don't worry, I will tell him where you are as soon as I see him."

The dark, dreary day that I could see outside added to my gloom. Rain splattered on the windows and brought back the terrible memories of the blood-shattered windshield of our van.

Father Black introduced himself, then said, "Lawrence, you have been through some tough times with the loss of your family. We are going to do our best to help you heal."

He handed me a bag. "Here's your father's medical kit. He wanted you to have it."

I cradled it to my chest. It felt reassuring. I stared at the floor, bewildered with all the new changes that would be coming.

Mrs. Mayor sat next to me and reached over to touch my head, but I leaned away. She sat upright, put on her black glasses, and took out her clipboard.

Mrs. Mayor said, "We're going to take you to your new home."

As we bumped along, I folded my arms in front of my chest and thought back to the accident. My mind was muddled, but I went over the words from Dad. "Be better than me, Lawrence." That shouldn't be hard to do. After all, he wasn't what I thought he was. The pieces of the puzzle were coming together. Doctors didn't travel like my father had. He was a part-time husband, part-time father, and full-time liar.

CHAPTER 4

GOD'S HOME

I remember that first day in God's Home. I was lying alone in the boys' room on a top bunk. There were two bunk beds and four small dressers for clothing. A card table was in the corner with four chairs. Dazed, I curled up, pulled my knees to my chest, and quietly cried alone.

After a couple of hours, a ruckus of kids entered the home. I wiped my sleeve across my face, got up, and sat on the edge of the bed, my feet dangling in the air.

A big dark-skinned kid filled the doorway. He was a hulk, with a coal-black bushy afro. He wore an Oakland Raiders football jersey and carried a silver and black backpack. The kid's mouth was a crooked grimace. "Get off that bed!" in a deep unfriendly voice. "It's saved for my cousin when he gets here."

"I, I, I was told—" I stammered.

The largest kid I had ever seen threw down his backpack, lurched at me, grabbed my legs and started trying to pull me off the bed. I flipped over on my stomach and held on to the back crossbeam with all my might.

I heard more boys come into the room. They shouted in unison, "Get out, get out, get out."

My hands slipped to the mattress as he pulled. I dug my fingers into the cloth edge, scared that he would rip me off and beat me up. I felt a second set of hands grab my pants legs. My pants started to slip down, I couldn't do anything but hold on. Soon they were down around my knees. Someone laughed and grabbed my underwear with two hands and jerked them down. I felt red-faced with hot cheeks.

A kid shouted, "Light that ass up, Bull."

I felt a hard whack on my naked butt, then another and another. More hot cheeks. Thwack! Thwack! My mind was in chaos and I didn't know what to do. Yet I held on with all my might, unable to speak, stifling my tears, refusing to give in.

"He wants another helping, Bull," another boy laughed.

"Let me give him a little," a higher pitched voice said.

They were in a frenzy. I was terrified, yet held on to the bed with all my strength, trying to save the tattered remnants of my pride. I summoned my strength and kicked my legs back and forth, trying to get free. I had almost retrieved my legs when each leg was grabbed again and this time the jeans were pulled off from my left leg. I was naked. One leg was pulled left and the other right.

I must have resembled the wishbone at a rowdy Thanksgiving feast. It was all I could do to stop from being jerked off the bed. I was barely hanging on. My goods were dangling down toward the floor while my rear end was staring at the ceiling. Everything was in plain view. The boys broke out laughing. I was humiliated.

Then I heard a girl's voice. Even today, as an adult, my face grows hot when I remember lying there with everything exposed when she entered.

"Oh, Dios Mio! What are you doing? Leave that kid alone! Mrs. Altee!" she shouted. "You guys are gross!"

"You bullies vill leave the new boy alone. Go do your homework and leave him be," I heard Mrs. Altee bark from the hall.

"Mrs. Altee, they pulled his pants down," said the girl.

"No, we didn't," Bull bellowed. "He took down his pants and flashed us." Every boy burst out laughing.

"Bull, do your homework before dinner," Mrs. Altee hurried toward the room.

"I'll get you, Whitey," Bull threatened.

"You vill get no one, Hassan," Mrs. Altee said.

"Go do your homework," she ordered Bull.

I yanked up my pants and retreated to the back of the bed, hiding my head under my pillow.

CHAPTER 5

You Can if You Think You Can, March 1975

The next morning, noises woke me up. I pretended to sleep until the other boys left. I got out of bed, dressed, and slipped into the dining room. There were seven other residents sitting around a long table eating cereal. There were three boys and four girls.

I was the only white kid. I tried to be inconspicuous as I slid in through the doorway. The boys had their backs to me and didn't notice, but the girl with the angelic voice from last night spoke up, "Hola, Lawrence, I'm Christina."

I immediately blushed, still embarrassed from the night before. But I remember how she looked—she had a soft gentle face and grinned at me with kindness in her eyes, tan skin, long shiny black hair, her bright eyes the color of tanned leather, rich and brown. She gave off an aura of strength and fearlessness. I knew she had seen everything God had given me, but she looked at me as if she was seeing me for the first time.

Christina pointed at the boys. "These banditos better leave you alone or I tell Mrs. Altee." She made a threatening face pointing at the other boys. She was a bold one.

Mrs. Altee entered from the opposite doorway with a tray of toast. She noticed me and said, "Ve vant you to sit. Sit, eat." She pointed to a vacant chair beside Bull. I sat there, haltingly, warily spooning my cold breakfast. I was hungry but didn't taste a thing.

I glanced to my left to make sure Bull wasn't planning to attack me. Every time, Mrs. Altee left the room, one of the boys pointed at me as if to say, "I'll get you." Christina glared at them.

"I'm gonna punch you in the face when you fall asleep tonight," Bull whispered with a creepy zombie voice. He made good on his promise. I was in mid-dream and was startled with a hard crack to my face. "I told you I was going to punch you in the face, motherfucker."

From that night on until Bull left the house, I slept away from the front edge, with my pillow over my head and my face toward the wall. On some nights when Bull came in late, if I didn't wake up, he would stand on his bottom bunk and punch me in the back of the head. It always gave me a migraine the next day, but I knew not to tell on him.

As we finished breakfast that first morning, Christina came around the table. She glowered at Bull and asked me, "You walk with me to school?"

I nodded yes, afraid to speak.

The other kids all rushed out, but I left the room last behind Christina.

"Where you from, Lawrence?" Her voice was so musical, like in church when they sing *Amazing Grace.*

"I'm from Miami."

"How long are you here for?"

"I don't know, but hopefully not long. I have a friend and a step mom who might adopt me. How long have you been here?"

"Bout three years."

"Three years?"

"Yes, my mom went missing and my aunt cannot adopt me, she already has too many kids and is watching my little sister."

"Where is your dad?"

"I don't know, somewhere in Mexico, I think."

"You gotta stick up for yourself, or they push you around. They pollo unless they are in a gang." She made a chicken sound and flapped her arms. She may have been tough but she sure was pretty.

Christina walked me to my first class. My teacher was a thin dark-skinned lady who was unusually tall and very proper. "I'm Miss Jabbar. Sit in the third seat, Lawrence. We've been expecting you. I see you have excellent grades from your last school. We're glad you're here." I was the only white person in the class. I felt as if I was under a microscope.

At 11:00, we ran outside to the large fenced-in playground. I looked around for Christina but couldn't see her. Finally, I found a picnic table in the back, sat down, and opened my book, *A Connecticut Yankee in King Arthur's Court*. I pretended to read but peered over the top of the book to see if I could locate the bullies. Not seeing them around, I started to relax. I thought about Slim and Buddy. I daydreamed of running across the beach, throwing the ball. I missed them so much.

That afternoon, after school, Christina and I were summoned to the office. Slim stood there. He reached down, grabbed me, and lifted me into his arms. I felt safe for the first time in two days. He hugged me tightly.

"Christina, this is my best friend, Slim," I said.

Christina was shocked when she saw his eye. She stared for a couple of seconds before she forced a smile. He reached out to shake her hand, she lightly placed her hand in his but pulled away quickly.

"Let's go to the playground," Slim said.

"Can Christina come?"

"Sure, bwoy, any friend of yours is my friend." I loved his accent. It felt safe and homey.

We walked out the door. "I have surprise," he said as we ambled behind the building to the parking lot. There, in an old red pickup truck was Buddy. I ran to him as fast as possible. I opened the door and Buddy jumped all over me.

"This is my puppy Buddy." With pride, I showed him to Christina.

We ran to the field and played for an hour. Buddy really loved Christina, and she was so excited to have a dog to play with. I threw his ball and we all chased it. Christina tripped over Buddy and they rolled around in the grass. She giggled a lot.

At 4:30 P.M., Slim and Buddy said they had to go—they climbed back into the truck. But, before they left I had to ask—"Can you adopt me? Can we bring Christina?"

"I called the adoption agency bwoy and they say that an unmarried person cannot adopt children. But, don't worry, I have always wanted to get married anyway."

They drove off, but not until promising to come back on the weekend.

Christina and I walked across the field toward home. "He nice and I love Buddy, but what happened to Buddy's ear? And what happened to Mr. Slim's eye?"

"I don't know. I found him at the pound, he was going to be put to sleep but I convinced my parents to adopt him. Slim has some kind of skin problem. I'm going to be a doctor and cure both of them."

"And I will be a nurse and help you."

"Why don't you be a doctor with me?"

"No dinero. I be the nurse and help you."

"You can if you think you can, and you can't if you think you can't." I repeated what my father had told me so many times. "My father told me it was the absolute truth."

The following afternoon, Mrs. Mayor called me to her office. I perched on the edge of a big chair in her office. She had a stack of papers on her desk. She opened an envelope and began reading out loud. I didn't understand all the legal stuff, but I heard my father's name a few times.

"Lawrence, your father did not have a will. Unfortunately, everything went to his wife. She has refused to make any arrangements for your adoption and has set aside no money for your care, or even your education. This is not for you to worry about now. We will tackle that problem in a few years. You are safe here. Do you have any questions?"

I shook my head.

"Go back to class. You will be fine." I left, not knowing what the future would bring. Moreover, the last thing I was feeling was fine.

That Saturday, Slim came to school and took Buddy and me to the field to play. Christina saw us and ran over to chase balls with us.

After thirty minutes, we were tired and joined Slim, sitting at a green wooden picnic table. Slim had a dog bowl and a container of water. He put the bowl down for Buddy and poured water in it. He gave Christina and me a juice box each and we sipped and enjoyed the day.

"You would be great padre, you have to find wife," Christina insisted.

"The ladies not that easy to catch. They keep getting away from me."

"You so bonito, they like you as much as I do when they know you." She went over and hugged him.

He smiled broadly and enfolded her. "You as sweet as sugar cane."

"You go to church to find a good wife," Christina said.

"Yeah, Mon, I go by there tomorrow and pick out one from the crowd." He laughed. "You there, pretty lady, step on up here and marry me."

CHAPTER 6

CHRISTINA AND SLIM, MARCH/APRIL 1977

In the mornings, Christina and I walked to school together. She babbled on while I listened and observed. She knew the family histories of the kids and why they were in God's Home. She pointed out Lily, whose parents were in prison for selling drugs and stealing cars. She mentioned Jimmy and Davonna, brother and sister, whose parents were child abusers and could only visit under court supervision. They never came anyway.

Freedom, a three-year-old girl, was found wandering the streets of Miami at 5:00 AM DCF removed her from her grandmother's home and brought her to us for safekeeping.

Christina and I became close friends. In the evenings, we studied in the small home classroom while the other kids watched TV. She even planned for our futures. "I'm gonna go to college one day and buy a big house. The Air Force recruiter comes to God's Home. I'm getting a scholarship."

On Sundays, we went to church together. She sang in the choir. She often looked around and pointed out prospective mates for Slim. "Lawrence," she whispered, "that lady is muy caliente. Slim will like her."

The days were warm and sunny and filled with studies and school projects, but Saturdays were the highlight of our week. On Saturdays, Slim came to see us, with Buddy of course. On the playground and fields with Slim, Buddy and Christina, I belonged to a family and felt complete and whole. During Slim's visits, Christina became quite interested in his personal life. She was always probing him, "Are there any single ladies in the hospital?"

"They look for handsome mon. I'm not handsome enough."

"I know some senoritas in our church. Come Sunday." But Slim didn't come to church.

In July school was out for summer, and Slim and Buddy came to see us more often, as Slim had some days during the week when he didn't work.

One of the days, Mrs. Altee made a picnic lunch and we played outside all day. When we stopped to eat, Slim had an announcement. "I met a nice lady at work. We go out to movie tonight." Christina was all over him with questions about this mystery woman.

Slim replied, "I got to ask her all of these questions before I can tell you the answers. All I know is that she work at the hospital and my friend set us up on a date."

The following Saturday, as soon as Slim drove up in his red truck, Christina was all over him like white on rice. "Where's your senorita? When is she coming? Do you like her? Does she like you?"

"She doesn't want any children." Slim hung his head. Then he smiled. "Oh well, there are plenty of seas in the fish. I go to church with you and just pick the lucky lady out of the crowd," he laughed.

We didn't expect any more progress until he drove up the last Saturday in July, with a dark-skinned heavy-set woman sitting next to him. Slim introduced Rawanda. She was a quiet lady, wearing a long colorful dress.

Christina asked her a thousand questions, including, "How many kids you want? You want a boy and girl? When will you and Mr. Slim get married? Will we be in the wedding? Do you want to adopt us?"

Rawanda answered, "I don't know," and "Maybe" to every question.

Rawanda had a tan-colored fan and she sat at the table waving it in front of her face. She wiped her handkerchief across her brow while we chased around with Buddy. When Buddy ran up to her, she crinkled up her nose and shooed him away.

Christina ran to our house and brought back a tall glass of iced tea for her. Rawanda accepted the tea, wiped her sweaty brow and fanned all the harder.

At 1:00, Rawanda said, "I forgot about an appointment that I have."

Mr. Slim hugged us both and promised to be back next week. They drove off and we never saw her again.

Christina and I never tired of dreaming about Slim finding the right lady, marrying and adopting us. In August, Slim started talking about another woman he met through a friend.

Later in August, Christina announced, "Sergeant Staunton is taking us to an air show." That following Sunday, about eight kids from the home piled into his blue van and we rode to the beach. Slim and Buddy walked up just as a fighter jet roared overhead. Grandfather had called it "The Sound of Freedom" and that roar stirred my soul.

I told Sgt. Staunton that I wanted to go to medical school. He said he would help to find an ROTC scholarship for me. "We need docs who fly, flight surgeons," he said. "If you study hard, the Air Force will definitely find a place for you. You too, Christina."

That summer was great in another way; Bull and his cronies were gone for the entire time to football camp.

In September, we returned to school.

CHAPTER 7

FAMILY MATTERS, SEPT. 1997-DEC. 1978

At the start of the next school year, Mrs. Mayor worried about my propensity to be a loner. She was worried that I didn't mingle with the other kids or the school staff enough. She sent me to see Dr. Friend, the school psychologist. I saw him every month.

By the time I turned eleven, I had settled into God's Home and stabilized in the system. I studied at school, read two books Slim bought me, *Call of the Wild* and *Adventures of Huckleberry Finn*.

That winter was the coldest on record, and we nearly froze. For the first time in my life, I experienced snow. I received my first long-sleeve shirt, a blue checked flannel shirt. Christina pulled me into the boy's closet by the collar. "It's a year since I seen my sister and she hasn't called me in three months. Something's wrong." She leaned closer. "I'm worried."

"Where's your sister?" I was so close that I could feel her breath.

"She's with my Tia Gloria in Liberty City."

"Call her."

"They don't have no phone. What you think, we rich?" she whipped back.

"I say we sneak out and go to see her." I wanted to be tough.

"You help me." It wasn't a request. She put her hands on her hips and looked ready for action.

"Yep. Let's ask Slim to take us there."

"He can't help. He stay out of trouble, so they let him adopt us."

"Then we sneak out tonight after everyone goes to bed." I was amazed at my brashness. I knew my only friend needed my help. "I know how to do it. Follow my lead. Be ready tonight after lights out. I'll have my knife and back-pack, you get a flashlight."

"I got Ritz crackers and cans of tuna in my closet. Bring your coat," she whispered.

My stomach had a knot all day as we went through our classes. Finally, I met Christina during lunch, and we sat at the corner table. We put our heads together to speak without the other kids hearing. I felt like Sir Galahad, help-ing a damsel in distress.

That afternoon, I secreted my thick gloves in my pockets, found a coil of rope and a long screwdriver just in case. I didn't know in case of what. I stuffed our equipment in my backpack with my Swiss army knife and silver wings.

I was fast asleep, still in my jeans and flannel shirt, when I felt her hand cover my mouth. I slid down the bunk bed, slipped on my tennis shoes and zipped up my secondhand parka.

I tiptoed behind her, past Mrs. Altee's office. I saw her purse on the table and opened it. There was a twenty-dollar bill right on top. I had never stolen anything in my life and I reasoned that I would give it back to her as soon as I could. The clock showed 11:43 PM as we crept out the front door. There was a bright silver- blue moon. The cold wind slapped me awake and I pulled my hood up. My breath fogged. Excited and scared, I had never done anything like this, and I had never been this cold.

As we strode along, I slung my arm across Christina's shoulder. She squirmed away. "Shhh! Don't touch me." She pointed. "Keep quiet." Gave me a look that could freeze a pan of boiling water.

By the schoolyard fence, she held up her hand. "We'll go over by the road in the back."

"I scouted it out. There is a better place by the side where the fence is cut. It's hidden from the road."

I pulled back the chain link, she squirmed through and I followed. A sharp barb caught on my coat, and I wiggled around, loosened it, and crabbed sideways. I brushed off some dirt that smelled suspiciously like dog poop and stood next to her.

"The road's over there. I saw a guy hitchhiking yesterday."

We trudged on the right side of 27th Avenue, staying away from the road and streetlights. After half an hour, Christina and I were tired and cold.

"We can hitchhike, I can protect you." I held out my knife.

She pushed her long hair under her Miami Dolphins cap and I stuck out my thumb. Cars zoomed past. After another half hour, we headed toward lighted golden arches. My lungs burned from breathing the freezing air. I pulled open the door and we went inside to light and warmth.

Christina ordered a fish sandwich and I had a Big Mac™. There was one other customer, a kindly-looking older man wearing a hat that said, "I LOVE GRANDPA." We sat at a corner table in the back by the bathroom, two tables behind his booth. He was clean-shaven and wore a jacket and tie over a white shirt. He had a bright oval face like Santa Claus, and wavy grey hair. He walked to the front, poured a cup of coffee, strolled by, and sat across from us. He said, "Brrr. It's cold as an ice box out there. You kids are out late."

A police cruiser pulled up outside. I nudged Christina to let her know that the cop was coming in. "Can we sit with you?" she asked.

"Of course." We quickly moved from our chairs to sit in his booth.

The cop strutted in, scanned the room, pulled up his coat so we could see his gun, and ordered some coffee and apple pies. He looked over at us and smiled. We looked like a family out for a late dinner.

I remember being afraid of the cop. This was my first foray out of adult protection. I was trying to be manly in front of Christina, but underneath, I couldn't fool myself. I felt anything but manly.

The cop car lights flashed blue and red, and the cop ran out the door, sloshing his coffee over his coat. The car sped off.

"The kids call me Grandpa Tim. Where you guys going on the coldest night in Miami?"

"We're going home to Liberty City," I lied. Christina kicked me under the table. I looked at her and she mouthed, "Shut up, stupid!"

Grandpa Tim said, "I live there on 69th Street. I don't remember seeing you around my block. Hey, you look cold. I'll buy you a hot chocolate." He rose and went to the counter.

Christina leaned close. "He seems nice."

"He's old. Maybe he'll give us a ride," I said.

"Shut up," she whispered as he came over with two Styrofoam cups.

He sat across again. "Thank God my car has a heater. My family bought it for me. They are very godly people." He crossed himself and Christina perked up.

"Are you Catholic?" she asked.

"Yes, I am, and I have six grandkids, three boys and three girls." He pulled a wallet from his pocket and fanned open a set of pictures. "I'm just returning home from visiting my sick granddaughter."

"I'm sorry to hear about your granddaughter," Christina said. I could see the doubt drain out of her face."

He smiled gently and stood. "I'm going to the men's room and then I have to leave. I can give you a ride home if you want." His voice was soft and comforting.

He went through the door to the bathroom.

"What you think?" Christina asked.

"He's very nice. It's too far to walk. I have my knife."

She grabbed my backpack. "Gimm' the knife, I'm sitting in back."

He returned and we huffed outside to his car. It was a nice white Cadillac. Smelled like a pine tree, had very wide seats and a great heater. He drove south and babbled about church and God and helping children.

He asked for the address from Christina. "Just let us out at the church on 17th Avenue. Our house is just around the corner. My mom don't know we sneaked out."

I chimed in, "Dad is a cop. He would be really mad if he knew we were out." I sat in the front and took off my gloves to warm my hands on the heater vent. Rubbing my hands together, I turned and winked at Christina.

She sat all the way back in the seat behind me. She hugged her arms around herself. "Come up here with us," Grandpa Tim said. "It's warmer." He gazed up at the rear view mirror.

"I'm fine," she said. I turned the heater vent so it pointed toward her.

He drove down a main road, and when he came to a red light, Christina said, "Turn here. This is 17th Avenue."

He turned, the car rattled over potholes. In the darkness, there were empty beer bottles and old cans on the side of the road. Near a 7-11 store, four guys stood warming their hands around a barrel with a roaring fire. The reflected flames made the men look like red-faced demons. I saw one of the men with a paper bag. He brought it to his lips and passed it to another.

"That's the church," Christina said.

I glanced forward and saw a large white church with a tall steeple with a lighted cross. Bright lights flooded the parking lot as we entered.

"Stop. Let us out here," Christina said.

"I have to turn around," he said. He drove a few hundred yards. "I'll turn around in that alley." He turned into the dark alley. He drove to the back behind the church where it was dark. He slowed to a stop by a dumpster. I heard the electric locks engage. He jammed the car in park, turned in his seat, and grabbed Christina by the left arm.

I jumped back in my seat, stunned.

She tried to jerk her arm away. "Let go of me!"

"Come up here and sit on my lap. I won't hurt you." He turned to me and snarled, "Get in the back and don't say a fucking word."

I didn't move, paralyzed with fear. He slapped me in the face with his left hand and used his right to hold Christina. I cowered back. He pulled Christina half over the seat.

"Get up here, or I'll beat the shit out of you." His eyes bulged out.

Christina grabbed for the door. He pulled her by her neck. She flew over the seat. He snatched her by the hair and turned her face to him and put his mouth over hers. Her right hand made a long and fast filleting motion at his face. I saw the blade. It flashed in the light and slit his face long and clean from his left ear to his bottom lip. His blood spurted everywhere and soaked his clothes immediately.

He took his hand off Christina and grabbed his face. I felt around for the door lock, finally located it, pushed the button and heard the lock pop up. She scrambled over me, jerked the door handle and we tumbled onto the gravel. She pulled me up, I stood, and we ran.

"You little bitch, I'll kill you," he shouted.

I ran as fast as I could, caught up to her as she turned the corner, and we ran down to the 7-11. She folded the knife and handed it back to me. She was amazing. When it counted, she was courageous. Some damsel in distress!

She bolted inside the door and I followed. I put my hands on my waist, bent over and panted for a minute until I caught my breath. I raised up and saw she had blood all over her coat. I pointed, she pulled her coat over, covered the bloody part and panted loudly. I looked out the window and saw the Cadillac race past. "There he goes," I whispered. She ducked.

I walked to the coffee urns and got some hot water and chocolate. I mixed them and gave her the cup. She smiled and took a sip. She blew over the top and took another sip. "He might call the police and tell them that we robbed him just to cover his tracks. We can walk to Tia's house, not too far."

We jogged down the street, staying in the dark shadows. At her Tia's small bright green house, she led me around the side. She rapped lightly at the back door.

After three more knocks, a little sleepy-eyed girl opened the door. Christina grabbed her and hugged her for a long time. Christina pulled back and had tears in her eyes. She ran her hand through the little girl's black hair, the same shiny color as hers. She buried her face in her hair. "This is Angel, my sister."

We tiptoed through the kitchen into the living room. There were kids asleep everywhere, on a lounge chair, another on a frayed couch and one on the floor. A baby was asleep and stinking in a crib in the corner. We followed Angel into a bedroom where there were two other kids sprawled over the bed. I curled up on the rug and promptly fell asleep.

There was hugging and screaming in the morning when they woke me. A short, heavy woman was holding Christina up and dancing around the room. She was singing and crying at the same time. "Nina, Nina, Nina," she said. Christina grinned and laughed. She put Christina down and looked her over. "You gotta clean up. You a nasty mess."

"We attacked last night, this his blood."

"Oh, Dios Mio! What this?" Tia said.

Christina told her the whole story. "We should call the cops," I said.

"No, we're not supposed to be out of the home. We sneaked out to check on you, Tia. You haven't called in months. Nobody came to visit."

"I lost my job. Husband gone. These kids to take care of." She spread her hands and shrugged. "No dinero.." She pointed to a closed door, "Cousin Julio is in there. He broke parole. No can call."

Tia looked over at me. "I find you clean clothes."

After showering, I realized how hungry I was. I got dressed in Levi jeans made for a 100-pound kid and I probably weighed 75. She gave me an old t-shirt that was clean.

The house was tiny but clean and well kept, except for a few toys and things dragged around the house by the kids. Christina took a seat at the table in the kitchen and I sat next to her. To my left, in a high chair was a little baby, fussing to eat but unable to reach his bowl. I pushed the bowl a little closer to him and he grabbed the spoon and proceeded to shovel in an oatmeal looking substance.

Christina was holding Angel on her lap. "You can be our foster parent, yes?" she said to Tia Gloria. "We live with you? I work and clean, we'll be no trouble."

"Nina, Nina," she shook her head. "I tried," she looked sad. "DCF say my house too small. I need two more bedrooms." She held her hands up, spread apart. "What can I do? Maybe next year."

"Please, Tia Gloria, just me. Lawrence will go with Slim. I get a job and help pay for everything."

"No can do. You gotta return to the home quick. I promise I take bus to see you. I bring Angel. You go home today or police come. I don't need no police. Julio"…she pointed.

Christina buried her face in her hands and cried. Angel cried.

After breakfast, Tia Gloria called a nephew to come and take us back to the home. We arrived back at 11:00 AM and sneaked through the fence. Christina told Mrs. Altee that we had started an early morning exercise program, and we were out running. Our secret was safe.

A month later, I was hopeful again. "I know a Jamaican lady who just came to work in the kitchen." Christina spread her hands. "She the bomb." She grinned. "Lady makes the best jerk chicken and she is cool."

I was reading her mind.

We gathered up our books and left the playground for the night.

The next day, Christina brought me to the back of the school cafeteria. She cupped her hands around her face, and I did the same as we looked through the screen door. "That's Miss Charmaine," she whispered, and she pointed to a golden honey-colored, robust and very curvy lady. She wore a long flowery dress.

"She looks nice. You think she'll like Slim?"

"Look at her legs," Christina said.

I cupped my hands again and stared. Charmaine bent over to pick up something and her dress pulled up in back to show the bottoms of her legs. There were the same pasty white markings as Slim had around his left eye and hands. In later years, I would come to find out in med school that it was vitiligo, like Michael Jackson had.

"She has the white spots like Slim." I said, stating the obvious.

"Yes, let's get her to meet Slim, when he brings Buddy."

That Saturday, Buddy, Slim, and I were throwing and chasing a ball in the field when Christina and Charmaine walked up carrying paper plates with cookies and jerk chicken.

"Mr. Slim," Christina called." We got some snacks for you guys. Miss Charmaine made the chicken and I helped with the cookies."

I saw Slim glance up at Charmaine. He smiled wide, whether it was for her or for the chicken and cookies, I did not know.

Slim nodded his head to the new lady. "Oh, bwoy, real Jamaican Jerk." He picked up a piece and chewed with a big grin on his face. His face radiated pure joy. "This the real deal, you know how to make the chicken, pretty lady."

She walked up to him, large and in charge. "I from Kingst'n. I better know. Have more."

Christina grabbed my arm and ran off for me to chase her. I followed her with Buddy, laughing the entire way. During the next few months, every Saturday when Slim brought Buddy to visit, sure enough Christina and Charmaine would join us with more jerk chicken. I looked forward to Saturdays all week.

As Christina and I hoped, Slim and Charmaine fell in love and married later that year. "We don't need a big wedding. We save the money to help pay for our big family." When Slim came on Saturday, we asked about the progress he and Charmaine had made to adopt Christina and me. They had completed the paperwork and were going through the interview process. It looked like Christina and I would be out of the house before long.

After six months of paperwork and interviews, the decision came down. Christina and I were not culturally compatible for Slim and Charmain to adopt. The state said it was better for us to stay in the home. My world was crushed, and I cried every night for a week, in my bed.

CHAPTER 8

WOODSTOCK, NOV. 1982

The end of November was unusually warm. On days that Christina and I were not together, I sat alone at my favorite picnic bench at the extreme rear of the playground. The school bordered on government property. It was on the edge of a forested area with stately oak and pine trees that provided an area of safety and solitude. An eight-foot fence surrounded the playground, kept the children in place while the large trees that arched over the fence provided shade for the kids who played beneath them. On the other side of the fence was an over-grown area the kids called the jungle. The wild area was full of paper trees, old growth pines, a tangle of vines, and deep sawgrass.

Often, I sat in the shade of the trees, with the warm breeze in my hair and the sunlight on my arms, reading favorite books and listening to the melody of songbirds. In the distance, I would hear the other kids playing tag.

A faint whiff of jasmine reminded me of Mom's perfume. It brought warmth to my heart. Thoughts of Mom reminded me of my life plan. I'd go to medical school like my father. But unlike him, I would have a family and remain faithful to them forever.

A slow motion on the ground caught my eye; a bright green garter snake slithered across the grass toward a yellow fluffy object three feet away. I stared down at it. At first, I couldn't determine what the fuzz-ball was. Then a yellow beak came into view. It was a tiny fledgling, it peeped to get the attention of its mother, unaware of the snake.

Instantly aware of the danger facing the helpless bird, I jumped to the side, reached down and grabbed the little tweet just as the snake flashed by my hand.

Feeling like a hero, I cuddled the fledging to my chest for heat and love. His soft, scared eyes looked into mine. For the first time in a long time, I felt important. Smiling tenderly at this little creature, I cupped the bird in the bottom of my T-shirt. He stopped peeping and settled in, accepting me as his new protector. I knew he belonged back in his nest, but my need for a friend was greater than my need to do what was right for him.

"I'll call you Woodstock," I was thinking of the bird in the Peanuts cartoons.

When the bell rang, I hid behind a trashcan, cradling Woodstock. The wind gusted hard, and I doubled the fabric, protecting my fragile friend. Then I left the schoolyard without drawing any attention to myself. Back at the house, Mrs. Altee confronted me. I walked in, bending at the waist, holding Woodstock hidden and protected.

"I have a stomach ache," I said and went directly to my room.

From the top shelf of my closet, I took down my old shoebox with my family treasures, the portrait of our family, my silver pilot's wings, Swiss army knife, and nine dollars.

A washcloth was a perfect liner for the shoebox, providing softness and warmth. I found a small plastic medicine bottle lid and filled it with water from the bathroom, so Woodstock would have something to drink. Dipping my index finger in the water, I let it drip into Woodstock's open beak.

When I heard Mrs. Altee leave in the van, I placed Woodstock in the shoebox, cut holes in the lid and hid it in the back corner of my closet. I went outside and brushed around in the dirt where there were flowers. I found two juicy earthworms. I brought them into my room and cut them into small pieces with my knife.

Woodstock was waiting in his little bird home for dinner, so I stabbed a piece of worm with the toothpick from my Swiss Army Knife and fed it to my hungry friend. Woodstock tilted his fuzzy head back and opened his beak. I repeated this four times and then gave him another drink of water from my finger-faucet.

When I heard the kids in the hall, I kissed him on his little bird head. He looked at me and let out a peep. I hid the box back in the closet behind an empty suitcase and closed the closet door. Then I jumped on my bed, crawled to the back corner and pretended to sleep.

After lights out, I lay in my bed, waiting for everyone to sleep. When the house became quiet, I cautiously climbed down and tiptoed over to the closet. I crept as slowly as I could. The thumpity-thump of my heartbeat sounded so loud, I was sure the other kids could hear it.

I feather-fingered the closet door. It gave out a small squeak, and my heart stopped. After a few seconds, I finished opening the door. With my pen flashlight between my teeth, I pulled the lid from the box. Woodstock got a drink from my finger and four tasty segments of earthworm. He made a loud PEEP! PEEP! and my heart leaped. Bull stirred, making a snorting noise. I turned off my light, covered Woodstock with my hands and held my breath.

After two minutes, Bull was snoring. I tucked my bird back in the box, closed the door, and tiptoed to bed. I couldn't wait to show Buddy, Christina, and Slim. I lay awake most of the night, scared that Woodstock would peep.

The next day, I could not get my mind off Woodstock. In my daydreams, Buddy, Woodstock, Christina and I lived with Slim and Charmain. I thought of my little friends and me as the heroes who would stand by each other to fight for good in the world. There I was on top of a hill, holding the flag of honor with Buddy at my side and Woodstock perched on my shoulder. All the other soldiers cheered us on, and my heart filled with pride.

After the other kids left for school, I quickly removed Woodstock from the closet and fed him. Before I put him away, I whispered in his little ear. "I promise, I will love you forever." Just as my mom had done to me, before she died.

I left class for recess, saw Christina, and walked with her toward the playground. "I have a secret," I told her.

Just then, "Hey, Bull, I heard Anthony say you were gay," Gonzalez yelled out.

Without thinking or warning, Bull punched Anthony in the mouth. He knocked Anthony to the ground, broke out two teeth, and left him lying there bloody and unconscious.

Washington laughed and Bull yelled, "One punch knockout, motherfucker."

I ran over, bent down and picked up Anthony's head. I glared up at Bull, but was too afraid to say anything. I turned back to comfort Anthony. He hadn't seen the punch headed for him. He was just coming to—unaware of what happened.

Mrs. Altee ran out to see about the commotion. "What happened?" she asked breathlessly, as she went to her knees.

"He just fell down on his face and knocked his teeth out. I rolled him over to help him," Bull said with a straight face. "Isn't that what happened?" he asked the crowd.

Not one of us disagreed, and I was ashamed. I was no hero. I was a coward, and Anthony was an easy target. From then on, Anthony never knew if Bull would do it again. Bull would sometimes flinch at Anthony as if he were going to hit him, or he would point at him and stick up one finger. Other times, he would look at him and say "One punch, Hop Along…" and laugh his head off. Anthony walked with a limp from some childhood illness, and Bull loved to remind him of it.

Christina and I walked to the back of the playground. "I found a baby bird," I said.

Christina scoffed. "You got no bird and now is no time for jokes. Anthony just got knocked out."

"We should try to get Bull kicked out of here without him knowing, but I do have a baby bird."

"You got no bird."

"Yes, I do, and I will show you after school. He's in a box in my closet. He sleeps all day."

"A box?"

"I'll show you after class," I said, just as the bell rang.

At 3:00 PM, I raced out. Christina called to me, "Wait up. I want to go with you." She paused. "Let me get my gym shoes. I have to bring them home."

We hurried to the gym, and she found her locker, unlocked it and retrieved her shoes.

We were the last to leave, and we laughed, held hands and ran together. I could hardly contain myself with excitement. When we made it through the front door, there was no one in the family room, but I heard shouting from the back of the house, where my room was. I raced as fast as I could. Bull, Washington, Gonzalez and several other kids were sitting in a circle, laughing and pointing. Bull looked up at me.

"Hey!" Bull shouted with a sneer on his face. "I found a bird in the closet, check it out." I knew something was wrong. I felt like there was a hole in my stomach. I looked down and my shoebox was open on the floor. Bull was holding my father's long, sharp, surgical scissors in his right hand. I jerked them out of his hand and saw pieces of little yellow feathers between the blades. The kids parted, and I saw his little yellow body on the floor. Woodstock's eyes looked lifeless and dull.

'You want to hold my new bird?" Bull asked.

I bent down to pick Woodstock up. I saw drops of blood on the floor and he was missing his wings.

I was stunned.

"You killed Woodstock?" I fell to my knees, tears streaking down my cheeks. When I picked up his little lifeless body, he slipped from my fingers, fell to the floor, and landed flat on his back with his legs sticking straight up. Bull and his buddies burst out laughing. I picked him back up and cupped my hands around his tiny ruined body. My heart was aching. Tears ran from my eyes.

I opened my hands and looked at my sweet helpless little friend I had tried to save. "You shithead fuckface," I screamed. "You murdered Woodstock." I jumped up and stood defiantly with the scissors in my left hand and the crumpled body of Woodstock in my right. I trembled. I could feel hate grow inside me like a cancer.

Washington came behind me. "Shut up, asshole!" He thrust both arms at my back, knocking me forward. I tripped over the empty box and fell toward Bull. I put out my hands to stop my fall, and the scissors went up, straight up, and stabbed Bull's chin. He looked shocked. Blood spurted from his throat. Bull screamed for Mrs. Altee.

Washington punched me in my right kidney, and I doubled over in pain. Christina grabbed one of Bull's trophies from the top of his dresser and swung it like a baseball bat. She hit Washington in the stomach, breaking the trophy and causing Washington to throw up all over Bull. Mrs. Altee came in right at that moment.

That's the moment I knew I loved Christina.

The paramedics came and took Bull to the hospital to get stitches. Bull acted like he was going to die, howling like a baby. Christina and I looked at each other and smirked.

We told Mrs. Altee what Bull had done and she believed us. They moved Bull and Washington to a house for older boys, and although we saw them at normal school functions, they didn't live with us. Whenever possible, we avoided Bull like the plague.

I was not punished for the gouge on Bull's chin. From that point on, I would make a point to stare at the jagged "W", then look away and stare again. I knew it annoyed Bull, but I acted as if I didn't know I was doing it.

With Bull gone, and the threat of nightly face punches over, I slept like a redeemed man and woke early, grabbed a quick breakfast, and ran out the door. I raced to my class and buried myself in my books. Most afternoons, I went to the school library to study, read a favorite novel, or spend time with Christina.

CHAPTER 9

A PLEDGE TO BULL (1982-1985)

"Lawrence, don't forget about your meeting with Dr. Friend after school today," Mrs. Mayor said.

She added, "Did you hear that Christina got adopted?"

Adopted! That word hit me like a big boulder. "Christina is leaving?" I would not be able to see Christina that night as she had a study group.

The next morning, Christina limped into the dining room. I dropped my spoon. She had a bandage on her head and tape over her jaw. Her skin was pale. I mouthed, "What happened?" She opened her lips to speak. A front tooth was missing.

"Christina, your face."

She moved back from me, held her fingers to her lips. "Later."

I gobbled down my cereal and waited by the door. She crooked her finger, beckoning me to follow.

She no longer smelled like flowers, more like iodine and peroxide.

"What happened?"

"Tia Gloria got a new husband. They have a bigger house and room for me." She looked away, avoiding my eyes.

"What happened to you?" I repeated. "Why are you limping?" She looked like she had been in a car wreck.

"It's nothing," she mumbled. Then she winced when she put her left foot down, stumbling. I held her around the waist.

"What happened to you?"

"I don't want to talk about it." Christina sobbed, shuddering in fear or pain, I did not know.

I hugged her for all I was worth. My only friend in the world was hurt. She was leaving. *What would happen to me without her? I love her and need her.*

I was half carrying her as we stumbled behind the school building. I helped her down to the picnic bench and sat beside her, our backs to the table. I enfolded her and wiped the tears from her cheek.

She shivered as if she was cold, but it was ninety degrees.

"Christina, what's the matter?" I touched the bandage on her head. She flinched.

"Don't touch it. It hurts." She had a thick gauze on her left hand.

The bell rang. I didn't move. I couldn't leave my friend. My heart ached for her.

"That fucking Bull. I hate him," she whispered.

"Bull? What about Bull?" My heart raced.

"Nothing."

"It was Bull? Bull did this?" She nodded; my mind saw blood. "Bull beat you up?"

She looked at the ground, put her hands between her knees, and shuddered again as she spoke. "Bull raped me."

She collapsed against me, reached around my neck, and held on. *I will get a gun and shoot him.* I held her for all I was worth. *No, shooting would be too good for him. I will make him suffer.* "Someday, somehow, I will make him suffer for what he did."

I turned her face up to me. She looked hurt and sad.

"You have to tell the cops," I said.

"I can't. He knows where my sister lives. He said he would kill her. Promise you don't tell. Promise me." Tears smudged her cheeks.

"I promise," I said. "What does Mrs. Altee think? What did you tell her?"

"Mrs. Altee found me and called the ambulance. I told her that I was running, tripped on the sidewalk and landed on my face. She didn't believe me, but I stuck to my story."

"I'll kill him, I promise you."

"No. We'll kill him. We will kill him."

My mind flashed to the blood on my knife. I knew I would find a way to get Bull back. I had no doubt.

Mrs. Jabbar came around the corner. "Christina, have you been crying?"

"I'm just sad to be leaving my boyfriend," she said.

Even in this tragic situation, when she called me her boyfriend, I must admit, it made my heart beat faster.

Bull came around the corner with a smug look on his face. "I thought I was your boyfriend," he winked.

I saw Christina look at me, hopeful I would do something. "Get the hell out of here, Bull," I said. To my core, I hated the bastard.

"We don't need your help here, Hassan," Mrs. Jabbar barked.

Bull strutted away, but not before letting out a hearty laugh.

Christina stood and left with Mrs. Jabbar. In my mind, I hatched my plan. I found out later that day that my plan would have to wait. Bull was off to college on a football scholarship.

With Christina adopted, my mind turned to studying, reading and spending a lot of time alone. I waited for my life after the home to start, eager to get out.

Almost every weekend, Slim, Momma, and my old and tired dog Buddy came to see me. Occasionally, they picked up Christina and she came with them, but I could feel us growing apart.

Slim did his best to be a real father to me. He was reliable, kind and honest. Looking back, it brings tears to my eyes to realize the sacrifices he went through. I was someone he didn't know. Yet, he did his best to teach me manly things, how to treat a woman that you love, how to be kind, yet strong, and most importantly, the unforgettable impact of a genuine smile that shows you are happy to see someone. I looked forward to my times with them more than anything. They were my family.

In my last year at God's Home, Sergeant Staunton arranged for me to attend ROTC after school. From then on, three days a week, I met my ROTC flight. The ROTC instructors taught me the history of the Air Force and military traditions. I spent countless hours marching across the drill pad.

Occasionally, I saw Christina. She was at a different high school, also in ROTC training flight. That year, she visited me less and less, but we still talked on the phone. Towards the end of the school year, she met a boy at her school. I was crushed. Over time, I came to accept that she had moved on.

When I graduated high school, I had the option of staying at God's Home until college started or I moved out. I called Slim and he invited me to spend the summer with him. I loved the freedom and it gave me a chance to show Slim and Charmain how much I appreciated them. Slim still worked as an emergency medical technician, primarily dealing with car accidents and injuries at homes. During the summer I stayed with him, he worked the day shift, which gave me the opportunity to handle all the work on the farm. Buddy would follow me around until he got tired and then he would find his way to the palm tree next to the lake and take a nap. Although Slim's farm was small, there was weeding of the garden, fixing the fences, mowing the grass, tilling the soil and working on the house and small barn. In the evenings, Slim, Charmain, Buddy and I would sit in the living room, eating a delicious dinner, talking and watching game shows.

When the day came for me to leave for university, I packed up my clothes, said my goodbyes to Charmain and Buddy and hopped in Slim's truck. As he dropped me off in the parking lot, he handed me an envelope with $500.

"You work hard and I want you to have this."

"I can't take it—you have done so much for me."

"You take this money—we want you to have it."

I felt embarrassed, but he would not take no for an answer. "Thank you and I will see you when the semester is over."

"Ok, but you call soon, we want to hear all about school."

I gave him a big hug, grabbed my duffel bag and made my way to the housing office.

CHAPTER 10

EAST MEETS EAST, SEPT. 1985

A pretty brunette lounged on a lawn chair and stared at me. Her spine arched inward as she raised her face to the sun and stuck out her perky breasts. I picked up my pace and strode by in a hurry to find my first dorm room on the campus of Atlantic State University. Excited, I bounded up the three steps of Brice Hall. Grabbing the brass handle, I heaved the door open as though I had been there before.

Temporarily blinded by the change from the bright sunlight to the dim hall, I took the room assignment form out of my pocket. Mr. Ebert at the housing office said that they tried to match people who have commonalities, but if it didn't work out, to let him know. He mentioned that I had been matched with two Japanese students who were also pre-med.

First stop, my room to drop off my meager belongings and look around. There was no sign of my roommates. Next stop, check out the library.

It was dusk as I made it to the library, a colonial mansion style with four enormous columns. The entire entrance was brightly lit and inviting. The smell of old leather welcomed me. I flashed back to my first visit to a library, as a five-year-old with my father. Dad had pointed to the stacks of books and said, "You can have any book you want."

I ambled through the stacks and looked at the numbers and placards that indicated subject matter. I searched through the section labeled Science and found my way to the chemistry section. It didn't take me long to locate last year's edition of my *Fundamentals of Chemistry* textbook. I pulled the book from the shelf and wandered around.

Behind the stacks, there were six polished mahogany tables with bright lamps, each with a green shade. I felt invited to sit and learn. I sank into a soft leather chair that felt like my mother's embrace. The leather chair smelled of age and learning. It drew me deep into its world, making me feel content. I settled back, adjusted the lamp and opened Chemistry 101. The first and second chapters drew me right in to the basics I would need for the study of chemistry. After an hour, I started Chapter Three to learn about molarity and Avogadro's number. I felt confident I was on my path to becoming a doctor.

I read that valence was the definition of the number of atoms a single atom could connect to. The thought occurred to me that valence could be applied to people and their ability to form bonds with other people.

"People have valence," I whispered. My original family members were like three atoms with incredibly strong bonds that kept them connected, despite the death of two of the people. I smiled at the thought that the three of us danced like atoms around one another, unbreakably bonded together for eternity.

Then I thought of Bull and how popular he was, circled by his group of followers. He must have had a valence of twenty or thirty, as everyone seemed to want to bond with him. I wondered what happened when several high-valence people came into the same room. Were there thousands of instant bonds that formed the group into one cohesive solid?

After reading a little longer, I decided I was closer to helium or neon, a noble gas with a valence of zero. But neon gas can shine brightly, and I knew my future would be bright.

Maybe I was destined to go through life with few significant bonds. The thought crossed my mind that half of all the people I loved had died. Mom and Dad, I loved them with all my heart, yet they died. Maybe I had the valence of death.

A bell chimed, and I looked up at the clock on the far wall, astonished to see it was already 11:00 PM. Still only halfway through Chapter Three, I decided to take a break and stretch my legs. I glanced about the room and saw two young Asian men seated at another table. They were reading the current edition of the same chemistry book I was reading. I wondered if they were my roomies.

The men looked similar, they had warmish tanned skin, coal black hair, and intelligent thick gold wire-rimmed glasses. Both wore navy blue sports coats and polka dot bowties. They had to be incredible nerds. I knew they would be smart and naïve. They were from my zero-valence tribe and would certainly not be part of the in-crowd.

I stopped for a moment behind a stack where they couldn't see me, but I could hear them. I listened, realizing they were speaking a foreign language, probably Japanese. I ambled to the front of the building and noticed a toilet and a little break room with soda and snack machines.

Inside the break room, I closed the door, put a buck in the machine, and selected Dr. Pepper®. My change rattled in the dispenser, the door opened, and one of the Asian men meekly entered, giving me a slight head bow. I smiled and nodded.

"I am Hideki, pleased to meet you." He spoke English very well.

"I'm Lawrence, pleased to meet you, too."

"Will you show how?" He pulled out a handful of coins.

I took two quarters and inserted them. "What do you want?"

"Same as you."

I pointed out the Dr. Pepper® button and waited for Hideki to push it and retrieve his drink. "Dr. Pepper®."

"Doctor?" Hideki looked puzzled by the name.

"Just a name. Hey, are you taking chemistry?"

"Sure, all Americans say sure, Sure I am take chemistry."

"You any good at chemistry?"

"Sure, I'm good but my brother best."

The door opened, and the other Asian entered with a scowl on his face. He aimed his black beady eyes at his brother and said something. "I must go," Hideki said.

"Wait, is this your brother?"

"Sure. He is Atsushi. His name means industrious."

I bowed my head as Hideki had, and reached out my hand. "I'm Lawrence. Glad to make your acquaintance."

Atsushi took my hand in both of his and pumped it up and down very fast. "Glad to meet you," he said.

"I think I have been assigned to your room." I pulled out my slip and showed them the room number.

"Please. We are happy," Atsushi said. "We study and then go to room later."

CHAPTER 11

BUDDY TOO, SEPT. 1985-JUNE 1986

I joined the brothers at their table. We focused on our solitary studies. First, Atsushi fell asleep, then Hideki. I was determined to stay up longer and study harder. Around 4:00 AM, I laid my head down on the wooden table.

Someone nudged me, and I sat bold upright and stared into the face of the librarian. The brothers were gone. "Do you have class soon?" she asked. The librarian helped me check out the chemistry book.

I grabbed up the textbook and backpack and ran from the hall of learning. In the bright sunlight, I jogged to the student union, grabbed a muffin and a Dr. Pepper®, and pulled out my campus map, running to the chem building.

Out of breath, I came through the eight-foot-tall double wooden doors and found myself at the top and back of an auditorium. Looking down, I thought the room could house four or five hundred students. I moved to the side and sat in the last row, way up on the top right. Peering side to side, I searched for a glimpse of my roommates. I heard a loud bell, and a man in a black graduation gown entered from the right and walked directly to the podium at center stage.

"I am Doctor Pauling Stanford, your professor for Inorganic Chemistry 101. For those of you in pre-med, I will be your professor for the following six semesters, all the way through senior biochemistry, so get used to me." His voice was amplified and high-pitched. He smiled, all the time reaching around in his black briefcase. He wore an old-fashioned blue and green-striped tie under his robe. His hair was long, brown and uncombed and looked like a bird's nest on his head. He had an unkempt goatee.

As Professor Stanford squeaked on, I looked around the room at my fellow students. In the first row, in the center, were Atsushi and Hideki. Each had his notebook out, furiously writing everything the professor said. One of them- I wasn't sure which- had a tape recorder on his desktop, obviously collecting every word.

After class, I went to the student union to eat lunch. I was wolfing down a tuna sandwich when I saw Hideki enter and walk toward the food line. I waved him over. We ate without speaking.

As I was leaving the cafeteria, my eyes met Christina's. My heart skipped a beat. She waved me to come over. It had been a few months since we talked and more than six months since I had seen her.

"Hi, Lawrence." She was reserved.

"This is Juan, my boyfriend." She motioned to a tall, handsome, dark haired Latino. "He is a freshman here, too."

He reached his hand out to shake mine. I offered a limp not-too-interested handshake. I made some small talk and excused myself, saying I had to meet my roommates. I was happy for Christina, but it was hard to see her with another guy. I didn't want to hang around with them.

I headed back to my room to study Chemistry.

After cramming my chem book for seven hours, I slammed the cover shut, finished for the night. I stood and walked around, reached my arm overhead, and flexed my torso to the side. I giant-stepped away from the window and glimpsed an 8 x 10 picture on Hideki's desk. It showed a loving handsome family of five, elegantly dressed. It reminded me of the family I once had. In the picture, I saw meticulously dressed, stolid faces in front of Mount Fujiyama, snowcapped and mist covered. The arrangement was odd, the two boys stood together to the left of their mother but left a space for another person. The picture looked off balance, and reminded me of the missing-man formation of airplanes.

My eyes were drawn to the girl on the right. Her rich black, luminous hair, pulled back in a tight bun framed her delicate, creamy white face. I stared at her jade green eyes. She took my breath away.

A sound startled me. Hideki entered our room and saw me pull my hand away from the family photo.

"My family."

"Yes, I hope to meet them someday." I picked up the picture. "Will your sister come to school here?"

"Aimi, my sister? No. She will attend school in Japan. She will not leave the family. She will marry important man to join our two families. We have one older, big brother. He could not be there. He was away."

"What do you mean, away?"

"In jail, but he is out now." I knew I had intruded.

Day after day, that first year, I spent countless hours bent over my textbooks. I studied to exhaustion, then walked around to clear the fog from my mind. Inevitably, my gaze fell to the enticing face of the lovely Japanese girl, and I felt a desire for her building in me. A glance, immediate warmth, and she carried me away from my brain-clouded study freeze to a warm safe place in her arms.

At the end of the year, the phone rang, which it almost never did. It made me jump. I ran over and snatched it up. The old familiar voice came across crisply. "I got to talk to Lawrence Leo, Mon," Slim said. A feeling of relief swept over me, and I sat on the floor with the hand piece against my ear.

"It's me. Man, have I missed you."

"Lawrence, the semester is over. Such long time since we have seen you. When you come home? Buddy misses you. Farm needs your young hands. We come to get you."

It was 6:00 the next morning.

Knock! Knock! Knock! I rubbed the sleep from my eyes, and opened the door for Slim.

"Early worm catches the bird." He smiled.

I hugged him as a son hugs his father. He was a little grey and starting to hunch over at the shoulder, but the sparkle of life was still in his eyes.

"My bag is packed, I can't wait to see Buddy." I hefted my bag.

"Buddy has a surprise for you. He is in the truck."

It was still dark and hard to see, but I scanned around and found the old beat-up Ford silhouetted against the sunrise. The windows were cracked open, and a golden-brown fur-covered face gazed through. Buddy's nose stuck out, and he barked the minute he saw me. He still wore the spiked collar I'd given him all those years ago when we were both pups. I grabbed the door handle, locked. Buddy pushed on the window, trying to get out and touch me. Slim came up, pulled out his keys, and unlocked it.

I reached in just as Buddy leaned into my hands, hugged his paws on my shoulders, and licked my face like I was a popsicle. My heart melted as I picked him up and hugged him hard. He was heavy, so I put him on the ground, and we walked around the truck to the passenger side. Buddy walked with an old age limp, dragging his back right leg. I rubbed his head, knelt to kiss and hug him. Slim threw my bag in the back. I reluctantly let him free, but Buddy could no longer jump into the truck.

I picked up Buddy's front legs and put them on the floorboard and then boosted up his back legs. He whimpered and struggled and made his way into the truck. I got in, and Buddy crawled onto my lap. He smelled of flea soap. I wrapped my arms around him. Slim started the truck and drove south. Buddy was so close to me that it seemed he was trying to get inside my skin.

"You wait for the surprise."

"Tell me now. Why do I have to wait?"

"Buddy will show you." Slim laughed.

It was an awakening drive with the sun peeking over the eastern horizon and the warmth of the day enveloping us. My shoulders relaxed, and I looked closely at Buddy. His old hang down crinkled ear still gave him a devil-may-care expression. His fur was grey around the eyes, he was stooped in the shoulders, but he still exuded life with his flickering, licking, loving tongue and wagging tail.

We drove in silence. I luxuriated in the closeness of the two creatures in the world who really mattered to me. Since the day of my parents' death, Slim and Buddy had been my rocks, my reality, and my stabilizing family. *I couldn't make it without them.*

Driving up the dirt road, I saw the little lake with the tall palm tree Buddy loved to nap under during hot summer days. When chores were done, I would lay with him, my head propped on his back for a quick nap. I cherished those times.

Slim stopped in front of his farmhouse and we jumped out. I rushed in to see Charmain. She was large, soft, cuddly, and smelled like home in her red and green muumuu. I hugged her for all I was worth, and she hugged me, cried happily, like I was her long-lost son.

"Buddy got special treat for you," she winked.

"I heard."

Buddy nudged me from behind toward the living room. "He want to show you." Charmain waddled through the door into the living room.

There was a cardboard box on the floor in the corner with a soft, gorgeous retriever pooch inside. Buddy was sitting up next to the pooch with his tail wagging like a windshield wiper in a heavy rainstorm.

"That's his wife, Ellie."

"I always knew he was smooth with the ladies." I grinned at my canine ladies' man.

I walked over to pet her and glanced into the box. Inside were six puppies that had the same golden fur color as Ellie.

"All the neighbors love them puppies and want one." One had a black nose that wiggled as if smelling in its dream. "That one we call Buddy Too, check out his ear," Slim said. "We keep him for you."

Buddy beamed proudly, stuck his nose in the box, and pushed Buddy Too into my hands, licking his head. I scratched the puppy's funny ear, and he opened his eyes and captured my heart.

I played with the dogs and their puppies all morning. In the afternoon, I helped Slim go to the farm store and get crates to package his tomatoes and parts to fix his tractor. It was the best day I had in months. I felt relaxed, carefree, and happy. The thought even occurred to me that I might take a year off from university to just relax here with everyone that I loved. I knew that was not possible. I had to finish college.

Later that evening, we sat down to a sumptuous dinner. All year, I had eaten sloppy joes and hot dogs at the Student Union cafeteria. Now Charmain fed us jerk chicken, corn bread, butter beans, and the works. I licked my fingers when I was done.

Slim turned serious. "Buddy has been sick and hurting." He turned his head to the side. "You see he can hardly walk." He squeezed his lips together. "I can't say it."

"What is it, Pop?"

He had a tear in his eye, and he turned away. "Buddy old and hurting, but he want to see you one more time."

He walked around and placed his hand on my head. "Buddy love you, Lawrence. He want to show you his puppies."

I felt a lump in my throat. "He is tired but he looks well to me."

"He very sick. I am sorry."

Charmain buried her face in her hands and sniffed. "I love Buddy, we have him ten or eleven years. Both you our sons."

I sat on the floor beside a drowsing Buddy. I petted his head. He looked up at me with those warm brown eyes, as if to say, "It's okay. You're here."

He tried to get up when he heard one of the pups yelp. I went over to them, and he stumbled and stood beside me. He nuzzled the puppies and Ellie, paying special attention to Buddy Too. He stared into my eyes as if to say, "I waited to see you one more time. I wanted to show you my boy."

I hugged him close and thought about our times together on the beach, at the farm, he was the last living connection to my parents. I loved that dog.

I had a troubled sleep. In the morning, Buddy didn't wake. We buried him under the palm tree by the lake he loved. I cherished the studded collar as a memento to him and all that we had been through together. His loss was great. I felt no shame crying. For the next three days, Slim, Charmain, and I burst into tears at the drop of a hat, one of us often setting off the others, like yawning. He was the sweetest of souls I had ever met. Without him and Slim in my life, I would have become so depressed that I might never have come out the other side.

I spent the rest of the summer with Slim, Charmain and Ellie, one by one, all of the puppies were given away, except Buddy Too. I enjoyed the break from the rigors of study. The hours of pushing a wheelbarrow, cutting grass, carrying feed, hoeing weeds, and picking tomatoes relaxed my mind. I slept to dreams of the beautiful Japanese girl I had never met and could never have.

I started calling Slim "Pop" that summer and Charmain "Momma."

CHAPTER 12

FIRST TIME, APRIL 1987-1993

"Hup, two, three, four. I don't want'a go to war," I shouted along with the other cadets in my formation. We were a group of sixteen in two files of eight. We marched for our Drill and Ceremonies course. The drill pad was a black-topped parking lot. We cadets called it Corregidor, after the forced death march during World War II. In the summer, the pad radiated heat. If it was 100 degrees outside, it was 115 on the blacktop, making the soles of our boots squishy and soft.

I was almost finished with pre-med. A few weeks later, I would go into medical school full-time. I was preapproved for a full scholarship from the Air Force that would allow me to spend all my time concentrating on my studies.

Hideki told me, "Our family is coming for graduation."

"Is your sister coming?" I was trying to restrain my excitement, but I just had to know.

"Yes, she coming, don't be funny guy, Lawrence," joked Hideki. "She leave with my parents to go back home, too."

"I was just asking. I have been staring at the picture of your family for almost four years, and I have never met any of them."

"They know all about you and want to meet you in person."

"I'm thinking about asking to be stationed in Japan after graduation. I have never been outside the U.S. and everything you have told me about Japan sounds wonderful."

"You would love it. It is most beautiful country in the world." Hideki's pride radiated in his face.

My mind was filled with the beautiful dream of the Japanese girl in the picture, Aimi. Her image lived in my heart and my soul. She was my destiny.

Two days later, the phone rang. Hideki picked it up and spoke in Japanese for a few minutes. His voice turned to a disappointed tone. His parents would not be coming for graduation. "My father is an important surgeon and one of his patients is not doing well."

"I am sorry to hear that, will your sister still be coming?" I hit him with a cheeky grin and a glance from the side.

"My sister will be staying at home." He gave me his big brother, protective look.

We graduated without much fuss. We still had medical school to go.

I spent the summer back on the farm with my family. Buddy Too was just like his dad and he followed me everywhere, and when he got tired, he would sleep under the palm tree, next to his dad's grave. Momma and Pop loved having me around, and I enjoyed being needed. Life was as good for me as it had ever been.

"The phone for you," Pop called out the front door. I hopped off the tractor and jogged to the kitchen. "It's Christina, she going to Basic Training," he said. He turned back to the phone. "Bye, Christina, you gonna do great. Come and see Momma and me; you gotta meet Buddy Too."

It had been over a year and a half since I had spoken with Christina. I was glad to hear her voice.

"Hi, Christina."

"Hi, Lawrence, how are you? I miss you, it has been forever." Her sing-song voice stirred my senses and reminded me that I was a man. "I am going to basic training soon, and I missed talking to you."

We spoke for thirty minutes and promised to keep in better touch with each other. She said she would come and visit the farm as soon as she could.

During the summer of my junior year of medical school, Christina had twenty days of leave from her assignment and came to stay with us on the farm for a long weekend. She had grown even more beautiful. On Sunday, Momma and Pop went to the store, and I found myself alone with Christina.

I was in the kitchen pouring lemonade, preparing to mow the grass when she walked in.

"Can I have a glass of lemonade?"

"Of course." I filled the glass with ice and poured the lemonade, walking over to her. I handed it to her, and as she took the glass, she leaned in and kissed me on the lips. I put my arms around her waist and pulled her to me. We embraced and kissed, and passion took over. We fumbled to my room, fell on my bed and made love. It was the best two minutes of my life. I had finally lost my virginity. I apologized to Christina but she just laughed.

"Don't worry, you'll get better. Don't let this change our relationship. I have to fly back tomorrow, and long-distance relationships never work. If we are meant to be, then the timing will work out for us,"

Although this stung a little bit, I was relieved to hear it. The reality was that I still had one more year of medical school and then all my Air Force Training. It would be impossible for me to visit her in Ohio, and I didn't need the distraction of trying to hold onto a long-distance relationship.

Momma, Pop, Buddy Too, and I took Christina to the airport for her flight back. I walked her to the gate, and she looked me deeply in the eyes and said, "Finish school, take care of Charmaine and Slim, and I will see you soon."

I missed her already. I wanted to get on the plane with her, but I knew I couldn't. Two weeks later, I was back at school, studying for all I was worth to finish my last year of medical school.

CHAPTER 13

MEETING AIMI AND HER FAMILY, 1993

"Sure, you come to dinner," Hideki said as he stood by the window in our room. He opened his arms wide to hug me. "My parents hear all about you for eight years and never meet you."

He handed me the blue dinner jacket and red tie. "You wear the power tie. You impress parents." He grinned.

In a few minutes, we three new doctors raced up to Nick's Steaks and Stone Crab Restaurant. The façade was sparkling with clean windows and hunter green awnings. One window had a large menu posted but no prices. As we walked through the front door, I spied a wooden cage with a pair of white doves rubbing their beaks together. One cooed at me as I gazed around the room. This was the best restaurant in Miami, armed with rows of rich leather chairs that reeked of old money. Dark green curtains enveloped the walls, reminiscent of wealth and luxury. White linen tables were accented with the illumination of vanilla scented candles. The waiters were dressed in tailored tuxedos, spoke with English accents, and were known to act as a gentleman's second in delivering surprise engagement rings, a specialty of the house.

While we strolled past the doves, I jostled Hideki, and we chattered back and forth. I pushed him, then Atsushi, happy to have med school behind us. Hideki spied his parents. He jabbed me in the ribs and put on his adult face. I became silent and assumed a stiff stance. Atsushi toned down his behavior to that of a humble son of a respectable Japanese family. Hideki stretched his back straight up to his full height, assumed a businesslike posture, and shepherded me to the table in the back center of the room.

My attention was drawn immediately to the breathtaking beauty sitting beside her mother, the girl in the portrait, the girl of my dreams. Her midnight-black hair glistened in a bun, yet strands hung down and framed her face. Two silver sticks held it all in place. Her hypnotic jade green eyes made my heart beat faster. They say a photo is worth a thousand words, seeing her in person was worth a thousand photos.

In the puzzle that was my life, she was the missing pieces of me. It truly was love at first sight, or at least, first meeting.

Hideki noticed me staring and grabbed the front of my jacket. Bowing deeply at the waist, he pulled me down with him. He turned us to the side, directing our greeting to his elegantly dressed father. Dr. Herito gave a small nod and a soft smile in recognition of his sons and did not look at me. Out of the corners of my eyes, I couldn't help but glance at his daughter.

Hideki bowed again, but not as low. "Father, may I present Doctor Lawrence Leo?"

Dr. Herito stood, he had wispy silver-black hair, combed over to cover a bald spot. His eyes were black and penetrating. He was dressed in a finely tailored three-piece black suit with a knife-edge in the trousers and a sparkling white shirt with a gold fob hanging from the watch pocket.

"Very nice to meet you, Dr. Leo. I have heard a great deal about you over the years. My wife, Mrs. Herito?" He swept his arm to the right. She wore a silver and red kimono wrapped with a sparkling golden obi. She and Aimi were already standing, fussing over the boys in an excited group hug.

Their embrace ended and as Mrs. Herito looked my way, I bowed as they'd taught me. I took a chance and glanced up at the Joan of Arc doll again. She peeked at me, her eyes flew away in another direction. Mrs. Herito smiled and gave a small polite bow back.

"My wife does not speak much English."

As I rose, Hideki put his arm under my chest as if to help. Standing straight, my eyes fell on his sister. I sucked in my stomach and blurted out, "This must see your bister you told me about."

Hideki moved around, smiled at my mistake, and said, "This is my brilliant and talented sister, Aimi."

"Please, everyone, have a seat," Dr. Herito said.

As I bounded toward the seat closest to Aimi, Dr. Herito intercepted me and pointed to the chair beside him. "Sit here."

I felt like a scolded puppy.

"Ahhm, Congratulations," Dr. Herito said. His words brought me back. Everyone had noticed my staring.

"Thank you, sir, "I said, looking back at Aimi and marveling at her sparkling jade eyes and delicate nose. She blushed, turned her face toward her mother, and whispered something.

"My sons did very well," he gloated. "I am sure you are aware."

"Yes, sir, they are brilliant."

"They have my brains. They will be magnificent surgeons."

Aimi spoke very little but when she did, her English was excellent. "What kind of doctor do you plan to be?"

"I am joining the Air Force to become a flight surgeon and will be moving to Japan. Your brothers have told me all about your country, and it sounds wonderful."

"Yes, it is beautiful. We will be very happy to show you."

After dinner, Dr. Herito picked up the check. I was relieved at his generosity. I wanted to ask Aimi to take a walk in the moonlight but didn't know how, until Atsushi cleared the way.

"This is South Beach, world known for style and grace. Even Versace lives here. Perhaps Lawrence would show us?" He grinned at me.

"I used to come here as a kid." I was trying to act sophisticated. "Would you like to walk along the beach and have dessert?"

"Sure," Hideki said, and his father nodded.

"I read about the Clevelander," Dr. Herito said.

We strolled out into the warm tropical evening. A gentle breeze washed over us, and a perfect silvery moon lighted the way east to Ocean Drive. My heart wanted to walk beside Aimi and hold her hand. That was not going to happen, so I walked in front, on the curb side, with Dr. Herito. Aimi and her mother followed, and the two sons brought up the rear.

Ocean Drive was one hundred feet from the beach, with sidewalk cafes and beautiful old cars parked along the palm tree-lined street. There were laughing couples jostling past the tables and chairs, holding hands in the moonlight.

"There is Versace's house, and the famous Clevelander bar," I said. We took an open table on the sidewalk. I held the chair for Mrs. Herito and angled to sit beside Aimi.

Dr. Herito looked around. "These colors are unusual, no?" He pointed to a pink and green edifice.

"We have many cultures from the islands. They love the bright greens, reds, blues, and everything else in the rainbow." I turned to look at Aimi and smiled, "We are very international," I added, thinking I would impress them with our multiculturalism."

The server brought us coffee and tea. "Key lime pie is the Florida specialty. I recommend it."

I invented excuses to look at Aimi and talk to her. I pointed to Orion's belt and said, "There is Cupid's arrow, aimed down the beach." Feeling a little too smart for myself, I turned to her father. "The sky is most beautiful out over the ocean."

"We have an ocean in Japan, Lawrence." Dr. Herito rolled his eyes. "And a sky and moon as well."

I grinned, not knowing what to say. He appeared to be one of those guys who always had to have the last word.

We finished our dessert and drinks. Just as I was about to suggest a stroll on the beach to put our feet in the ocean Dr. Herito squashed my plans, "It is late and we are tired, please take us back."

"OK, we are not far." Because I wanted to extend the evening, I turned north instead of south. We strolled past the tourist area where the streetlights ended. Clouds covered the moon, making for a dark passage. I tripped over some trash on the sidewalk.

"This place stinks like a sewer," Herito said. A rat or feral cat scampered away in the dark, causing Mrs. Herito to let out a little shriek and jump.

I tried to get my bearings. *Where the hell were we?* I turned west, hoping to find Collins Avenue, but I must have made a wrong turn. We walked past darkened stores with boarded-up windows. We searched for bright lights.

"Where is a taxi cab?" Herito grabbed my arm.

I said, "We go west and south, and we'll get there in five or six…"

"You're lost," Herito said.

Mrs. Herito said something, and the doctor stopped us. She picked up her foot and rubbed it. "We must find a telephone and call a taxi," Dr. Herito said.

After another three blocks, I saw the bright lights of a main thoroughfare, and pointed. "There is civilization."

We emerged from the shadows into a bright street. I scanned for a street sign but couldn't find one. I saw a cop about three blocks ahead. He was in the middle of the street, directing traffic. We headed toward him.

Atsushi shouted, "There's a phone booth," he pointed, "across the street." He jumped off the curb to race across the four lines. An enormous city bus barreled at him.

"Atsushi, stop!" I yelled and reached for him. He had looked the wrong way. The bus brakes squealed, and I smelled burning tires. The thud sickened me.

Mrs. Herito screamed, "Atsushi!" She covered her mouth with her hands.

Aimi screamed.

Doctor Herito pushed past me.

Atsushi's crumpled and bloody body lay half in the road and half on the sidewalk. I fell to my knees beside Dr. Herito, just as the cop ran up. "I have an ambulance coming," he said.

I bent over to check Atsushi's pulse, but Dr. Herito pushed my hand away and glowered at me. "I am the doctor here."

Herito examined him. There were obviously severe injuries to his right leg, and probably his head. He lay unconscious.

Hideki and I stood while his mother and Aimi cried.

The ambulance skidded to a halt with lights blazing, reminding me of the night my parents were killed. Dr. Herito helped them gurney Atsushi. He glared at me and sped off in the ambulance. The cop summoned a cab for us, and we returned to the restaurant. Hideki drove his father's rental car to Miami General Hospital.

Everything changed that night.

CHAPTER 14

TAKING CARE OF ATSUSHI, 1993

The charge nurse told me they were in the operating theater. I sprinted up to the viewing area. Inside, Dr. Herito and Hideki were leaning over the short balcony wall, transfixed on the surgical team bathed in lights. In the center of the whole ordeal was Atsushi. I touched Hideki on the shoulder, but he shook his head no. He moved his eyes surreptitiously to the left, indicating his father. Dr. Herito turned and saw me.

"Get out of here. This is your fault," he spat the words.

"I tried to save him," I responded. "He ran in front of the bus."

Hideki stood and hustled me out the door. "Lawrence, leave us alone. My father is in no condition to talk. He is distraught, thinking he is losing a son. Go, I'll calm him down."

"Go now and tell Aimi and my mother that we will be out to see them as soon as we can."

"Gajin!" Dr. Herito yelled.

I dashed back to the waiting room. It was crowded with thirty or forty people clustered in small family groups. I saw Aimi and Mrs. Herito sitting in a corner huddled together. Aimi looked up with fright on her face. "Did you see Atsushi?"

I shifted from my left foot to my right. "Yes, he looks pretty good."

Mrs. Herito blurted out something in Japanese, and Aimi answered, "Mother wishes to see Atsushi. Where is my father?"

"He is with your brother, watching the operation. They will not let you in to the viewing area because you are not a doctor. Someone will come and speak to you as soon as possible." I took a breath and looked around. "Would you or your mom like a drink or a snack?" I pointed at the vending machine.

"Sure, a Coke." She forced a small smile. I pointed toward the machine, and she preceded me there. Trying not to slouch, I sucked in my stomach and puffed out my chest.

"I am so sorry for the accident."

"It is not your fault. My father is just upset." Her smile was gentle and fleeting.

I shifted my feet, cleared my throat. "I'm so sorry for what happened."

She touched my arm. "Lawrence, do not blame yourself."

I couldn't keep my eyes off her cute dimples. "Thank you." I spied a hot beverage machine. "Can I get your mother a cup of tea?"

She walked beside me. "Mother would be most thankful."

I took the paper cup and delivered it carefully to Mrs. Herito. She smiled at me as I handed her the tea. Her eyes were teary. We sat there for half an hour, and then I suggested a walk. Mrs. Herito told Aimi to go with me.

We strolled into the main lobby. I spied the gift shop and led her there. "I want to get your mother some flowers."

"Mama-san would love that."

There was a book section that had a great international selection. While I looked through the flowers, Aimi thumbed through the books. She spent some time with one, and I went over to see her. She saw me and held a book toward me.

"This is a famous book you should read, Lawrence. I am trying to write like this." She flashed the cover to me. "When you come to Japan, you will understand us better if you read *Some Prefer Nettles.*" She handed it to me.

"I don't read many novels, but medical school is over, and I want to learn more about your country." I opened my wallet and saw my picture of my mother, father and me those many years ago. I wished to have a family with this wonderful woman.

We strolled back across the lobby and into the waiting room. I handed the pink carnations to Mrs. Herito, who smiled and thanked me.

I started reading *Some Prefer Nettles*, but couldn't concentrate. Aimi tapped her feet, and Mrs. Herito wrung her hands.

Hideki flashed through the doors. He was breathing hard. He spoke rapid Japanese to his mother. He turned to me.

"Father wishes Mother and Aimi to come to the room with Atsushi." I stood up to go with them, but he stopped me. "He said you were not to come. Sorry, he is upset."

"I understand. Please tell him I am very sorry for what happened."

As they hustled out the door, I felt dejected and beside myself. I walked outside and remembered the interns' dormitory, where I knew they would welcome me. I entered and saw the intern on duty and explained the situation. He assigned me a small room with a cot, desk, and lamp. Simple but functional.

I called Mrs. Cheney in hospital administration, "My roommate Atsushi Herito was hit by a bus…"

Before I could finish she interrupted me, "I heard, I am very sorry, he's listed as stable but critical. He's in the ortho recovery, fifth floor. Mandy Richards is the charge nurse, and you know how good she is."

"Thanks, Mrs. Cheney."

I decided to wait a few hours before trying to see Atsushi. I lay down and contemplated the situation. I had finally met Aimi, but in the process, I had pissed off her father and was being blamed for the accident.

After pacing for three hours, I couldn't wait any longer. I had to hear about Atsushi. I dialed the room number and Aimi picked up.

"Aimi, it's Lawrence. How is your brother?"

"He is sleeping, he is stable and not in any immediate danger. He woke up in a lot of pain, but his tests came back and he does not have brain problem. I cannot talk, my father will be back soon."

"Aimi, I am glad your brother will be fine. I am terribly sorry about what happened to him." I stood and paced around the room. "I know the timing is terrible but, I have to see you again and talk a little."

"Lawrence, we have tickets to go back tomorrow. I don't know if Mother and I will go home or stay, but my father is staying until Atsushi is better."

"Is it possible to see you before you leave?" I paused and held my breath.

"I don't know, but I wish to see you before I go."

My heart jumped. I froze. "You can't leave tomorrow. I'll come up there."

"No, don't come up. My father will be angry."

My fingers tightened on the phone. "What can I do to see you?"

"Tomorrow morning at 6:00 AM, I will be writing in the hotel lobby. Come there. I must go, Lawrence. Good-bye."

The abrupt hang-up took me by surprise, but she wanted to see me and I was on cloud nine. I lay on the bed and thought about the evening's events and Aimi. My feelings for her were real and strong. I could not let them go. This love is what Elizabeth Barrett Browning meant when she wrote, *How Do I Love Thee?*

Christina had been stationed at Wright Patterson Air Force Base in Ohio. I needed to talk with her. A sleepy voice answered, "Hello, Captain Gonzalez."

I was relieved. "It's Lawrence. How are you?"

"Lawrence, is everything okay?"

"I'm fine. Nothing's wrong. I just need your help."

"It's almost midnight. Are you drinking?"

"No, I'm not. Listen, you were always honest with me, and I need help with a girl."

"A girl?"

"I met someone and I really like her."

"I'm happy for you. I'm jealous, why are you calling to tell me?"

I spent the next thirty minutes burning a hole in her ear, talking about my feelings.

I ended by saying, "She's my roommates' sister. I just met her. She's from Japan and is wonderful. I'm falling for her after our dinner last night. But her father and brothers don't want me to have anything to do with her."

"Last night? What? Are you crazy? Cool your jets. You only know this girl one night and you have fallen in love with her? You don't know anything about her."

"You don't understand." I shook my head. "I might love her."

"Take your time." She let out a long sigh. "Your whole life has been in the orphanage and school. Experience life, see the world, and don't fall in love with the first pretty skirt."

"I thought you would understand."

"Listen next month, I get thirty days' leave. Let's do something together, take a trip, see the sights."

"I can't. I'm working eighty hours a week as an intern."

"Okay, but don't do anything before we have a chance to talk."

"OK, I appreciate you letting me wake you up."

"I'm always on your side. I'm always your best friend."

I wanted to change the subject. "By the way, how's the Air Force? How's Ohio?"

"Lawrence, it's too late and I'm too tired to talk about the Air Force. Call me tomorrow and I'll tell you everything. Get some rest and I will, too."

I wondered if I was just desperate to find love.

CHAPTER 15

Hopeless News, 1993

I called a cab to take me to her hotel. As we drove through town, the cab hit pot-holes. Hanging from the mirror, the little Puerto Rican flag waved red, white and blue. The driver jammed on his brakes at the entrance to the hotel. Bright moonlight illuminated my wallet – thank God the ride was only ten bucks, but the driver growled at me when I gave him a measly one-dollar tip.

"Hey, I'm short. I'll hit you next time."

I entered the glass doors into the lobby. The garden ambience was enhanced with all the green palms and red hibiscus flowers. Every surface and corner had some tree, bush, or flower that brightened the air. The place had an aroma of natural perfume.

I scanned the room for Aimi. I didn't see her but spied a coffee pot by the concierge desk. A uniformed cop was filling his cup as I walked up and nodded. He grunted and left. I filled a Styrofoam cup, added two sugars, one creamer, stirred, and sipped, allowing the strong rich coffee to warm me.

I headed over to the elevators, trying to exude a confidence that said I belonged. I paced in front of the stainless-steel doors, glancing at my watch. Every time the elevator bell chimed, I tensed up. After ten minutes, my watch said 6:04. I thought about calling up but decided to wait in a brown leather chair.

After a few minutes, I heard the elevator stop. The doors parted to form a silver picture frame. Centered in the back of the car was a vision in all white that drew my eyes, like magnets, to her. She was an angelic image, jeans, a snowy silk blouse, and pure white tennis shoes, her glossy black hair cascading across her shoulders. It took me a moment to recognize Aimi in American clothes. My heart rate went into overdrive.

Everything moved in slow motion as if I were underwater, watching the scene unfold. She came to the front of the elevator, placed her hand on the door, and scanned the room. Then I rose and waved to her.

"Hi, over here."

"Lawrence, it is nice to see you." She gave a small nod. "You are so good to my brothers, I almost feel like you are my fourth brother." She sounded sincere, but no way did I want to be her brother. I took her laptop from her hand to carry it for her.

I gathered my thoughts. "Can I get you some coffee?" I pointed to the pot. "They have it over there. Maybe tea?"

"Tea would be nice. Thank you." She smiled.

We walked over. "You said you're a writer. Can I read your work sometime?"

She blushed. "I cannot show anyone. Just beginnings of college student. They are not ready." Finding a pot of hot water, I put a tea bag in a cup and poured. I pointed at the sugar and cream. She picked up a packet and emptied it into her cup. I nodded to a secluded area I had seen earlier, partially hidden behind bushes.

We sat in the alcove with soft lights. Pictures of moonlit seascapes were hung on two walls. She put down her tea and opened her laptop. Inside, there was a yellow legal pad lying across the keys. She touched the pad. *I wish she would touch me with those delicate fingers.* She kept the pad facedown, put it to the side, and turned on her screen. MS Word came up, then a page full of writing. "I will tell you one story I wrote last month, but don't laugh at me."

I shook my head.

She read in a soft voice. My heart raced, wanting to be near her, and my mind wandered all over her body. I didn't hear much of what she read, despite making a concerted effort.

Then she said, "I wrote this line I really like and that says how I feel."

I looked into her eyes

"Trust is the sugar in the bakery of the heart. Life without trust is cake without sugar." She looked up and into my eyes. "What do you think?"

"Trust is the sugar of a relationship? Is that what you mean?"

She laughed, "No, trust is to a relationship like sugar is to baking a cake. The relationship cannot be complete or even appreciated without trust." She became serious. "Lawrence, women require trust."

I cleared my throat. I needed to reassure her that I was a person of trust. "My father, on his deathbed, revealed that he had a wife and it was not my mother. I was devastated. My father made me swear that I would never be unfaithful. His last words were, "Be faithful to your family, Lawrence. Your wife and your kids. Be better than me."

A small thoughtful frown covered her mouth. "I am sorry to hear about your father."

"Thanks, it was a long time ago. The point is about being trustworthy."

Her lips parted slightly as she raised her cup, the lips I wanted to press into mine.

I moved over and sat next to her. I must have gotten too close, because she shifted away. "Aimi." I had to clear my throat again. "I am the trustworthy person for you."

"Lawrence, how can we be together?" I am not the girl for you. My mother and I have to go to Japan this afternoon."

"Today?" I spread my hands wide. "You can't…can't leave today."

"I must. My parents have already decided whom I will marry when I am done with university. Lawrence, family obligations call on me to obey their desires."

"You can't." I struggled for the right words. "I am joining the Air Force and coming to Japan. You can't marry anyone else until you give me a chance."

"You are a fine man, and I am sure you are very nice. But I do not know you, and I must follow family traditions. I do not like it, and my grandmother hates the idea of arranged marriage, but Father says I must."

Cold washed over me. Aimi stood and excused herself. She left her laptop on the table and walked across the lobby. I felt like the rug had been pulled out from under me; my mind was a whirl. She never really said she liked me, was I in way over my head? Was Christina right? Was it just my need to have someone close to me? Was I just infatuated? But my heart felt like more than infatuation was wrapped around it. I had to think of something.

I knew I could make Aimi mine if only I had a chance. She thought of me as a brother, which made me shake my head. Wanting to write down her address in Japan, I picked up the yellow pad. Turning it over, I was elated to see my name surrounded by hearts.

I wanted another cup of coffee. I picked up her laptop and pad and walked toward the pots. I met her halfway. "More tea?"

I heard the elevator door open and a shout. Dr. Herito huffed over and grabbed Aimi by the arm, pulling her away from me. He spoke roughly to her in Japanese. She hung her head, blushed, and walked into the elevator. Dr. Herito snatched her laptop and legal pad from me and scowled as the elevator doors closed. *She is leaving and her father is mad at me again. I can't seem to catch a break.*

Back at the interns' dormitory, I was exhausted. I fell asleep immediately and slept like a log until 1:00 PM. Even then, my eyes burned and I was groggy.

Calling up to Atsushi's room, I found that the family had been there but had left earlier, *they must have gone to the airport.*

The nurse said Atsushi was recovering fine and sleeping. I showered and rushed out the door to grab a cab. I had to say goodbye.

I ran through the doors into the JAL terminal and down the concourse looking for the Tokyo flight. I ran and ran. It must have been a half mile and the terminal was packed. There were scores of people tugging rolling suitcases in an endless parade. I found my way to Gate 33C and saw the plane pulling back from the jetway. I was shattered. I'd missed my chance for the woman of my dreams.

She was going back to a loveless marriage to some rich guy. I hung my head and trudged back through the terminal, immersed in the misery of missing my chance for true love. I would never see her again.

CHAPTER 16

MUTUAL ATTRACTION

Three days later, unshaven and disheartened, I wandered down the corridor of the orthopedic recovery unit and opened Atsushi's door. I placed *Some Prefer Nettles* and *Shogun* on the table – I had finished reading *Some Prefer Nettles* the night before and just started *Shogun*– and stared at him. He was connected to the O-scopes, which registered normal heart rate and high BP. His wrist felt warm, and the pulse was strong and reassuring. *Old friend, you are going to make it, but I don't know if I will.*

I pulled his chart from the foot of the bed. In the OR, Atsushi had undergone femoral stabilization with an intramedullary nail in the longest bone in his body. In recovery, he was prescribed nonsteroidal anti-inflammatories for the wound, and opioids for the pain. After extensive physical therapy, his prognosis was full recovery within four to six months.

"Lawrence?" He surprised me by mumbling my name.

"Atsushi, let me look at you." I pulled back his lid and stared into his eye. "Move your right hand." He wiggled his fingers.

"Lawrence, you are no ortho. When was the last time you shaved? You look like hell."

"No, no," I shook my head. "I'm just checking you out, buddy. Can't have you limping for the rest of your life. What's your name?"

"Dr. Know-It-All," he laughed, "You look like an unshaved street bum." He coughed.

"I've had a couple of days off and have been lazy."

"Where is your sister?"

"Buddy, they went home two days ago," his words tweaking my heart. I felt down and all alone. Disguising that I felt dejected, I grabbed the plastic water pitcher and poured him a glass. "Are you sure you're ok?"

"Me ok? You ok? They did not leave, they changed plans."

He flopped back. He had a crooked grin and haughty, laughing eyes. "Now I know why you not around for the last two days." He grabbed the side of his head. "Migraine." He glanced down at the traction supporting his leg.

"Aimi is still here?" Hope coursed through my veins. But I knew that I had to play it cool.

"Let's check you out better." I had to find out more. "So, your family didn't leave?" I pulled out my light and looked into his eyes. "Wiggle your right toes." He did so. "What was your college major?" *I have to see Aimi.*

"I majored in coed physiology," he coughed. "I plan to examine every nurse at the hospital. It may take some time."

"Quit fooling around? Is Aimi really here?"

I was so engrossed in listening for an answer between his laughs that I had not heard the door open. "Snap your fingers. What is your brother's name?"

"My brother is Slacker." He smiled and looked behind me. I twisted around and found Dr. Herito and Aimi standing in the doorway.

"What are you doing here? Leave at once," Dr. Herito said.

Atsushi spoke, "Seriously, Papa-san, Lawrence performed a full examination. I am fine. Right, *Doctor* Lawrence?"

"Atsushi, my friend. I'm no surgeon. Your father is."

"Listen, I'm fine." He waved his hands and snapped his fingers at the same time. "Just get me some food. I haven't eaten in a week."

"You have head trauma," Dr. Herito said. "Don't be so impetuous, my son. I will speak to your physician." He huffed out of the room.

I smiled at Aimi, and Atsushi noticed. "Lawrence, take Aimi, get real food. I'm tired of lukewarm oatmeal and watery tomato soup. Italian sub with double meat." Mrs. Herito glided in, gave me a small smile, and placed her hand on his forehead.

"Are you sure?"

"Yeah, a supersized Dr. Pepper™ with fries and lots of catsup."

Picking up my books, I looked to Aimi. She smiled, shrugged, and walked out the door with me following. "Come. Lawrence." She waved me forward. "We can get him food."

In the elevator, I tried to stand very close to her. She pulled back.

"Atsushi told my father that the accident was not your fault. He said you reached out and tried to stop him when he looked right. My father was mad the other morning because we met without a chaperone and without telling him. I told him that I explained the situation to you, and that I am already spoken for."

My heart sang, maybe not so much for Dr. Herito's understanding as to be near this beauty and to continue my quest. *She may think that she is spoken for, but until she marries him, I am not giving up.*

"I am very happy that you are staying." The doors opened into the cafeteria.

While in the food line, Aimi said, "We will stay in America until Atsushi is released."

Sitting in the chair across from her, I scooted it nearer. I tasted my Dr. Pepper™, trying to come up with something to say.

"What are you reading?" She looked at my book.

"Well, I finished reading *Some Prefer Nettles*, it was excellent, thank you for the suggestion. I am half way through *Shogun* by Clavell, a great Australian novel about Japan." I turned the cover of the book to her.

She looked at it reverently. "My professor said that I must read English more. A good book?" She turned her face up to me. Her green eyes sparkled and her dimple flashed.

"Of course, it's fantastic. Here, you can have it." I held it out to her.

"No, you are not done with it."

"Please, I would love for you to read it." I sensed she was not comfortable with our interaction. I wanted her to take my book, a way of accepting me. I cleared my throat. "Oh, take it. I have read it before."

The uncomfortable pause engulfed me again. Thank goodness, her mother padded up to us with a broad smile. She took my hand in both of hers. Mrs. Herito spoke in Japanese and Aimi interpreted.

"Mama-san says that Atsushi explained you tried to stop him from running into the bus. He said you almost got hit yourself. Mama-san thanks you humbly." Mrs. Herito had a motherly warmth in her eyes. She sat beside Aimi, and I got up to get her a cup of tea and a donut.

When I returned, mother and daughter were having an intense discussion. Mrs. Herito pointed for me to take the chair across from her.

Sitting beside her mother, Aimi looked my way and said, "We will spend each day nursing Atsushi in shifts. Father will start at 10:00 AM, when the doctors are there, so he can speak to them and thus assist my brother best. Hideki will take over and stay until 3:00 or 4:00 PM to help him walk and perform physical therapy. In the early morning, when I normally write anyway, I will stay in Atsushi's room with my computer. Mother-san will come at meal times to supervise his diet and recovery. It is a good plan. No?"

I nodded. *I will get to be with you every morning.* After fifteen minutes, we left the cafeteria, and I stopped by the elevator to say good-bye. Mrs. Herito reached up and held my head in both hands. She smiled at me, and I could see a hint of love, or at least a hint of like in her eyes. I gave her Atsushi's sandwich and drink, and they left. I returned to the interns' dormitory to catch some Z's.

I must have been more tired than usual because I slept all evening and awoke at 5:00 AM, I showered, cleaned up, and read the newspaper. At 6:00 AM, I strolled down the hallway to Atsushi's room.

The charge nurse smiled at me. "Atsushi is doing well."

"Is he awake?"

"He wasn't fifteen minutes ago, but his sister is in there."

I smiled and continued to Atsushi's room. His door was ajar. I silently pushed it open. The room was dimly lit, and Aimi was sitting at a desk facing the window overlooking the lighted Miami skyline. I crept past the sleeping Atsushi and stood behind her, loving the tranquil sight and the feeling of closeness. The lights and full moon were breathtaking. An enchanting jasmine aroma wafted up from her, putting me in a trance. I stared into her shiny black hair. The reflected lights sparkled like stars and blended perfectly into the city scene through the window. I imagined us walking on the beach in the bright sunlight, kicking at the water lapping at our feet. Darting around in front of us was Buddy, running into the waves, chasing his old ratty, green tennis ball.

I felt a surge of hope, like the world would be a better place. She surprised me. She twisted around in her chair. "Hi, Lawrence. How are you?"

"Nice to see you." I felt a magical attraction to her and wanted to say more, but she was a little bird I didn't want to scare away. "I was checking on your brother."

She looked over to the bed. "He is resting. His leg is not hurting so much."

Still fearful of frightening her away, I decided it was the appropriate time to leave. "I have to return to my rounds. Hope to see you later." She waved absentmindedly.

Over the next two weeks, I invented all variety of medical pretexts to stroll down the fifth floor and into his room. I examined Atsushi's chart and leg. My heart ached to touch and kiss Aimi. She often worked, absorbed in her writing, barely noticing me. On occasion, she lowered her book and asked about an obscure word or how I was doing. These moments gave me strength as I went about my business. When she didn't look my way, I stole glances at her and caught whiffs of her perfume.

A day later, when I woke, I had an hour to kill before my shift. I hurried down the corridor of the fifth floor. Atsushi was awake, and Aimi was by the window. She was sitting on the couch with her legs curled up under her, reading *Shogun*. She wore a long white summer dress and the white running shoes. Her hair was sparkling black and up in a bun, adorned with a white scrunchy. I had meant to walk away without bothering her, yet, somehow, I found myself standing in front of her, staring. She glanced up at me. A hint of a smile crossed her face.

"Morning." I smiled back. "I did not mean to disturb you."

"Good morning," she said.

"And how does your writing go?"

She fluttered her hand. "Just so-so. But I am enjoying this book you loaned me. Japan is more like *Some Prefer Nettles* than *Shogun* now."

"I'm glad you like the book." She was acting nonchalant toward me.

"When you come to Japan you will see much different culture."

A therapist walked in.

Atsushi called out, "Lawrence, give me a hand."

I went around to the side and helped him adjust his pillows to change angles. The white-smocked physiotherapist began exercising Atsushi's leg and rubbing his hip. Atsushi groaned.

Behind me, I heard, "Rarence, happy you see." It was Mrs. Herito.

"Mrs. Herito, you speak English?"

She laughed and said something in Japanese to Atsushi. "Mother is trying to learn English. I am helping her, and she asks for you to help sometime, also," Aimi said.

I stood and bowed to her. "I would be honored."

"You son, no bow, Rarence."

"Mom, it's L-Lawrence." Aimi emphasized the letter L. "Law-Law- pronounce the L."

I smiled. "That is a very tough sound for Japanese."

Later that night in bed, I thought of the way the bright sunlight danced across Aimi's face. I replayed our conversation, trying to find a hint of love in her words. I couldn't remember if she had said *I hope you come to Japan* or *when you come to Japan*. I twisted in my sheets, wondering if she were sending me a signal. Finally, I leapt out of bed and prepared for my daily rounds.

Early one morning, I walked into Atsushi's room to find Aimi staring out the picture window at the skyline. I walked around the bed to stand next to her and admire the view.

"Hi Lawrence, Atsushi has gone to physical therapy and will be back in a little bit."

"Ok, I have a little while before I need to start my rounds. Do you want to get a cup of tea?"

"No thank you, I just finished one."

Not wanting to leave her, I quickly pivoted to small talk. "What are you studying in college?"

"I study to become a teacher." She put her hands together. "I love children."

"I think you would make a great teacher. Probably you can teach your own children as well."

Casting her eyes to the floor, she mumbled, "I will have children perhaps." Her brow furrowed. "The man my father wants me to marry has four grown children. He does not want more." Her eyes were sad.

"What a crime to deny you children, you're young and vibrant. Children would make you complete."

"This is not to be," she shrugged. "My father has decided."

My eyes burned. "I want to have children. We can have children together."

She turned to face me and put her finger to my lips. "I like you, Lawrence, but my father has decided. He will not allow me to think otherwise."

I took a small step closer to her, and she did not step away. I put my hands on her hips and she flowed into my arms. I hugged her. *If I kiss her, she will feel my love. Do I dare kiss her?* Her eyes were somewhere between wonder and gentle love, and for the first time, I saw golden flecks in them. I ached to kiss her, knowing that I could lose the chance forever. My heart raced, my palms were sweaty, and longing became unbearable.

I kissed her. Her lips were smooth as a rose petal, soft as a lover's whisper. She looked surprised. Then her eyes relaxed. She closed them and melted into my arms. The warmth of her body sent a current through me. She reached up, put both arms around my neck and hugged me into her. I was warm and safe and full of hope.

I placed my hand on the back of her head, and my heart swelled. I was floating. I heard her murmur, "Mmmmm." My left arm was around her waist and I touched her bare skin. I cuddled her in. Her taste was romance, her smell flowers, and she felt like forever. I wanted to stay connected with her for the rest of my life. I would never let go.

Enwrapping her delicate body made me feel big, like a knight in shining armor protecting my maiden. She looked into my eyes, and I kissed her again. She reached up her hand and caressed my face, then pulled my head closer and kissed me. I felt her need. I felt love. Her eyes grinned at me in agreement.

The door behind us opened. "What is going on here?" Dr. Herito asked. "Daughter, get away from that gaijin."

I jumped back, but I kept my fingers touching her arm. I had gained new resolve and was determined not to cower in his presence. She made me strong.

"I love Aimi. I want to have a chance to get to know her better. I want children, she wants children."

"Get out. Aimi is spoken for. She not marrying you."

She moved from my side, stood directly in front of her father, and calmly said, "I am not a child. I am grown woman." She bowed her head in respect, and I heard her voice, soft and full of hope. "I want to make my own decisions. I want children."

Dr. Herito turned bright red. "Do not speak so in the presence of this gaijin." He turned to me. "Go, or I will call security."

I turned to Aimi and mouthed, "I love you." She smiled and I left.

The next morning, after a long restless night, I went to Atsushi's room as always. On the desk was an envelope. My name was written on it in her delicate left-slant handwriting. I picked it up, and Dr. Herito entered.

I put the envelope in my pocket.

He looked a mess, hair uncombed, and suit wrinkled, rare for such a meticulous man. He hustled to Atsushi's side.

"Sir, I have to ask you something."

"Not now, Lawrence. No. I know your trick. It will not work."

"Sir, I love your daughter. I am an honest man, true…"

"Well, she is gone home to Japan. You will never see her again."

My mouth gaped. I was stunned. "Dr. Herito, I love Aimi, and I think she loves me."

He looked at me with blood in his eyes. "You know nothing of honor or love. Aimi is marrying a Nissan."

I glared at him. "She's gone?"

"Do not think about my daughter. She is spoken for and will be married very soon." He stormed out.

I headed back to my sparsely furnished apartment. Feeling alone, I took off my lab coat and threw it on my bed. The envelope slid out of my pocket and glided to the ground. With all the commotion, I had forgotten to read it.

Overcoming reluctance comes easy to an orphan because we know rejection and loneliness. So, I faced my fears and picked up the note, turning it over to examine it in detail. The paper was fine linen, warm in my fingers. I smelled a whiff of jasmine emanating from it.

Dearest Lawrence-San,

I am sorry about the circumstances of our parting. Papa-San is sending me back to Japan today. He does not want me to ever see you again. This is pain to my heart, as I have feelings for you. I am in a difficult position as family demands I marry traditional Japanese. I wish to see you again, but it is not possible. Do not tell my brothers about this letter.

    If you wish to write to me, you can send a letter to my girl-friend.

Yumi Sanoka
White Lotus House
24-123 Istanoku
Tokyo, Japan 227-0038
Deepest Respects,
Aimi

My face was hot. I jumped up and paced around the room. *She has feelings for me, she wants to see me again, but is held back by her family. I will get stationed in Japan and then worry about winning over her father.*

All night, I dreamt of Aimi and our life together. I was so excited. I woke at 4:00 AM to write her a letter.

Dearest Aimi,

I found the letter you left for me. I am so happy that you have feel-ings for me. I understand that your family has plans for you, but I am persistent, and I will win your father over. I have never felt this way about another person in my life. I want to see you as soon as I can. I will do anything to get to Japan and spend time with you. You are beautiful, and I wish to know you much better and see you more often.

I will be leaving to start my Air Force training in the next month. Training lasts for twelve weeks and then I will receive my first assignment. I will try to be stationed in Japan. If I cannot, I will come to Tokyo on leave to meet with you. My heart sings for you, my eyes dream of you, and my soul burns to know you better.

I miss you already.

Lawrence Leo
Lt. Lawrence Leo
General Delivery
Wright Patterson AFB, Ohio

CHAPTER 17

WING-MAN, 1997

The aircraft slammed down on the runway at Wright Patterson AFB, knocking me into the side window. I seized the armrests. Another passenger gasped. The tires screamed with agony, and the smell of burning rubber permeated through the ventilation system. The officer sitting next to me sweated profusely through his blue Air Force uniform. Tall and thin, with tanned skin the color of a worn saddle, his chest was covered in medals. His large head was roofed in curly black hair. An enormous watch, bright silver aviator sunglasses and wings and gold major's leaves completed his uniform.

He spoke with a slow southern twang. "Shiiit, partner, what a landing."

"Geez, do Air Force pilots always land like that?" I asked.

"Partner, we say any landing you walk away from is a good landing. If you can use the equipment again, it's a great landing."

I retrieved my bag and followed. He strutted like an athlete. We joined a long line of passengers deplaning from the military jet. As we passed the open cockpit door, the pilot - with an apologetic look on his face and captain's bars on his shoulders – was standing there saying good-bye. Behind him, slinking down in a seat turned toward the open door, was a second lieutenant.

Major said through the open door. "You almos' broke my back, Lieutenant. Did you log three landings for those last two bounces across the runway?" He had a broad smile.

As we descended the staircase onto the tarmac, my seatmate introduced himself, "I'm Bob Kimball. Call me Chuck."

"Lawrence Leo, a new flight surgeon." We shook hands.

"Welcome to our humble abode. I'll give you a lift to the BOQ."

"What's that?"

"That's your new home. The Bachelor Officer's Quarters, or as we like to call it, Disneyland, Ohio."

Chuck raced his truck across the base and took me to the Orderly Room. I checked in and received my schedule and a package of instructions outlining life for the next twelve weeks in the Aerospace Medicine Primary Course. I was taking classes in Aviation Medicine, Military Customs, and Courtesy.

Later, I sat at the desk in my Q room and wrote Aimi another letter. I decided to tone down my enthusiasm. I didn't want to scare her away. I had an overwhelming feeling that this was the best chance I would have to find my soulmate.

Chuck came to my room and looked around. "Partner, this is kind of bare. You'll get better digs when you graduate. Don't be a barracks rat, let's go to the O' Club. I hear there is a gaggle of nurses starting training in your class. Let's go bag some chicks."

I followed Chuck into the Officers' Club. "All the new students go to the Rathskeller in the basement where there's a great DJ and cheap drinks."

From behind, I noticed that Chuck had a John Wayne swagger as we ambled up to the bar. He looked to his left where six young women in civilian dresses sat at a wooden table.

Chuck beamed at me. "Partner, in Air Force talk, this is a target-rich environment."

"I don't, I don't know about…"

"Quit your babbling. You're my wingman. When I cut one from the pack, you back me up and take her wing-woman for a ride. Help me get her alone." He winked.

Chuck walked over to the table and said, "Howdy, ladies. I'm Chuck, the official welcoming committee to our luxurious Officers' Club. First drink's on me."

He pulled up a stool next to the cutest blonde and straddled it. He raised his arm in the air, pointed his index finger to the sky, and made a circular motion to the waiter nearby. The waiter hurried to the bar to retrieve a round.

Blondie regarded Chuck with a mischievous turn of her head and said, "Well, thank you. Are you a general?" She smiled sweetly with a nod to her girlfriend.

"No, ma'am. Just a humble major. But I am an instructor on this here very base."

A dark-haired woman looked me directly in the eye, pulled an empty seat closer, and pointed to it for me to sit. My heart fluttered, she reminded me of Christina. I felt hot. I lowered my eyes; my first instinct was to look for a place to escape. I sat down instead, just as the drinks arrived.

Dark Hair leaned in, "I'm Maria, a new nurse."

"Hi, Maria. I'm new here too. Just learning the ropes from Chuck."

"Chuck seems to be quite the dude."

He stood with the blonde girl, and they strolled to the dance floor. I wondered if I should ask Maria to dance. Two of the other girls got up and danced together. Maria took my hand and pulled me to the dance floor. I felt like everyone was staring.

"Loosen up, Cowboy. We're just dancing."

She was right. I was tight. I relaxed and did my imitation of the moonwalk across the floor.

"There you go," Maria laughed.

In ten minutes, I was sweating. The DJ announced a break, and we walked back to the table. When we sat down, she pulled her chair over closer and stared into my eyes.

She reminded me of Christina. Hispanic complexion, black hair, dark eyes and similar perfume.

"Where are you from, Chris…Maria?"

"I'm from New Orleans, and I have been stationed here for three months. I miss Cajun food, you know, we love crawdads, okra and cornbread. Where you from?"

"I'm from Miami. This is the longest trip I ever took. I think I'm going to like it." I smiled at her and she smiled back. We drank gin and tonics, and I ordered a second round.

Chuck shouted, "Barkeep, make 'em doubles, we got a lot of time to make up for." He was swapping spit with Blondie. The music had changed to Marvin Gaye's "Let's Get It On."

I asked Maria to dance. She snuggled into my chest. She placed her hand on the small of my back and pulled me to her. All too soon, the music ended, and we returned to our table.

Chuck jumped up and grabbed Blondie by the hand. "Darlin' let's play some pool." I grabbed Maria's hand and we ran to the long green table. "Rack 'em, Cowboy."

I racked while he ordered drinks. "Doubles," he said again.

Maria snatched a cue from the wall stand. When she bent over the table, I could see down her blouse, and any chance I had of looking away went out the window.

During the third game, and the fourth or fifth gin and tonic, I lined up a shot and got dizzy. I felt like I was about to fall over. "I've had enough."

"Me, too," Maria said. "Let's get out of here. I have an apartment off base."

We jitter-bugged to the bar, and I paid my tab. We strolled out to the parking lot, where she had a new red Mustang. She opened the door, and I turned around and planted a strong wet kiss on her. "That's the tiger I want in my tank," she said.

We went to Maria's apartment, and I had a drink while she excused herself. She came back into the living room wearing a peek-a-boo white negligee. She turned down the lights, and my heart raced. Her dark skin peeped through the lace, and a whiff of flowery perfume made me catch my breath. *Christina.* We made love. At 3:00 AM, she drove me back to the BOQ, and I passed out.

WHOOP-WHOOP-WHOOP! An alarm screamed that kicked me awake and brought adrenaline flashing through my body. I ran out into the hall in my pajamas – thank God I had gotten rid of the Spider-Man ones- and met a flood of other students. There were emergency lights flashing in the hallway and red EXIT signs illuminated over the staircase. The students shuffled to the stairs and went down.

Someone yelled, "Who the fuck calls a fire alarm at 4:00 AM?"

On the lawn of the building, the fire marshal had a bullhorn up to his mouth. "This is a test of the fire evacuation system. Assemble here and after roll call, you will be permitted back into your quarters." I recognized some of the other people on the lawn from my flight.

"If you think this has been an amazing night, Partner, wait until you see what I have planned for tomorrow," Chuck shouted to me across the lawn.

CHAPTER 18

SURVIVAL TRAINING

I completed the Aerospace Medicine Primary Course by concentrating on the problem of restricting antihistamines for aviators prior to flight. This became my advanced area of study. In addition, I spent a great deal of time researching other medications prohibited before flight.

We were required to endure a short course in survival training. Survival School was necessary because flight surgeons, though not pilots, fly on missions every month. In this capacity, we face the possibility of bailing out over hostile territory and navigating back to friendly areas. For this course, we spent five days sleeping outdoors in a tent in a forest a few miles from the base. The instructors showed us how to navigate with a compass and find our way using the stars.

Beholding the stars made my heart beat faster thinking that Aimi could see the same celestial bodies. On cold nights, these thoughts warmed me up, inside and out.

Back at our base, I saw Chuck in passing. He seemed to have a great number of smart comments to make, referring to the nurses and our one night out. I found his comments cheapening and so I avoided him.

Several weekend nights, I stayed with Maria – nothing serious but lots of fun. I felt guilty. I was thinking of Aimi when I was alone. When I was with Maria, I thought about Christina. My head was confused, my body was stimulated, but my heart was Aimi's.

After AMPC, I sortied to flight training at Shephard AFB, Texas. This phase of training started with the "G" familiarization segment. I jumped on the High-G chair, tightened the lap belt, and spun at a fantastic rate until the chair reached eight G's. While spinning, I was told to lift my hand and operate the controls. The pressure was astounding. I couldn't lift my hand or hold my head up. My neck felt as though it would break. Despite the strain, I passed my high G test.

The advanced students warned me of the second segment of training, the altitude chamber. Students called it *The Chamber of Horrors*.

Wide-eyed when I arrived, I was greeted by Sergeant Washman. The students secretly nicknamed him Washout. He explained that our training would include night orientation, spacial disorientation, high G's pressure breathing and egress procedures.

"If you are going to panic in an airplane, my job is to have you fail in the chamber now. I will teach you how to handle high altitude pressure, so you can survive. That way, no one is hurt, and you can walk away with some of your dignity intact without damaging an Air Force airplane."

Nine students, two instructors, and I were seated in a long altitude chamber with four small round windows. The thing is like the inside of an aircraft fuselage, or submarine. It's painted a dull green with a few baseball-size windows. The big pressure door slammed home with a deep metallic clunk, and the locking wheel spun closed. Washout told us to don our oxygen masks and test the airflow. Mine was good, so I was ready when they signaled they were removing some air and taking the chamber up in altitude. I heard many pressure valves swish open and closed, then saw a large altitude gauge – the red dial pointed to 1,000 feet.

The instructor pulled a valve and leveled off, the pressurized air swished through the pipes. "Take off your oxygen masks," he said. There was no degradation in breathing. I felt fine.

Donning our masks, we went to 10,000 feet and repeated the exercise. The air felt thin, but I was still able to breathe.

At 15,000 feet, when I removed my mask, I took three breaths and felt light-headed. After a minute, I felt dizzy, the room was spinning, and my vision was blurry. Washout instructed us to replace our masks and raised the altitude again.

At 18,000 feet, my right premolar started to throb. I thought it was nothing, so I didn't say a word to Washout. At 21,000 feet, the tooth throbbed like a jackhammer pounding on me. I signaled to level the ascent off. The signal to level was to hold my right hand out in front of myself with the palm down and move the hand side to side to catch the instructor's attention. By that time, I was sweating so much, my shirt was drenched as if I'd been caught in a rainstorm. The pain was unbearable. The instructor noticed me struggling, and came over to ask, "What's the problem?"

"My tooth is burning a hole in my mouth," I spoke over my internal microphone for the first time.

"Do you have a filling?"

"Yes, that's what hurts, but I don't want to quit."

"It's called Dental Barotrauma," he said, signaling the other instructor handling the controls.

"We'll take you down to the air lock. Go to the dentist, and he'll replace your filling. Then you can complete this flight tomorrow."

The dentist replaced my filling, and I completed training without any further problems.

The Chief Medical Assignment Detailer asked for my dream sheet. I filled it out immediately and sent it in, listing my three top choices for my first assignment.

#1 Japan

#2 Japan

#3 Japan

I wasn't surprised when I received orders to Yokota, Japan.

Looking at the gleaming C-141 Starlifter, I thought – *This is the most important journey of my life. This IS my life.*

CHAPTER 19

BULL SWAGGERS BACK, JAN. 1997

"Flying across the Pacific in an Air Force C-141 Starlifter is like being chained down to a bed-o-nails in an insane asylum," the sergeant sitting next to me screamed over the roar of the jet engines. "These military planes are incredibly noisy."

I was in the 150-foot-long cargo hold of the primary airlift airplane that jetted to my new assignment at Yokota Air Base outside Tokyo, Japan. The uncomfortable web seats made my butt fall asleep and shoulders ache. The bare interior had damn little insulation. Without the insulation, the flight was shivering cold and rock concert loud.

Two passengers joked about starting a fire in the cargo like they heard happened on a Russian military jet flying over Siberia. "All them Russkies died," the sergeant said. "A hundred less we got to kill," he joked.

I heard, or rather felt, the engine sound decrease, and the nose of the big jet declined earthward by three degrees. We prepared to land. The aircraft descended for fifteen minutes as I looked out of one of only six round windows. We slid downward through a grey layer of concealing clouds that looked dirty and cold. As I gazed into the clouds, I could see Aimi's beautiful face. I wished I could see her as soon as we landed.

A tap on my shoulder startled me. The loadmaster pointed to his seat, made a buckling signal, and used his hand to show we were landing. I buckled in with a red canvas seat belt and pulled it tight, wondering if it was as safe as civilian belts in commercial aircraft. We landed in a rain shower. I dodged drops and ran into the passenger terminal shivering, alone and wet. Maybe I had made a drastic mistake coming to Japan and chasing an impossible dream.

I reported in at the Hospital Squadron Orderly Room. My present location was now officially recognized. I raced to the Base Post Office to see if there was any mail from Aimi. Jumping up two steps at a time, my heart pounded when I asked, "Any mail for Captain Leo?"

"Let me look," the young airman said. "Got nothing for you, Captain."

I retreated to the bachelor office quarters to set up my room. I had only the clothes in my suitcase. I put those away neatly in a drawer and walked to the Base Exchange. I wondered why it was called an exchange. *Maybe, some old-fashioned hold over from Civil War days?*

I passed a row of hearts set up for Valentine's Day, and remembered it was almost my thirtieth birthday. I bought the biggest heart to give to Aimi, if I ever found her. I wondered when and how I would see her again, and if we would be a couple. I fell asleep, my heart aching.

In the morning, I followed another new doctor around for in-processing. We had to bring our appropriate records to Base Finance, Personnel, and the Education offices. I checked to make sure that the monthly allotment of ten percent of my pay would still go to God's Home. After lunch at the BX snack bar, we went back to the orderly room for base orientation.

There were about sixteen new (mostly E-1's and E-2's) eighteen-to twenty-year-old kids and I was a brand new captain. We sat in desks in a small classroom to wait for the ordeal to begin. "How long does this in-processing last?" I asked the guy next to me. "When do we practice medicine?"

"A couple of days. In the meantime, we have stuff to do, and you have to get a license if you want to drive a car over here," the guy said.

"I didn't think about that. I'll need a car. I know some people here, and I want to drive and see the country."

A sergeant with a diamond sewn on his sleeve came in. I had learned that the diamond showed he was a first sergeant, in charge of discipline. He shouted, "Room, atten-shun!"

We all jumped up and stood at attention. I thought this was rather childish, but knew formal introductions were a routine part of military customs when a senior officer entered the room. I stood erect, looking straight ahead, and heard someone marching with taps on his shoes, making a grand entrance designed to impress us.

I stared straight ahead as a tall, burly black man marched to the front of the room, his sparkling shoes making tap-tap-tapping noises all the way from the back. "At ease. Take your seats."

Oh, my God! I'd recognize that voice anywhere. It's that son of a bitch, Bull. I can't get away from that asshole.

Standing in the back of the room, wearing my aviator sunglasses, I was hidden from his sight. I glanced at him. He was wearing his dress uniform adorned with four rows of ribbons, brightly shined US insignia, and two polished major's oak leaves. He was wearing aviator sunglasses and stood rigid and tall, towering over all of us newcomers.

"I am Major Hassan, the Base Chief of Police. I command the Security Police squadron and all the personnel in it." He paced back and forth. "I have the full authority to execute the duties of my office as I see fit. While stationed here, do your duty and stay out of trouble, and you will have no problem from me, but step over the line and I'll have your ass in a brace so fast, it will make your head spin."

He looked over at the sergeant who screamed, "Atten-shun!"

We jumped to attention while Bull tap-tap-tapped out the door.

I reported to the hospital administrative area, where I was introduced to my new supervisor.

"Hi, I'm Bob Kennedy. Welcome to Japan." I glanced at the eagles on his collar that made him a colonel.

Dr. Kennedy explained that he was the head flight surgeon. "There are only three of us flight surgeons, the other docs are standard specialists found at any regional hospital. We have our own office in a Quonset hut by the flight line. We don't get embroiled with all the machinations in the hospital unless there is a disaster that inundates the staff. Come with me. I'll show you your new digs."

I sized up Dr. Kennedy. He was an older physician-grey, balding, and portly. He had a sparkle in his eyes that made him seem much younger that his fifty-five years.

As we walked across the base to our office, Dr. Kennedy explained, "We are just like civilian docs. Use my first name, unless we're around patients, then call me Dr. Kennedy. It sounds more professional."

Bob made me feel relaxed and comfortable. He showed me to a small office furnished with government grey desks and leather chairs. It still managed to look warm and nice. There was an old wooden propeller clock, centered over the door. It was gorgeous, but had a loud tick-tock. Bob sat in the easy chair and motioned me behind the desk. "If you have any questions, I am here for you."

"Thanks, Bob, you make me feel welcomed. When do I start?"

"Now. You start now, Lawrence, from this point forward. But the hours aren't tough, the patient load isn't much, thank God we're away from the base hospital. There are only two flying squadrons, and I'll introduce you to the guys tonight at the O' Club. They're great."

"Thanks. How about going off base? How does that work?"

"Any time you are off duty, you are free to go wherever you like. There's a medical exchange program with Tokyo General that pays an extra $4000.00 a month. I'll make sure that you get a chance at that income."

At the O' Club, Bob introduced me to all the flyboys in green "pickle" suits. I had never felt more welcomed in my life. They brought me beers and slapped me on the back.

"Lawrence, I'm flying Monday at 0700," a captain nicknamed Animal, said. "Cool training mission where we drop cargo out of my C-130. You have to fly four hours a month. This flight will get half your requirement out of the way. Come with me."

I looked at Bob.

"Sure, Lawrence, go. I'll cover the office."

"A couple of us are going to a Tokyo club later. Come with us," Animal said.

"Uh, I don't know. I'm just getting settled."

"Oh, come on. We'll get you home and back again to Mama Bob," Animal chuckled.

We went back to my BOQ to change clothes. I wanted to see Tokyo and start looking for Aimi. I put on the rumpled shirt and slacks and found Animal.

"I don't have a lot of clothes. I need to go shopping."

"We can't have our coolest doc dressed like a wrinkled nerd. You're my size, grab a pair of slacks and a good-looking shirt. We want the geishas all over you. When they hear you're a doc, they'll go nuts for you."

"Listen, Animal. I have a girl in Japan. I have to find her."

"Yeah, I got a girl in Korea, and one in Singapore I can't find either. You're gonna' fit right in."

Then I heard tap-tap-tapping coming down the hall. "Inspection in ten minutes," someone shouted.

"What is that? Friday night inspection?"

"Throw your stuff on and let's get out of here. That's the asshole from the Security Police Squadron. Stay away from him. The geisha girls say he's a sicko."

CHAPTER 20

LOOKING FOR AIMI

Dr. Kennedy reminded me of a kindly old grandfather. He laughed at my constant daydreaming and frequent preoccupation with love. I overheard him phoning his wife, "I smell love in the air. Cupid touched that young doctor. I'll bring him around home for you to meet."

I followed Dr. K through his front door. His wife hugged me as though she had known me for life. "You're cuter than a bug's ear. Too bad my daughters are already married." She grinned at me. "Come, I want to hear all about you."

I followed her to the kitchen. She pointed at the table and chairs. "Sit, eat." She placed a heaping plate of golden fried chicken and mashed potatoes in front of me.

"Wow, these look great."

"Tuck in. We don't hold to ceremony when it comes to dinner around here."

I was embarrassed to eat so much, but it was the best meal I had had since Momma's jerk chicken—nothing beat Momma's jerk.

After dinner, we retired to the living room for apple pie and coffee. "Your fried chicken was great, and this apple pie is delicious."

"You make me blush, young man." She grinned. "Have another piece and tell me about this woman you are in love with."

I told her about Aimi. "I love this girl, but I'm worried that she hasn't written back. I have probably written her six times in the past four months. Not a word from her."

"Japanese families are very traditional. They probably do not want her to see you," Mrs. Kennedy said.

"Yes, her father has made it very clear that he doesn't want me near his daughter."

The next day, I asked Dr. K., "What was it you said about an exchange program with the Japanese hospital?"

"Twice a week I work at Tokyo General and help handle their non-emergency cases while they do the big things." He had a wise grin and twinkle in his eye. "They pay $1,000 a week. I'll get you in if you…"

"I would love that. It would give me a chance to check up on my old college roommates. Can you?" Of course, I planned to look for Aimi.

"Tuesday," he rubbed his chin thoughtfully. "I'll see about starting you next Tuesday."

After a tediously slow week, like watching stones grow, as my Japanese friends say, I dressed to venture into Tokyo. I wore white slacks and a blue dress shirt covered with a jacket. I was on a mission to find Aimi, following the single lead I had. I pulled out the note she left for me and stared again at her friend's address. At the taxi stand on base, I walked up to the first green cab and showed the driver the address. "Can I hire you for the day?"

He was a middle-aged man with a warm and inviting face. "Please, to come in. I work on the base for many years." He stood and opened the back door. "My daughter marry American officer. He wonderful husband, three kids." He pointed to pictures on the visor above the passenger side.

"That's nice. Beautiful children. What does he do?"

"Husband pilot. They stationed in states now. I visit North Carolina in July. Miss my grandkids. What you do?"

"I'm a doctor," I said. "I met a Japanese girl in America. I am trying to find her."

"I help you."

I gave him the note I had with Aimi's friend's address.

As we drove on, I gazed admiringly at the wonders of my beloved's country. The bullet train flashed by at the speed of a jet, the wind rocking the car. I daydreamed that I took Aimi on the train to a country retreat where we kissed and loved each other all day.

After a short ride, filled with sights I had never seen, architecture that was new to me, and a culture I did not understand, we came to a cross roads. The driver rounded a corner and stopped at a ten-story apartment building. There were Japanese figures written on the door.

The driver pointed to the door. "There, I wait here."

My heart skipped a beat. I pointed to the door. "There? That is the address of the apartment?" The driver nodded.

I held my breath and approached. I felt dizzy, light-headed, and outside myself. A bank of buttons lined the wall. I reached for the bell but pulled back, unsure. I turned, walked ten steps away, and looked back. I ignored the butterflies in my stomach, spun around, bravely climbed the three steps, and pushed the center button.

The speaker came to life. "Konnichiwa."

"Yumi, is that you?" I shouted.

A man's stern voice responded. The driver ran over and spoke like an auctioneer babbling at the speed of sound. The voice came back and said something. The driver pushed a different button, and a female voice came on. My heart pumped sunshine through my veins.

My driver turned to me, "Yumi here."

"Lawrence, is that you?" the speaker crackled.

"Yes, yes, this is Lawrence."

"I Yumi. Aimi not here. Aimi no can see you."

What did she mean? "I have to see her. I came all the way from America to see her. Please help me, please."

"Her father kill me. I no can help. Sorry." The speaker clicked off.

My world shook. But something kicked in. I wasn't going to give up. Aimi was the woman of my dreams and worth fighting for—dying for.

"Please let me up for just a minute. I have written Aimi and she has not written back."

"Yes, I got your letters and gave to Aimi. She no can write back, she made up mind."

"Please just let me come up, I want to talk with her on the phone and hear from her."

I felt enormous relief when the door buzzed. I entered a dark foyer with a tall wooden staircase directly ahead. A door squeaked open some floors above, and the same voice called out, "Lawrence-san, up here you come."

I vaulted up the stairs three at a time. A tiny, black-haired girl waited on the landing for me. She wore jeans and a T-shirt that said, "I Heart NY." After five flights, I was out of breath. I bent over at the waist, put my hands on my knees, and panted. I caught my breath, straightened up, put my hands over my heart and looked at the girl.

"Hi, I'm Lawrence."

"Hi. Lawrence, good to meet you. I'm Yumi. Please to come in."

"I'm so sorry." I bowed deeply. "I am honored to meet you."

"You are gentleman." She laughed. "Aimi tell me."

She put a teakettle on a small gas stove. We sat at a low table in the center of the room. "I have chairs—let me get." She walked out of the room and returned with two folding chairs. She opened them, retrieved a card table from the closet, and opened it. The kettle whistled. Yumi returned to the stove and poured steaming water into a teapot.

"Can you call her for me? Can you give me her number and I will call?"

"No. You must not call her. Her father arrange wedding."

She brought over two cups and poured. She excused herself, went into the other room, and shut the paper-thin door. I heard her on the phone. She was speaking slowly and deliberately, and then it changed. She shouted into the phone, and the only word I understood was "Aimi." She slammed the phone down and stormed back into the room.

"Hideki coming to see you. He explain."

We sipped tea for fifteen minutes. I tapped my toes, the muscles in the back of my legs twitched. I drummed my fingers.

"Where does Aimi live?" I asked Yumi.

"With father, not far." She was being evasive.

"Does she talk about me?"

"Hideki will be here…"

"But I think I love…"

"You wait. Hideki…"

I wiped sweat from my brow, placed my hands in my lap, and twiddled my thumbs. *You could cut the thick air with a Samurai sword. Where the hell was Hideki?"*

The buzzer sounded, and I recognized my college roommate's voice. Yumi buzzed him in and waited. Hideki entered, and I ran over to hug my old buddy. The frown on his face stopped me. "You are not welcome here."

"I don't understand. I thought…"

"You make trouble for my sister and family, go back to America. We do not…"

"I am here to see Aimi. I don't know why you are so…"

"Leave. My sister is engaged and you know that my father does not want you to see her."

"I know that your father does not like me, but Aimi wants to see me and I can win over your father."

Hideki made fists, pulled back and took a karate stance. "You have been told to leave, now leave before you dishonor my family."

"You know me. I don't dishonor. I love…"

"Get out of here. Get out. My sister does not want to ever see you. She engaged to marry. Get out!"

"Hideki, I am your friend. I mean no…"

"Shut up. You get out, I call my brother, Mamoru. He get you out."

"I'm so sorry, I don't want to cause any problems. I have fallen in love with your sister, and I promised her that I would find her when I get to Japan."

Hideki's face turned crimson. "Get out. Never come…" He swung and hit me on the jaw. I went down like a lead-filled, heart shaped balloon. I hit the ground with a thunk, banging my elbow on the wooden floor. I looked up and shook in anger and fright. Yumi pointed to the door.

"Go, Lawrence-san. Never come back."

I crawled backwards out the door. After I crossed the threshold, Hideki slammed it in my face. I stood and brushed off my jacket. I ran my hands over my body from top to bottom. My Members Only jacket had the left sleeve torn at the shoulder, and my elbow pained me tremendously. I looked around to see that no one else had heard the fight.

I stood at the door, glassy-eyed, confused and embarrassed. I was hurt and my heart was shattered. I closed my eyes as a tear leaked out. My stomach ached. I lowered my head down to my chest and managed the stairs slowly, one at a time.

This is going to be a lot harder than I realized. They want to keep Aimi far from me.

At the entrance, rain streamed down the glass window. I opened the door, quickly chilled by the wind and freezing cold rain that splashed on my face. I had lost the love of my life. My only chance for true love had been short-circuited by her family. I pulled my collar up and signaled the driver to wait while I walked down the block and cleared my head.

The cold wind and rain were oddly comforting. They fit my mood.

I stumbled west for a few blocks, the rain pasting my hair to my head. I walked on and shivered. My reflection in a store window showed a pathetic-looking drenched man with blue lips. I put my hands in my pockets. I shuffled along, feeling sorry for myself. The world was grey and the sky confused. Clouds swirled in all directions. I walked through puddles until my feet became numb with the wet and cold. I turned to head back to the car.

Fifty feet from the car, I heard a slight voice from behind me. "Lawrence-san?"

My heart swelled. I spun around and saw a woman in a trench coat with the collar up and a large rain hat. She took off the hat.

"Oh, my God. It's you, Aimi."

I ran to her and grabbed her in my arms.

CHAPTER 21

NEVER SAY AIMI

I buried my face in her hair, smelled flowers, and I wept, laughed, and did both at the same time. I was confused, but my eyes welled up, and tears flowed freely. I was glad for the rain that hid my tears. I tried to talk, but a lump in my throat stopped me. I squeezed hard.

Aimi stiffened up and held back. She pushed me like she was holding off a drunk at a bar. I felt her shudder. She was crying. "Lawrence. What are you doing?" She sniffed.

"Aimi, Aimi, I missed you—" I squeezed her tighter. She pushed back, looked up, and I bent to kiss her. She turned her head to the side. My heart fluttered. Her eyes were full of doubt and questions.

"What's wrong?"

"Lawrence, this cannot be. I must marry someone else."

My heart sank. "No, Aimi, I love you. And I know you love me."

She squeezed her lips together. I saw tears in her eyes. She looked at me. "This cannot be." She shook her head. "My father made the arrangements. I must marry Japanese."

"But, Aimi, I saw love in your eyes. Aimi, you love—"

She placed her index finger across my lips to stop me speaking, "This cannot be, Lawrence. I had a girlish infatuation over you. Mama called it puppy love. But I am promised to powerful family."

"I thought you had feelings for me."

"Lawrence, I cannot stand here in public with another man. I am promised. We must go to tea shop."

She hurried off and I followed, with cold rain soaking the back of my neck. She stopped in front of a small tea shop. I opened the door and held it for her. The smell of spicy tea and fresh baked goods and her captivating aroma of jasmine surrounded us. I stared in amazement at the pure beauty of her as she shook off the rain. She spoke to the woman, went over to the counter, and picked up a phone. She spoke rapidly for a minute, then hung up. I was numb and didn't know how to proceed. I wanted to press my love but was scared that I would frighten her off if I were too forward.

The grey-haired shop woman came over and said something in Japanese. Aimi answered, and motioned to a small table. I pulled out a chair and helped her remove her coat.

We sat and she said, "I have called Yumi. We must have a chaperone at all times."

"Yumi? I just left her apartment. I doubt she is going to be happy to see me again. I hope she does not bring Hideki."

"Yumi called me to tell me you had been to her apartment, she is a very dear friend, and she will come because I asked her."

I focused my eyes on her, and my heart glued to her heart as I took my seat. I tried to see her eyes, but she kept them downcast. I pushed up her chin to see her better, but she looked back down and whispered, "I cannot."

"I have missed you."

She placed her finger over her lips and looked up. I was drawn into her liquid emerald eyes like Napoleon was drawn into Josephine. A feeling of family forever and the deepest sea enveloped me and made me warm inside.

"You are most respected," she whispered.

"But I love—"

"Shhh." She put her finger to her lips.

The woman brought our tea in silence, and Aimi poured my cup first, then hers. I sipped without taking my eyes off her. I must have looked like a kid with a new puppy who couldn't stand to leave it alone. I reached to touch her face, but she moved back.

In two minutes, the bell tinkled over the door, and Yumi padded in. I stood and bowed to her. Yumi looked across to Aimi, who sheepishly nodded for her to come over. She took a seat, and the woman brought her a cup and poured tea, refreshing our cups as well.

We sat there quietly, sipping our tea for ten minutes. Aimi glanced up and I stared at her face. She looked away self-consciously. The woman came over and asked Aimi something. She shook her head no. She looked me in the eye and said, "The rain has stopped. Will the gentleman escort two ladies to the park?"

I stood and pulled back her chair. We walked to the door, bright sunlight enveloped the entire street. I held the door for them, they glided out, turned left, and down the next street. After five minutes, we came to a formal Japanese archway. Going through, it opened into a verdant, flower-strewn garden. We walked to a bench set off by itself.

"Lawrence-san, I have missed you."

I was tongue-tied. I picked up her hand to hold it; she pulled it back. Yumi gave me a stern look.

I felt so confused. "I miss you so much."

"Lawrence, this cannot be, you must move on."

A noise from behind startled her. "I must go now." Yumi stood, looked around, and waited for Aimi to stand, and they left the garden. They walked in the direction away from the teahouse to an entrance for the subway. I was one block behind when Yumi turned down a different street and waved good-bye to Aimi.

At the subway station, Aimi fled down the stairs, gone in ten seconds. Startled by her disappearance, I stood staring after her. I was befuddled, not grasping what had happened. Nothing made sense. I had arranged my whole life to be here with her, and she had rejected me. Yet, I had not been mistaken about the look in her eyes back in America. There was love then and a glimmer of love on the street, even when she was rejecting me. At that moment, I swore to make her my wife.

I came around the corner and saw my taxi but not my driver. I thought he must have gone for a walk and I continued to the car. I placed my hand on the door and felt a claw-like leather glove on my shoulder. I spun around. A tall,

Japanese man smashed me in the face with his fist. I fell to the ground, and a sumo wrestler-sized monster pulled me into an alley by my feet. I tried to kick my legs free, but it was impossible. As he dragged me into the alley, the back of my head banged the ground.

I heard a groan behind the dumpster; my driver lay battered on the ground. The bigger fiend pulled me to my feet, and the tall man spoke.

"You son of a bitch. You never see my sister." He punched me in the stomach, and I folded like a Japanese fan. I would have dropped, except the ogre behind me had his arms wrapped around my chest.

"You forget Aimi's name. Never let her name escape your lips, or I find you and kill you." He punched me in the nose, and blood shot everywhere. I couldn't see for the blood. He kicked me in the balls, pain I had never felt before and I fell hard onto the ground. He kicked me in the ribs for good measure. Then he jumped on top of me like riding a horse and repeatedly punched me in the back of my neck and head. I flipped over, flat on my back. He punched me right in the nose. My head slammed into the concrete. The pain was excruciating. I passed out.

Regaining awareness, I saw someone peeking around the corner; it was Yumi with her hand over her mouth. She ducked back when I saw her. He punched my nose again, and my head hit the concrete. "Say you never see Aimi. You never say her name."

"Fuck you," I said.

He punched me again in the nose. "Say, 'I never see your sister.' Say it."

I babbled, coughed. "Fuck you. I love Aimi." I scuttled away crab-like.

He jumped on me and strangled my throat with his hands. "Say I never see your sister," he spit out the words between his teeth and onto my face.

He reared back to hit me, and I shouted, "Fuck you. I love Aimi." He struck harder, and it felt like my orbital bone fractured.

I glanced over at Yumi, who had a terrified look on her face. She ran past the entrance and away. He hit me again in the nose, and I was woozy. "Never say her name."

The sumo wrestler kicked me. I heard a police whistle and the sumo wrestler said something to Mamoru who jumped off me and stood. Then he bent down and placed something in my pocket. "You call me when you want another ass beating," he laughed as he glared down at me.

Mamoru and the sumo wrestler walked away laughing. I whispered, "Aimi" as I slipped into unconsciousness.

CHAPTER 22

BRAVERY WINS

The taste of blood woke me. I felt horrible. I touched my face. *My nose must be broken.* I pulled my wet and ripped coat around my neck. I felt miserable, injured and alone. My heart was empty and my love was gone. I felt weak and inadequate and unable to protect myself. I didn't feel like a man. Self-disgust enveloped me.

A moan came from behind the dumpster. I moaned back, rolled over, and opened my left eye. It was puffed up, but it was better than the right one, which was smeared with blood. Through the haze, I saw my driver and crawled over to look at him. I got to my knees and examined him. He came to his senses.

"What happen?"

"Family of my girlfriend." Looking around to make sure they were gone, I examined his head and saw a purple contusion. We limped, arm-in-arm, back to his taxi.

"We have to go to the hospital to check for concussion."

"Tokyo Hospital close. We go."

He drove for a few minutes and pulled into the circular entrance of the emergency room. We carried each other through the doors. A nurse rushed over and helped us to an empty room. I opened my wallet with the Medical Emergency card that said DOCTOR in large bold letters in English and Japanese. The charge nurse asked if she could help me. "Yes, I'm looking for Dr. Kennedy from Yokota Air base."

A light went on in her eyes. "I find for you."

I heard my name over the speaker. I picked up the phone, and Dr. Kennedy's southern voice said, "Lawrence, they said you were injured."

"My nose is broken. Someone jumped us in an alley. I am hurt."

"I'll be right there." He hung up.

I was dazed when Dr. Kennedy ran into the ER and rushed up to me. Out of breath, he gasped, "What the heck happened to you?"

"I was attacked by my girlfriend's brother. They also beat my cab driver." I stood wobbling. Dr. K. grabbed my arm and sat me in a nearby wheelchair. He rolled me to the treatment room, where a nurse was cleaning up my driver.

After examining both of us, Dr. Kennedy said, "You have to stay here at least overnight for observation. The trauma to your head might be severe." He annotated our charts and settled me in a room before leaving.

What a migraine! The nurse gave me some ibuprofen to ease the pain. For a couple of hours, I fell in and out of sleep.

I dreamt Yumi came into the room and sat in the chair beside the bed. I shook my head. *This is not a dream.* She saw my motion and stood beside me, lowered her head and whispered, "Aimi come see Lawrence-san."

I tried to sit up to speak, but the pain knocked me back down. I put my hands on either side of my head and grimaced. She put her finger over her mouth. "Wait."

I tried to make my mind return to my safe place in Tahiti with Aimi, but the pain was tough. I squeezed my eyes shut, and I was in Tahiti.

An angel's voice interrupted our walk, "Lawrence-san, what he do to you?"

I looked up. There was a woman wearing a scarf covering her face. She unwrapped and I gazed into her jade eyes. She leaned closer to examine my bandages. I felt her breath and smelled her jasmine and it was really her. I still had a headache, so I knew she was real. "Aimi, you came."

Her face contorted in anguish. "What did he do?"

"I am happy to see you."

"It looks bad." She touched my bandages.

"Your brother told me to stay away from you or he would kill me."

"I know. Yumi told me that they beat you because you wouldn't stop saying my name. You are brave for me."

"I am not afraid. I will fight for you."

"It was Mamoru, my older brother. He is the protector."

"I love you, and I don't care who it was, they will not stop me from seeing you. Only you can tell me to leave."

She leaned down toward my face. "Lawrence-san, I know."

"You came," I grinned painfully.

"Lawrence, my father goes too far. He cannot make me a slave. You fight for me. I fight for you. My father cannot make me marry. I cannot let them hurt a man I have such feelings for."

I reached up, pulled her face down, and kissed her on the forehead. The tingle thrilled me. She held my head with both hands, turned my face and kissed me hard on the lips. "Lawrence-san, you truly love me?"

I peered into her eyes. "Of all the people in the world who are in love, mine is the strongest for you." She kissed me and held the kiss.

Her eyes lit up, glassed over. "You fight for me, I fight for you." She made a fist. "I will tell Grandmother what they have done."

My heart sang through the pain. "I love only you," I said. She gave me strength. I felt like crying at the same time.

I heard a cough and Aimi straightened up.

Yumi said something in Japanese.

Aimi looked at Yumi. "You are right, my father knows many people in this hospital. I must be careful." She turned to me. "Lawrence-san, you will be true and faithful, forever?"

"Forever, I promise."

She leaned down again and hugged me. In my ear, she whispered, "Lawrence-san, I love you, only you."

My heart raced, my face flushed and my soul sang. She loved me. I kissed her and held on tight.

She pried away. "I cannot stay longer. I give you my room phone number to call me. But you can only call late at night, after twenty-three hours."

Yumi stood by the door. "Hurry. Cover your face."

Aimi stood and wrapped the scarf around her head. She covered her face. The door closed, and I watched it for the longest time. My heart was full, and I was happy. The headache returned, and my nose felt like it had gone through a meat grinder. But I felt fulfilled.

In the morning, Dr. Kennedy oversaw the medical staff as they reviewed my test results and tested my mental faculties, checking for signs of a concussion. By 2:00 PM, I was ready to leave. He and I walked out and into his car. As he drove, I told him what had really happened with Aimi and how Mamoru and his sumo wrestler attacked me.

"I would stay away from them if I were you. Even though Japan is a sophisticated and developed nation, there are forces working in their society that we westerners don't understand. I suggest you stay away from her and her family."

"Dr. K., I am in love with Aimi and she loves me. I will figure a way to see her."

"Let's tend to your injuries and then we can talk about it," he said as we walked into the flight surgeons' building on base. We went into an examining room and I sat up on the table.

"Hand me your jacket and I'll hang it up," Dr. Kennedy said.

"I got it." I took off my Members Only jacket and walked to hang it. I missed the hat tree and the jacket fell to the floor. Dr. Kennedy reached to help me pick it up. A white packet fell out of the pocket.

Dr. Kennedy picked up the white packet. He turned over the glassine paper and glared at me. I was dumbfounded. His eyes squinted, and his mouth opened. "What the hell? Just what the hell is this? Cocaine?"

CHAPTER 23

COCAINE

"Lawrence, what the hell are you involved with?"

"Dr. Kennedy. It's not mine. Someone—"

"God damn it." He rolled his eyes. "Were you involved in some drug buy that went wrong? Is that what happened?" He stared at me.

"Bob, really? It must have been planted by Aimi's brother."

"Are you on drugs? If you need help, I will—"

"For Christ's sake, Bob, I swear I never. Test me!" I shouted, holding out my left arm. "I am ready for the blood test right now."

"I want to believe you."

"Stop," I said, putting my hands up, palm out. "I told you Aimi's brother Mamoru and a thug beat me up. Obviously, he planted the drugs at the same time. I swear to you." I slammed my hands into my leg.

Dr. Kennedy patted my back. "We will figure this all out." He sounded warm and fatherly. "I believe you, but to cover all the bases, let's conduct a drug test." He brought out a blood draw kit, took a sample and sent it off with the technician for analysis.

I put my head in my hands. I mumbled, "I really love Aimi." Dr. K. handed me a box of tissues. I wiped my face and sat back. I glanced into the mirror, shocked by my appearance.

"Lawrence, are you sure she is worth all of this trouble?"

Nodding, I wanted to explain—"I lost my parents when I was a boy and had no other relatives. I grew up in an orphanage dreaming of having a family of my own. Those were some miserable years. Finally, I met the woman of my dreams. Her father sent her back here, and I joined the Air Force to get over here and find her. She loves me, Bob. She really loves me."

Bob beamed. "I get it, I get you," he grinned. "I'm a true romantic and Mrs. Kennedy is the Cupid's arrow of the Americans in Japan. She'll be so happy to hear true love has struck, she'll be over the moon with joy." He came back around and took hold of my hand. "We'll figure this whole thing out and do what we can for you and Aimi."

"Thanks. Aimi came to see me in the hospital. She told me that she loves me. She wants to be with me. Her father wants her to marry some rich Japanese guy."

"Most Japanese families are like that. They think they lower their status by having an American mutt in their family. They call us *gaijin*, which is like the N-word for foreigners."

I walked over to the window and peered out. I bowed my head, leaned forward, and placed my forehead on the cold glass. "I don't know what to do."

"Oh, we'll figure it out. Listen, let me call Mrs. Kennedy. She asked about you. We'll go to my house, eat her fabulous fried chicken and make a plan."

Dr. Kennedy dialed his home number. "Hi, darling. There's a problem with Lawrence. He's here with me. Well, he's had a spot of trouble getting with the Japanese love of his life and needs your help—Certainly, he's right here. I'll put him on."

I took the phone. "Hi, Mrs. Kennedy."

"Lawrence." Her voice was melodic, smooth, and familiar. She had a slow southern drawl. "LARR-ENN-CEE, I know someone at every Japanese social club that is worth being part of. I will figure out which ones they belong to and we will get things going. This girl's family will be lucky to have you as a son. I'll be crying at the wedding."

"Thank you, I need the help." I felt better.

"Now come for a bite, and I'll plot a war plan to get your love for you," she laughed.

"We're on our way. I'm famished." I handed the phone to Dr. Kennedy.

"Okay, honey, I'll bring him home in a few. I have some processing to complete, and then we'll come directly there." He hung up and turned to me, "Good as done, my boy."

BANG! BANG! BANG! Someone hammered on the wooden door, startling us. I jumped up. Dr. Kennedy spun his head around with a "Now what?" look on his face.

The door opened, and Bull stood looking down at me, a good six inches taller and a hundred pounds heavier than my skinny 165.

Dr. Kennedy walked right up to Bull without hesitation. I had never seen anyone do that before. Dr. K. had no idea that he was dealing with a vicious rapist and a cruel bully who would gladly kill him if he wouldn't get caught. "What's the meaning of this? I am in the middle of attending to a fellow officer who also happens to be a doctor."

"I apologize, Colonel, but I am Major Hassan. We received an anonymous phone tip that Captain Leo brought cocaine into this facility, and I have the drug dogs here. I am sure it is a hoax, but you understand we have to be sure. Please stand back." He stared at me the whole time he spoke to Bob.

Fuck me!

Bull and two MP's walked through the door. A big German shepherd ran directly to the desk and sat down staring directly at the packet on the desk.

"What is this?" Bull shouted. The sound of his voice raised the hairs on my neck and gave me goose bumps. *I hate that son of a bitch.* The MP pulled her dog away, and Bull picked up the powder.

Bull glowered at me. "Either this is yours or his. Or were you selling it to him? Which is it?" I felt crushed.

"Wait a minute." Dr. Kennedy held up his hands. "This is a hospital. I was treating him, and this was planted in his clothes. I have already taken blood to show that he is not using, and I will have the results in a day."

"I still have to take him in. We received a tip; the tip was accurate. Cuff him and read him," Bull barked.

I placed my hands behind my back and lowered my head. Bull searched through my pockets and found nothing.

"That is not mine. It's a plant—"

"Yeah, you were a druggy at the home. You have the right to remain silent—" He read off a little card.

"I never used drugs, and no one ever said that about me." I stared straight ahead. Dr. Kennedy was watching me, not knowing if I was telling the truth or lying. He dialed the phone and spoke to the Base Commander.

Bull turned to me. "A racist and a drug user."

Dr. Kennedy interrupted. "Don't say a word, Lawrence. I will have you out of there in no time. As for you, Major Hassan, I suggest you be prepared to defend every one of those accusations with corroborative witnesses or face a court-martial. It is a crime to impugn the integrity of an officer. Are you prepared to produce witnesses?"

"No, but—eh, I just eh—"

"Then I suggest you shut up and do your job professionally!" Dr. Kennedy was on fire, sticking up for me like both my dads would have.

Bull grabbed the cuffs behind me and closed them tight. I winced, without giving him the satisfaction of crying out. He shoved me through the door. He led me on a slow procession through the office, using his voice as though there were a huge crowd of people he had to push his way through, when in fact there were five people in the office, a busy day for us. "Stand back, suspect coming through." He pivoted his head, making sure everyone saw me. He was clearly enjoying my humiliation.

CHAPTER 24

EVIL RETURNS

Bull pushed me into the military cruiser with the bubble gum machine on top. He had been an impediment to my existence since I first met him. He was the most evil person I had ever known and he enjoyed torturing me.

Dr. Kennedy followed us in his car, easing some of my tension.

There was an amazing vortex of disparate thoughts swirling through my head. *Someday, I'll get Bull. I love Aimi, she came to see me over the objections of her father. I can't wait to see her and call her tonight. I can't stand this Bull, fucking asshole. The drug test will prove that I am innocent.*

"Get out," Bull said with a sneer in his voice.

"Follow the airman into the lock-up behind the desk sergeant. We will take your mug shot and prints, and handle you like any other felon. You think just because you made it through medical school you can do whatever you want. There are still laws, and they apply to you. By the way, how's my old girlfriend Christina?"

I walked in steaming mad. Dr. Kennedy was right behind us. "Bob, watch what they are doing, don't leave me alone in a room with Bull."

Bull strutted up to the desk sergeant as the airman led me around the wall into a large room and removed the cuffs. Bull fingerprinted me and had me stand beside a wall as he flashed the mug shot camera. "Smile for the birdie," he taunted, holding up a little fake bird just like Woodstock.

I couldn't fucking believe it. "You are a special kind of stupid, Bull."

"It's Major Hassan to you, felon." There was venom in his voice.

"I'm an officer and a doctor."

"You're a drug user and a felon in my custody. Now shut up and get in that cell." He pushed me roughly and slammed the barred door.

"I want to see Dr. Kennedy," I shouted between the bars. He turned out all the lights and went out the door.

I sat an hour alone in the cell until I heard some arguing voices and then a full colonel came in followed by Dr. Kennedy and Bull.

"Hassan," said the colonel. "Release Dr. Leo. You know we don't do this to officers."

"Colonel, I found him with dangerous illegal drugs on his person, and he resisted arrest. This was for safety."

"You're full of it," I shouted at him. "I never had drugs; they were planted."

"At ease, captain," the colonel said while he pointed at me. "We are releasing you in Dr. Kennedy's charge while we investigate this entire incident."

"Sir, you can't release him. He's a danger to the base if he brings in more drugs," Bull shouted.

"Don't be so dramatic, Major. Dr. Kennedy will keep him under base detention until we sort this out." He turned. "Right, Bob?"

"Of course, Jack. He'll be confined to base until you clear him."

I was so happy to get out of the cell and out of Bull's evil clutches that I shook with relief. I entered Bob's car. "Thanks, thanks for helping me."

"You're welcome. Just stay out of Major Hassan's sight until we sort this out. Now, let's go home and have that great southern fried chicken I promised."

I was looking forward to seeing Mrs. Kennedy. She made me feel welcomed. Like Dr. Bob always said, she was 'sweet to the core, kind to the heart and apple pie all the way to her soul.'

Back at their house, Mrs. Kennedy set up the bedroom for me. There was a yellow, fluffy quilt on a queen-size white bed, and the room was done out in flowers and dolls. It smelled like lilacs and felt safe.

"Here's the phone, Lawrence," she smiled at me. "Works just like home. Call the lovely Aimi, and we will hold our breath till breakfast to hear about everything she says."

At exactly 11:01 PM, I settled down in the bed and dialed her number, holding my breath and counting every ring, ringgg-one, ringgg-two, ring-

"Moshi-Moshi," a soft voice answered.

"Aimi?"

"Lawrence-san?"

"Yes, I couldn't wait to call you. How are…"

"Wait, I close door." After a few seconds, "I must warn, my brother is not happy and will hurt you. Watch careful…"

"I know. He planted drugs on me."

"He bad man. I miss you. What your number?"

I gave her my phone numbers for work and the Kennedy's, and we exchanged dreams, hopes, and desires for thirty minutes. She re-confirmed her love for me. My heart sang and fluttered every time I thought that simple line; *She loves me.*

I explained that I couldn't leave base for a while.

She asked, "I come to see you Saturday?"

"Please, I would love that. Come as early …"

"Do you wish for children, Lawrence-san?"

"Yes, I would love children. You would make a wonderful mother for our children."

"Oh, I wish many children. We…I must go, someone come, I love you." Click!

CHAPTER 25

AIMI ENLISTS AID OF GRANDMOTHER

"You're driving me to drink," Dr. Kennedy said. "Quit fidgeting. Your incessant pacing is driving me crazy."

"I'm sorry, Bob. I'm just antsy."

"This should keep you on the straight and narrow. Major Hassan wants to see you."

A cold wave flashed down my spine. I called the area defense counselor, my lawyer, and asked him what to do.

"Have another medical professional, one you don't know, administer all known drug tests to you. That way we will have evidence that you are not a user."

"Why someone I don't know? Dr. Kennedy is the senior physician."

"Yeah, but they could claim conflict of interest. I will have a civilian medical facility analyze the tests as well as the base facility. That way we have separate independent analyses showing you did not use drugs."

After looking at all the test results, the prosecuting attorney determined that there was not enough evidence to pursue a legal case. Bull was mad and insistent that I be court-martialed, but thankfully, he was over-ruled.

I had to pick up the Dismissal of Charges from Bull. In his office, he said, "Arrogant people eventually make mistakes, that's when I catch them." He had a sarcastic sneer on his lip. "You better watch out, I have my eye on you. All the kids at the orphanage said you were a liar."

I snapped back, "I resent that, Bull, I am not a liar, but I know exactly what you are." I remembered, as a kid, being shocked awake when he punched me in the head. He would pick random nights to hit me, sometimes a month between punches. I slept on the top bunk, my face against the wall, as far away from the rail as possible, pillow over the back of my head. It didn't stop him. The whole time we were in the house together, he randomly woke me with a swift hard blow to the head that would leave me with a migraine the next day. Afterward, he would lay in his bed and laugh to himself. In ten minutes, he would be snoring like a log. I couldn't sleep properly for days.

The following Friday, I had fifteen flight physicals to perform, so I was busy the entire day. I slept well that night, dreaming of Aimi on the beach in Tahiti. I couldn't get her vision out of my mind. She had cracked my heart open like a walnut and climbed inside.

Saturday, I woke before dawn. Leaping out of bed, I showered and shaved in record time, then stood around twiddling my thumbs. I walked out to the end of the runway and watched the warm and pink sunrise. There was a squadron of F-15 fighters landing. The roar of the engines took my mind off Aimi for a short time. I felt at peace.

I walked back to the Kennedy house to wait. While strolling back, I decided that I needed to buy a car. Most of my friends had bought sports cars and liked to hot-rod around. I decided I needed a family car, perhaps even a station wagon. I laughed to myself, thinking about buying a family car as my first car.

At home, Mrs. Kennedy greeted me with her customary mama-bear hug. She smelled like fresh bread, all warm, soft and doughy. We had a casual breakfast and sat around talking, my anticipation of seeing Aimi growing by the minute.

"Stop pacing," Dr. Kennedy smiled in his fatherly way.

Expecting her at noon, I was surprised when the phone rang at 11:30 AM. Dr. K said it was the gate, and she was there waiting for me. I bolted out the door and ran the half-mile as fast as I could. I ran across the streets in the housing area, past the Base Exchange, and down the main thoroughfare. Someone slammed on their brakes and honked at me as I crossed against traffic. I raced as hard as I could all the way to the guard station, and there she was, fresh and pure white and edible. I grabbed her with both arms and wrapped myself around her. I held her and she relaxed on my shoulder. I could feel her shudder, and I was filled with joy.

"There is another young lady for you to sign in, Captain," the two-striped airman said.

I pulled back from Aimi and looked at the airman. He nodded his chin in the direction of another Japanese woman. She wore an American woman's white silk business blouse, and a pinstriped jacket. She looked so business-like.

"Lawrence-san, you know Yumi, of course," Aimi said.

"I am delighted to see you again," I said, "and so happy to see you, Aimi." I bowed a small bow. I had not expected Yumi to come with Aimi, and didn't really know how to act in front of her.

We strolled back along the route I had come. I was beside Aimi, with Yumi following discreetly about ten yards behind. "I am happy to see you. Thank you for coming."

"Lawrence-san, we must speak seriously. I hope you do not find me too forward, but I think we both know where we going. My family is getting suspicious. I postpone parties my parents have planned. Soon, I must tell them that I not marrying their choice of husband."

"I had not thought about what position this would put you in. I will make it all worthwhile in the end."

"Lawrence-san, Mamoru has been to prison. He hurt a man very badly who cheated my father. Broke his arms and legs with a baseball bat. He will do anything to protect our family and anything my father tells him. We must be smart and figure out how we can show my family that we are right for each other."

"How can I help you?"

"I don't think you can do anything, but I am going to tell my grandmother. She was forced to marry another man, not the one she loved, and she resented it whole life. Grandmother did learn to love Grandfather, and they had children and a wonderful life together until he died, but she felt she missed an important part of her youth. Grandmother-sobo says that the heart knows truth. I joke with Grandmother that she should try to find her old flame, maybe he is single, too."

I was happy for the rest of the evening. However, as would become our normal way of doing things, at 8:00 PM the girls had to go. We piled into Dr. Kennedy's black Lincoln Town Car and he and Mrs. Kennedy drove us to the front gate, where the taxi waited.

Aimi and I walked away from the others about one hundred feet, and had a short conversation about our next meeting. Over the eight Saturdays in a row that we met like this, it always ended with her saying, "I come to you next Saturday. I love you, Lawrence-san."

"Next Saturday, will you meet me at the Hidden Gardens? I have someone special for you to meet." I smiled at the invitation, knowing it was her Grandmother.

Little did I know how important this meeting would be.

CHAPTER 26

OBAA-SAN IN THE HIDDEN GARDENS

"Lawrence, call her Obaa-san. She is the revered grandmother of your most beloved. Bring to Obaa-san the lotus blossom." My Japanese doctor friend, Kaito, closed his eyes and nodded. "In our culture, that blossom grows in the muddy water, yet rises above the murk to achieve enlightenment. Obaa-san will understand that you, too, have risen above others to become a doctor. She will see that you are serious about her granddaughter. The lovely lotus has another meaning, also appropriate. The pure white bloom represents cleansing the spirit that is growing out of the murky water. These are all deeply meaningful in Japanese culture."

Saturday, I was excited to meet Obaa-san. I awoke early and ate breakfast. Dr. Kennedy said, "I was asked to work at Tokyo General this evening, but I have stand-by at the base hospital." He winked at me. "You could take my car to meet Aimi, and then fill in at Tokyo General."

"Thanks, Bob. I could use the money. Should I bring my medical bag?"

"Yes, and I always take the fly-away drug kit from the pharmacy with me. The bottles are labeled in English. In an emergency of the moment, if I am working on a patient, I don't need an interpreter to find the drug I require."

"Good idea. Thanks. I'd better get started."

Driving through Tokyo was a harrowing experience. Cars shot at me from all directions. Veering between swerving maniac drivers taught me the secrets of the kamikaze; bravery and stupidity. I pulled off the main Indianapolis 500 training road, on to a smaller kamikaze street. I circled the block and found an open parking space right beside the gate, but had a lot of trouble parallel parking Dr. Kennedy's behemoth town car. Finally, I got the Yank Tank into the spot.

Kaito had told me that I was being given a particular honor to be invited into the Hidden Gardens. They were especially close to the hearts of the Japanese. These gardens were closed to outsiders, except for one holiday a year.

At exactly 11:59 AM, I took the flowers with me, climbed out of the car, and tried to walk humbly into the garden. I was not practiced at walking humbly, but this time, I took small steps ambling through the wooden archway with my head bowed. "The proper attitude," Kaito explained.

The lotus blossoms in my hand had a light vanilla aroma. As I scanned the garden, I realized I was surrounded by jade green plants the color of Aimi's eyes. From the bushes, crickets and frogs called to their lovers and gentle leaves brushed my arms. A sword plant amazed me, thick, broad leaves with a single black flesh-ripping thorn on the tip. Every spike was filed down, so it could not stab visitors. Gentle and thoughtful people.

As I was following a bubbling stream around a bend, I saw Aimi. She sat on a teak bench with an older lady. When I spotted her, my face lit up, my pulse raced, and my eyes devoured her. Beside the two ladies, on the grass, was a small yellow bird that looked like Woodstock. I tiptoed toward them to make sure I didn't disturb the peaceful feeling that covered the entire garden. Behind them, wading in the stream and stalking its prey, was a tall pure white egret on yellow legs.

Aimi wore a long white kimono with green leaves and pink roses woven in the fabric. She was a vision of beauty and delicacy. As I approached, Aimi stood up and bowed. I bowed deeper and flashed my most humble smile. I hid my natural confidence. Kaito had said confidence was a turn-off.

Grandmother-sobo stood, and with her back straight, she was four foot nine inches tall. She had full, rich silver hair done in a bun that resembled a flower, completed with silver sticks to hold it together. Her lips broke open into a broad smile, and her intelligent chiseled face was laced with a roadmap of wisdom and experience. She said something so softly I had to lean in to hear her. She spoke in Japanese.

Aimi interpreted, "Grandmother is pleased to meet you, Lawrence-san. She wishes to walk around gardens with us." Grandmother held onto Aimi's arm, and slowly padded away following the stream. I tagged along behind for a moment. They stopped. "You walk with Grandmother, she wishes to feel your strength."

Grandmother said, "Kanaria."

Aimi translated, "Grandmother pointed to the yellow canary perched on a branch in a cottonwood tree. It is good luck from our ancestors."

I gave Grandmother my arm, and she placed her feather-light hand on my bicep and gave me a little squeeze and a funny cheeky grin. She walked gracefully, almost floating above the path. She whispered to me as we walked.

Aimi listened, then her face flushed, and she bowed her head and said, "Grandmother greatly appreciate lotus blossoms and say to Lawrence-san, 'Our love is like the lotus, murky start, but can grow to beauty.'" I smiled at Grandmother and nodded.

"Grandmother said Lawrence-san must be strong. It will be difficult to win family approval because they do not trust Americans." I looked back and Aimi blushed as Grandmother went on. "She said also, you must treat Aimi-san with love and respect, and above all, be faithful and honorable."

"Please tell Grandmother that I will always be honorable and faithful to Aimi-san. I promise I will never do anything but protect and admire you."

We walked on, and Grandmother named each of the flowers we passed. She picked up a red one that had fallen on the path and held it under my nose. "Smells like cinnamon," I said.

Grandmother stopped to examine a yellow blossom. She beamed. We continued until she stopped and watched the canary, as another one landed on the branch beside it. She turned to Aimi, then to me, and smiled an all-knowing smile.

"Thank you for showing me so much of your garden," I said. Aimi interpreted.

"Grandmother-sobo say she like you. Your heart is truth." She smiled gently.

"Thank you," I said.

I glanced at Aimi and back at Grandmother. She had a conspiratorial smile, a hint of knowing something that others did not know.

Suddenly, her face changed and flashed pain. Her skin turned ashen. I looked back at Aimi. Before I could react, Grandmother let go of my arm and grabbed her chest. *That's the Levine sign, I learned in med school, heart attack!* She collapsed to her knees.

CHAPTER 27

HEART ATTACK

I held her and dropped to my knees, laying her gently on the ground. My medical training kicked in. Fingers pressed her carotid artery. *No pulse. No pulse! CPR! Holy shit, she's dying!*

I crossed my hands to her chest and pumped for her heart. "Run to my car and get the medical bag and the medicine kit in the back seat. Run!" I fished in my pocket, tossed her the keys, and counted my sixth pump. "Grandmother is in cardiac arrest," I shouted.

I pumped and counted. In my mind, I went over what to do. Fear washed over me. Still no breath.

I pumped again until I got to thirty. *No breath, no pulse. Pump! You're losing her!*

Aimi was back in seconds, wild-eyed and panting. She carried the two cases. "Open the case." *This is bad.* Aimi looked frightened.

Aimi opened the case.

I pumped again and counted. After thirty, I opened the airway. Thank God. "She's breathing." I felt relief, but only momentarily.

Aimi looked dazed. I turned back. Holy smokes. Grandmother was conscious! She looked at me. I grabbed the medication bag and crushed an aspirin.

"Give me the water."

I lifted Grandmother's head and washed the aspirin into her mouth. "Swallow, Grandmother," I pleaded. "Call an ambulance, Aimi."

"Drink, Grandmother," Aimi spoke urgently, then in Japanese.

The ambulance team arrived. They efficiently strapped her down in moments. Aimi and I rode in back with her. We arrived at the emergency entrance of Tokyo General and wheeled her into a treatment room. An ER physician came in, made a quick examination, and left. A cardiologist came and took over. I went into the waiting room and found Aimi.

"How is Grandmother?"

"She is breathing and looks much better."

Ten minutes later, the ER doors flew open, and Dr. Herito bolted in with his hair all frizzed and shirt unbuttoned. He rushed to Aimi, speaking in Japanese. He glowered at me. His deep black eyes narrowed. He growled at Aimi in a low, dull, angered voice.

The cardiologist came over. He placed his rubber-gloved hand on my shoulder. "Very fine work, Dr. Lawrence-san, you saved her life."

CHAPTER 28

RESPECT AND HUMILITY

Dr. K came to Tokyo General to see me during Grandma's operation. It seemed that whenever we needed them, he and Mrs. K were there for us in those fledgling days of groping for true love. At Tokyo General, Dr. K was greatly respected for his fine medical ability, revered for his dedication, and trusted because he spoke flawless Japanese.

He and I rode the elevator to see Grandmother. He counseled that it would be better for him to examine her because he knew Aimi's father.

"This guy's a real hard nose. The young docs call him Toranaga, after the last Shogun. He's a stickler for doing things right and his way. He is also a shameless social climber. It is in their culture to be obsequious, but he takes it to an elevated level, showing phony respect to minor functionaries and social elites. The other local docs think he is humorous. They laugh behind his back."

I wondered what it would be like, seeing Aimi's father in Grandmother's room right after she had a life-saving operation.

"Bob, he ought to love me after I saved her life."

He turned directly to me. "Lawrence, do not take that high-handed attitude. The Japanese hate arrogance." Bob shook his head. "You have to show humility, modesty, and meekness to gain their respect. Watch the sumo wrestlers to see how the most powerful Japanese conduct themselves. Inside the ring, the Sumos look like rhinos, huffing, puffing, and stamping their feet to display power. Outside the ring, they are meek and mild, and therefore deeply revered by all. If you see them interviewed on the street, they act like gentle old grandfathers who would not hurt a flea. You would be wise to conduct yourself like the mighty sumo."

"Well, I never thought of it like…" I felt embarrassed, having him tell me something so obvious. "Bob, I'm sorry."

"That is why I am here, my friend."

I jumped off the elevator, strode quickly as if I was back in med school and late for an anatomy class. Dr. K caught up as I was about to open the door. "Stop," he whispered, breathing hard. "Here is how we do it in Japan, with respect."

He led me back to the nurses' station and spoke softly in Japanese. The nurse handed him the chart and he examined it, then gracefully passed it to me. "We do not barge into her room. We have the nurse precede us to make sure all is in order and to announce us. To do otherwise would be arrogant, and my young friend, that you are. Walk behind me."

Dr. Kennedy pulled my arm to get me behind him. When the nurse led us to Grandmother's room, she knocked softly. The door opened, we bowed, and entered in a most deferential manner. I followed him like an obedient Japanese wife.

It looked like an American hospital room but, was painted stark white and about three times the size. The focus of the room was an enormous picture window with the entire panorama of Tokyo in the background. I could see the mountains way out behind the city. I looked around and immediately saw Aimi at the head of Grandmother's bed. She didn't look at me, so I turned my head away. Her father was examining a heart-monitoring oscilloscope, and Dr. Kennedy bowed. I bowed deeply and stood behind Dr. Kennedy.

"Dr. Herito, it is a great honor to see you," Dr. Kennedy said, again bowing. "I understand that we have a patient related to you."

"Hello, Dr. Kennedy. This is my mother."

Dr. Kennedy was acting coyly, as if he did not know any of this. "We are honored to have the great lady visit our humble hospital. Though we wish the circumstances were different." He offered a small bow to the sleeping grandmother. "We sincerely hope your mother is well."

"She is in serious condition but pulled through the surgery without difficulties. I—" he emphasized "I" as if to say only he was good enough to administer care to his mother, "I have examined her. She is in the best hands, and I expect a full recovery." He seemed cold.

"I am delighted she is in such capable hands. May I introduce my young colleague, Dr. Lawrence Leo? Oh, I forgot, you already know Dr. Leo from college with your sons."

Dr. Herito glared at me. "I am acquainted with the impetuous young doctor."

"Impetuous, you say. Perhaps young, unrefined, and hasty. However, I was told he saved your mother's life? Perhaps I was misinformed." He turned to me with a question on his face. Unseen by Herito, he winked. "Did you not administer CPR to this woman as you told me?" He looked sternly at me.

Caught off guard, I said, "Yes, and I gave her an aspirin." I sounded like a jackass.

Dr. Herito smirked. "Your young friend did a competent job helping my mother. I'm sure any medical student could have done the same. I am thankful to him, but let us not turn him into the great heart surgeon, Dr. Michael Debakey. He was fast and helpful, that is all."

"Very well, I understand. If you can help him develop his medical competence further, I would appreciate it. He is my subordinate," he grinned. "He would gain greatly from your vast medical knowledge."

"Certainly. Now, if you will excuse—"

"The young doctor has some experience and a lot of book knowledge, but as you may know the proverb, "Better to spend one day with a great teacher, than a thousand days of study." Dr. Kennedy was convincing.

"I bow to your knowledge of my proverbs. Do you know the one that says knowledge without wisdom is like a load of books on the back of an ass?"

"Of course. In this case, Dr. Leo had both knowledge and wisdom. I am proud of him and hope you are, too." He smiled and kept up the pretense. "Is this your family?"

Dr. Herito made the introductions, and when I bowed to Aimi, I slipped her a little love note and wished her grandmother well.

We took our leave of the Herito family. In the hall, Dr. Kennedy said, "I will give you all my shifts for the next couple of weeks, so you can remain close to the family. Be extremely careful. Dr. Herito is the slickest physician I ever met. He will only be impressed by highly competent medicine."

I went back to the Flight Surgeons' Office on base to wrap up some needed work. Later that evening, I made my way back to the hospital to check on Grandma and see Aimi.

"Lawrence-san." Aimi rushed over to me, and I hugged her close. "Grandmother is doing fine. Papa-san says she will have a full recovery."

My heart raced. "I am so glad to see you. I am glad you are here." I beamed.

"I am to stay with Grandmother. There is a small family chamber beside her room. I will stay for the entire time she is here. We must be careful. My father is most angry." She looked teary, and spoke softly, "Father says I am forbidden to ever see you again."

A cold shiver ran over my skin, and the hairs rose up on the back of my neck, "Aimi, what will we do?"

"I do not know, Lawrence-san."

I walked down to the cafeteria and purchased tea and snacks for Aimi and me. We talked about her grandmother and the luck of us being with her when she had the heart attack. Aimi seemed relieved now that her father said Grandmother would be fine. After fifteen minutes, I had to return to my duties in the emergency room.

At 3:00 AM the rush in the ER slowed down, so I flew upstairs to see Grandmother and Aimi. There was only one night nurse at the station, and the lights were almost all out. I asked her about visiting Grandmother as a family friend and assisting physician, and she let me into her room.

Grandmother was breathing fine. I checked her monitors. Blood pressure was a tiny bit high, heartbeat strong, and breath rate where it should be for an eighty-year-old. I sat and looked at her for a minute, hoping she was recovering at the best rate possible.

After five minutes, I gazed out the picture window. The scenic wonder of Tokyo made me feel small, like a boy again. Leaning close was like stepping out into a galaxy of radiance, displayed in front of me as the eighth Wonder of the World.

Lights were everywhere. Buildings were illuminated as though a million fireflies had organized to make this incredible view for my pleasure. I saw the universe that John Denver immortalized in his music. This rivaled his view for splendor and beauty. "Rocky Mountain High" reverberated in my mind.

It was like a spread from National Geographic. Tall skyscrapers balanced each other in the foreground. Mount Fuji rose majestically in the background, the brilliant reflective snowcap visible for miles, perhaps even from outer space. I stared off into the night lights and dreamed of living in that fine city with my little Japanese-American family—Aimi, two almond-eyed children, and me.

I stepped back, returning to reality from the momentary flight to the stars, and looked for the door into the family quarters. It was at the back of the room, and I silently crept over to it.

Slipping through the door, I saw Aimi lighted by the glorious starlight and asleep in a pure white bed. Her proximity turned my heartbeat into a love Geiger Counter. The nearer I came to her, the faster it beat, pinging like a metronome, until, once again, my skin tingled in closeness.

CHAPTER 29

GRANDMOTHER SPEAKS TO HERITO

Dr. Kennedy gave me two weeks leave. I took a hotel room within walking distance of the hospital, near Grandmother and Aimi.

During Grandmother's hospitalization, I spent my time on the night shift to avoid Herito. In less than two weeks, Grandmother was alert, sitting up and giving me Japanese lessons. We spent evenings in the room telling each other how to say things in English and Japanese. When we would get bored with that, Aimi would translate and the three of us would sit and tell stories. My bond with Grandmother grew stronger by the day and our ability to communicate got easier and easier.

Often, Aimi and I would rendezvous late at night, after Grandmother fell asleep. We were able to secrete ourselves in her family quarters, hold hands, talk about our future, and the things we liked. "I wish to travel the world and visit all Seven Wonders."

"I want to take you to see them."

The extra time we spent together gave me a chance to understand her better. She loved flowers, but had bad allergies to many and was, likewise, allergic to bee stings. She loved animals, but she only ever had one pet, and that was a goldfish. When it died, she was so grief-stricken, she could not leave her room for a week. Most of all, she loved her family. She adored time at home surrounded by loved ones in a safe environment.

Some nights we played Japanese chess—called Go, read books and discussed our future. I loved our dreamy plans, but our problems were still vexing.

"How will we ever get married when your family will not even discuss it with us? We should just elope."

"We will not start a family by sneaking out like pirates in the dark. We will have a proper Japanese wedding. All of my relatives must be there. Grandmother-sobo has a plan to help us. She has already set the stage with my mother and is working on my father. She knows how. Tomorrow, when Father comes, she wants us to be here. She will tell him some things that will make him think about us."

I tossed and turned all night. I couldn't settle down. I tried to sleep, but my mind kept returning to the ugly, hate-filled face of Dr. Herito and his dislike for me. He was such a social climber that, unless the royal family adopted me, there was no way I could gain enough status for him to sanction our marriage.

The next morning, Aimi called and asked me to come to Grandmother's room to talk with her. Entering, I bowed to Grandmother, bent down and kissed her cheek. She grabbed my head, faced me to her and looked deeply into my eyes. She said something in Japanese. Aimi translated, "One who smiles is stronger than one who rages, Grandmother-sobo said to you, Lawrence-san."

Baffled, I turned to Aimi and kissed her on the cheek. As I held her, the door opened. Her father stormed into the room and saw us embracing. He shouted something in Japanese that reverberated through the room like the hurricane that had thundered through God's Home the second year I was there. Aimi jumped back and bowed her head like a chicken ready to have it chopped off. Grandmother said something short and stern, and Dr. Herito stepped back and looked to her with a sheepish face. I turned and Aimi was crying convulsively, her breath shuddering.

"Grandmother-sobo wishes her son to stay, so she can speak to him and future grandson-in-law," Aimi said, trying to catch her breath. I was happily surprised when she called me her future grandson-in-law, but I could see the muscles tighten in Dr. Herito's jaw. He looked like he could chew right through his stethoscope.

Grandmother spoke and Aimi interpreted. "When I was young, I fell in love with a boy from the neighboring farm. We were simple children.

However, my father would not allow me to marry a poor farm boy. My father wanted me to marry into a land-owning family of a much higher status. He wanted me to have a rich future. However, love does not respect money. My father sent me away to his brother in a fishing village. I separated from my love, and I was forced into an arranged marriage. No love.

I hated my father. Five years, I kept my baby and myself away from him. During those long years, I learned that my husband was a kind and loving man. I let go of my hatred, accepted my place in his family. But I never felt the same about my father. Even today I still resent him. He stole my love and he stole my choice."

"My son," she said to Dr. Herito. "If you turn against their wishes and drive these two apart, it will harden Aimi's heart, and she will resent you for the rest of your life. You must think carefully of the love of your daughter and treat her wishes with respect."

Dr. Herito listened intently but kept his jaws tight and his eyes in small slits. He turned his head to the side and looked at me with cloudy eyes. "This is my only daughter. I love her. She is my princess." He wiped his eyes.

I looked over at Aimi, and she had the same teary-eyed look on her face as her father.

Dr. Herito went to the bed, leaned down next to his mother, and softly wept. He reached his arms around her and held her tightly. She wept with him in humility and understanding.

Grandmother-sobo spoke again. "You have learned a great deal about your daughter this day. All of us know her kindness, but none of us knew her strength. Now we know that if we do not honor her love and her wishes, we will lose her to the man she loves and to his home in America."

We sat in silence for some time, settled down to a quiet and serene hospital room. Dr. Herito still did not make eye contact with me. I knew we hadn't yet won him over. I kept thinking of Dr. Kennedy's instructions. *Know when to speak.* I kept silent.

The door opened and Mamoru came in. "What is wrong? Why is he here?" He pointed at me.

He sprang toward me, and I prepared to take another beating, but Dr. Herito jumped up, right in Mamoru's face. He said, "Do not threaten your future brother-in-law."

The next six months spun by like a Pacific typhoon. We rushed to make thousands of arrangements for our wedding. I had to take classes in Japanese language, ancient traditions and various aspects of Japanese culture. Three nights a week, the classes were as intense as medical school. In addition to that, I also had to buy a complete civilian wardrobe to wear at the social events, numerous parties and our wedding.

I called home to Pop and Momma and gave them the exciting news. They were over the moon for me but could not come to the wedding. "I will pay for the entire trip for you and Momma to come," I explained.

"Money is not da problem, mon. We got to take care of the farm and feed the animals. We do everything. We can't wait to meet her. We love you and miss you so much!"

My old friend and roommate, Atsushi, entered the Herito living room and grinned at me. "Sure, you are truly to become my brother." He pulled me in for a man hug.

"Thank you, my brother."

Atsushi sat in the chair across from me. "Lawrence, I want to explain about the feelings of the brothers to you." He pursed his lips and furrowed his serious brow. "We always liked you, especially all those years at university. We gained respect for your hard work and dedication."

"Thank you. I too, respected your dedication and…"

He interrupted me. "Wait." He held up his hand to stop. "Let me finish. Sure we respect you at school, but when you became infatuated with my sister," he shook his head. "I become protective."

"I understand."

"No, you do not understand. My brothers and I wanted to kill you. I always liked you, but," he frowned, "my sister?" He threw up his hands. "We want the best for Aimi, you not the best. You are good, but never good enough for baby sister."

"I'll try to be good."

"Sure, you listen. Give me chance to explain. When you save Grandmother, and my father declare you family, you became a full member. You are truly my brother. You always friend. Great college study partner. Now, you brother."

I rubbed my cheek. There was still a tiny scar from the beating. "Even Mamoru thinks I am his brother?"

"Hideki, Mamoru, Lawrence and Atsushi, we are the four Samurai." He stood up like a swashbuckler pretending to draw out his sword.

I hugged him again. I had not felt such belonging in a long time, maybe forever. I belonged to this family. Warmth enveloped me, I felt whole. I was truly part of a family again.

CHAPTER 39

HERITO ASKS FOR HELP

"I'm telling you, Doc, my honeymoon was the greatest seven days of my life." I chuckled. "Maybe even the greatest seven days of anyone's life." My soul was as full of warmth and devotion as I could ever have imagined. The love and closeness I felt for sweet Aimi had never happened with anyone else.

"I have never known real intimacy with another human as I do with Aimi."

"It's an amazing maturing process, this love thing," Dr. Kennedy said. "Falling in love and committing to another human being has an everlasting effect on one." He had a smile on his face and a faraway look in his eyes.

"I feel different, happier. Part of something bigger, more significant than me."

"Mrs. K and I want you to stay with us until your house on base is ready." We took them up on their offer and set up a little love nest in their guest room on the opposite side of the house. The room was warm, soft, and comfortable. Inside our little nest, our hours there laying face-to-face, skin-to-skin and heart-to-heart were the most connected minutes I had ever had. Time stood still, and nature enveloped my soul. I cherish the memory of those beloved hours of 'baby-making' as Aimi called them.

"You will always be faithful, promise me." She needed my reassurance.

"I love only you and you forever," I pledged. She smiled warmly, kissed me deeply, leading to more baby-making.

One morning, Dr. Herito called.

"Lawrence-san, my mother is experiencing problems with her new heart valve."

"I am sorry to hear that Grandmother-sobo is in difficulty. Aimi and I will go to her immediately."

"That is not necessary. She has the best staff possible and is in no immediate danger." He coughed. "There is one way you can help."

"Anything."

"There is a drug that is approved by the American FDA. We cannot get it over here yet. Can you obtain it for her? It has shown great trial results in U.S."

"Of course. Give me the particulars."

I called Dr. Kim, my confidant, and asked his advice.

"I have relatives in Korea. I do it all the time. I order American FDA approved drugs, assign it to my aging father who lives with me, and give the drugs to the relative. You can use my father to order the drugs for Grandmother, and I will help you."

I called the pharmacy and placed the order in Dr. Kim's father's name. Friday, I went to the pharmacy, signed the prescription, and picked up the medication. I drove to the Kennedy house, got Aimi, and went to visit Grandmother-sobo. When we arrived, I gave the medicine to Dr. Herito and went to see Grandmother in her bedroom. She was on prescribed bed rest and looked grey and exhausted. She looked lifeless, her eyes were dull, and she hardly breathed or moved. I worried.

Dr. Herito entered and went to her bedside. "She is listless and worn out. Just as she was two days ago. Your medicine should help her enormously by increasing the flow of blood to the heart and lessening the strain," he said as he held her head up and gave her two pills with a glass of water.

Aimi took me outside to talk. "Lawrence-san, I am very worried. I must stay with Grandmother-sobo until she recovers."

We walked and talked for two or three miles around a grove of trees and started back. "I am so worried about her, she looks like a ghost," Aimi concluded.

My spirit sank as I realized she was right. At that moment, I realized that I loved Grandmother deeply, not just because of Aimi, but I loved her like the grandmother I never had. She was the one person who trusted me from the beginning. That lovely old lady was the reason we were together and so much in love. No matter what the consequences, I had to do whatever it took to help her recover.

We hustled back into the house, and I went looking for Dr. Herito, while Aimi returned to her grandmother's room. I found him on the phone in the dining room. He looked tired, and I realized what an ordeal his mother's heart problem must have been for him.

I sat beside him, remembering what Dr. Kennedy advised about me acting humble with a very senior physician. I approached the subject softly and tentatively. "Father-in-law-san, Aimi-san is concerned for her grandmother, whom she loves immensely."

"I have the same concerns. Her physician is doing everything possible."

"Do you think there is anything else?"

"Lawrence, she has the best heart surgeon in all Japan. I cannot supersede. He is a valuable and deeply venerated—"

"But did you see how she looks?" I asked.

"He is attending." There was a loud joyous shout from Aimi.

"Lawrence, come here," she yelled.

I jumped up and ran to the bedroom. Rushing through the door, I saw Grandmother sitting up. I ran to the bed, grabbing my stethoscope, but Dr. Herito beat me. He listened to her heart. He moved his instrument from her heart to her lungs, and then back to her heart, and a smile came over his face. He took down his stethoscope and proclaimed, "Her heart is stronger."

I was full of questions. "What happened? May I listen? She seems to have regained her color. How is this possible?"

Grandmother smiled and Aimi interpreted what she said. "Two brilliant doctors for son and grandson make me healthy."

Dr. Herito put his stethoscope on her chest again and listened all over, then pronounced, "She is very healthy. Before this time, Grandmother-sobo never took drugs of any kind. Your new drug from America increased her blood flow and improved her heart function."

Grandmother was delighted and seemed so full of life. She smiled and joked with us. "You saved my life second time, Lawrence-san."

We had tea at her bedside. She wanted to get up, but Dr. Herito would not allow her. He demanded that she return to the hospital for a check-up.

Aimi and I soon said our goodbyes and went home to the base. The trip was exciting because Aimi revealed that she was a couple of days late. My excitement coursed like the electricity from defibrillator paddles. Life was good. She sat close and we held hands. She smelled of vanilla and love and my happiness overflowed.

Perhaps a brighter future was in store.

CHAPTER 30

BULL HAS A DATE

I sat in my office, updating records, when a loud crack startled me. Someone kicked my door open. I jerked my head up and glared at Major Bull Hassan. He stood in my doorway wearing his mirrored sunglasses, his hands on his hips, puffed chest and a smart-alecky smirk.

"This is the greatest day of my life."

"Get out of here, Major."

"Look what I got." He held up a piece of paper. "I have the evidence right here. You're a felon, and you're going to Leavenworth."

He walked closer, towering over me, opening a bag of dried dates from his pocket. He flipped a date up high over his head, leaned back with his mouth gaping open, caught it, and smiled. He chewed like a cow. Saliva ran down his chin and he wiped it with a stained handkerchief.

"Felon? What are you talking about? I've done nothing wrong."

"Bullshit. You got a prescription from the base's pharmacy and transferred it to a Jap civilian." He spit the date pit on my floor. He threw another in his mouth.

"I have the hospital's copy of that prescription right here with your signature. By the way, the Jap FDA does not approve that drug, so this is a violation of their laws as well as ours. I will have to notify the ambassador." He grinned, spit the pit on my floor, then flipped another date in the air and caught it in his mouth.

"You might go to prison in both countries. That would be great, a bunch of tiny slant eyes beating the shit out of you every day."

I tried to inhale. *What am I going to do?* My skin tingled, and my stomach churned with fear. My face was on fire. I couldn't speak, couldn't breathe. I thought back over the years I had known Bull, to the horrible things he had done at God's Home. I remembered how I felt when he cut the wings off Woodstock. I hated him more when I recalled how he had raped, beaten and humiliated Christina.

"How did you find out?"

"The prescription cost over $2,000 per bottle. We are required to verify each one."

"I stopped by the patient address on the prescription. The old chink didn't know what I was talking about. He told me to call his son, Dr. Kim. Good old Dr. Kim rolled on you in about three seconds flat. All I did was offer him immunity to explain the truth to me."

"What do you want, Bull?"

"I heard you got married. Why wasn't I invited to your wedding?" He laughed. "I sure would love to meet your wife and get to know her." He looked at me dead serious. I had a sinking feeling in the pit of my stomach. Wanted to retch.

I can make this go away, but I am going to need something from her."

"Not in a million years," I said. He leered, spit out the date pit, and tossed another in his mouth. I had never liked dates, and now, I hated them.

"I was just kidding. I don't like Jap poontang. I'm gonna arrest you and see that you go to jail for a hell of a long time. You are a fucking loser, you've been a piece of shit your whole life."

"If my parents hadn't been killed, I would never have met you. Your parents threw you off at the orphanage because they didn't want you!" I knew I was going to jail, and it didn't matter. I would probably not see my baby until he or she was five-years-old. I would be an unemployable convicted felon with a dishonorable discharge.

"I am arresting you right now. It's just you and me back on the playground," he grinned and tossed up another date.

"You obviously haven't told anybody or you wouldn't have mentioned my wife. There must be something that will make this go away?"

"Yes, $100,000. Payable in one easy lump sum." He laughed.

He moved within a foot, towering over me. In a deep, penetrating voice, he growled, "Dr. Leo, you are resisting arrest." His face was full of disgust. "You little goody-two-shoes, you had every advantage at the orphanage. They all loved the smart white boy. Even that fag shrink wanted to adopt you. The great *white* hope." He bent down and whispered in my ear. "But now you've fucked up. $100,000 or jail."

Then he threw up a date and caught it in his mouth. I heard "Mumpf, mumpf." I looked upwards. He grabbed his throat and grimaced in panic. He tried to clear his esophagus, harrumphed and grumped deep in his chest. He looked at me, scared. His face turned ashen, his eyes flashed panic. He opened his mouth wide for air, but his windpipe was blocked. I knew at any moment the date would kick free and shoot out. He put his left arm on the desk and leaned against it, beat his chest with his right hand. Full-blown panic had set in. He signaled with his left arm for me to come over. He pounded his fist on my desk.

My medical instincts kicked in. I jumped up, went behind, and clutched him in the classic Heimlich position. Bull braced himself, ready for the big pull. I pushed my hips into his and prepared to lift two-hundred-sixty pounds and pull as hard as I could to force the air within his lungs to expel the date.

But I didn't lift and I didn't pull. He looked over his shoulder at me, signaling with his head for me to hurry. His face was scarlet. I kicked behind me, closing the door. His eyes pleaded with me. The veins in his neck bulged. He grew weaker. His legs shook as he lost control. I clutched him tightly, and when his weight became too much, I lowered him. I was careful not to dislodge anything. I heard the propeller clock ticking behind me. I never loved that clock more. His eyes were open, he was still aware, but weak. Tick, tock, tick, tock, one, two, three.

I lay Bull down as if I was preparing to perform CPR. He reached his arm up to put his hand in his mouth. I pulled his wrist to wrench his weakened hand away. He clutched on to my dangling crucifix, breaking the chain. I knelt on his arm and gave him a big happy smile. I opened his fist, retrieved my crucifix, and slid it in my pocket. "This is for Christina, Woodstock, and everyone else you hurt and raped." I saw, under his chin, the ragged scar in the shape of a letter 'W.' I loved that little Woodstock and was happy that I finally avenged him. I heard the clock tick again, tick, tock, thirty-one, thirty-two.

I placed my hands on his chest as Bull opened his mouth, gasping for air. His eyes bulged, and his face turned blue. *I promised Christina I would kill you.*

After a moment, he stopped moving altogether, sixty-five, sixty-six.

I felt his carotid artery. A whisper of a beat remained.

I waited another minute. One-hundred eighty-five, one-hundred eighty-six. I picked up the prescription he'd brought in, folded it, and put it in my pocket. A flight of afterburners lit and covered all sound with their blasts. Voices; Kennedy and someone else laughed, walking from the parking lot. I leaned forward, did pushups, I counted thirty, thirty-one and thirty-two. I pushed until I couldn't push any more. Sweat beaded on my forehead.

Looking into his fading eyes, I was now sure of what to do. I leaned close to his ear and said, "Bull, you must be proud of me. I did thirty-two pushups, broke my personal record."

Bull closed his beady eyes. I tested his arterial pulse, no pulse. Not the slightest beat. Tick, tock two-hundred-eighty-five, two-hundred eighty-six. I did eighteen more pushups. I went down on my knees again and assumed the CPR position at Bull's side.

As I applied pressure in the CPR motion, I violently put all my weight behind my hands, and made sure I felt a rib crack. The pit shot out of his mouth, the air rushed out of his body, and he took a breath. My heart jumped, he wasn't dead. *Holy Shit! I might get life in prison if this guy lives.* I waited to see if he woke up. Would he move again?

But he didn't take a breath, it was just an involuntary reaction, he was dead, he was blue, and I was nervous. I grabbed the date and jammed it down his throat as far as I could. I pushed so hard that I had teeth marks on my thumb and second finger. I took a scalpel out of my drawer and performed a tracheotomy. I slid the hollow tube of a pen between the cricoid cartilage and the Adam's apple of his throat.

"Help, help, help me!" I screamed.

Within thirty seconds, Dr. Kennedy flung open the door, and fell to his knees beside me. As I stood up, I looked out the window, and saw a Military

Police sergeant walking toward the window. Not knowing how long he had been there, I yelled at him to call an ambulance. He immediately got on his radio. What had he seen? Had he come with Bull? Did he know anything?

I leaned back. "I found him like this. Something's lodged in his throat, so I performed a tracheotomy. I've been pumping his heart and applying CPR for twenty minutes, but he was already blue when I found him." I wiped the sweat from my brow. "I need the paddles."

"You can forget the paddles. This man is dead."

Later that day I called Dr. Kim and explained that I found Major Hassan in my office, dead. He was clutching the only copy of the prescription. I had taken it and destroyed it. Kim said he had not told anyone else. Problem solved.

My mind turned to Christina, I had to tell her the news about Bull. The first chance I got I would call the base locater and ask them to find Christina for me so that I could call her.

CHAPTER 31

AIRMAN'S AWARD, NO BULL

Two weeks later, the medical review board made its ruling. "Major Hassan choked on a date, which lodged in his esophagus, fully obstructing his passageway causing death by asphyxiation. He died before Dr. Leo found him. Dr. Leo valiantly performed CPR for twenty minutes and performed a tracheotomy. Dr. Kennedy relieved an exhausted Dr. Leo. The fact that Major Hassan's ribs were cracked without dislodging the date is a testament to the severity of the obstruction."

Dr. Kennedy said, "I submitted you for the Airman's Medal for your heroic attempts to save his life."

"I don't think I am worthy." I bowed my head with a humble smirk. "Doing my duty."

"Nonsense. You applied CPR for twenty minutes and then wanted to hit the paddles to restart his heart."

The stress of potentially being caught caused me to have more headaches. When the Medical Review Board issued its findings, I was relieved. *I finally put that piece of shit behind me.*

Living with the Kennedys was fantastic, but after five months, it was time for us to move. The base assigned us a two-bedroom bungalow for our first house. It required extensive renovations and updates before we could move in. We were excited to have our own home with more privacy as husband and wife but would miss the doting and cooked meals provided with love by the Kennedys.

To prepare for the big move, Aimi and I had a great time buying furniture. She shopped endlessly for a crib, changing table, rocking chair, all the things that would make the baby's room complete. We had months before the baby would come, but the time flew by.

We were in the base furniture store. "I like this king-size bed," Aimi said.

I responded with a grin. "No, I'll get the queen-size so you can't get so far away from me."

She laughed. I tickled her, and we fell to the bed, giggling.

I showed her the catalog with all the neat American furniture, but she had other ideas. "We get very nice Japanese furniture while we are in this country. Make sure baby know heritage."

For our dining room we settled on a traditional low Japanese table. Aimi bought eight pillows, and she laid an oriental mat over the dining room floor. It was very inviting.

Aimi's mother knew a well-known Japanese artist and commissioned seasonal paintings of the Imperial Garden for us. The first picture was winter, featuring weeping willows covered in snow. Next to it was a picture of fall, with colorful leaves cascading into the river. Geese flew south in formation overhead. My favorite was spring with pink cherry blossoms that reminded me of the garden where we walked with Grandmother. The summer picture showed people rowing on the river, having picnics on the grass and enjoying the day.

We loved our time in our Japanese home. We grew closer and more loving by the day.

Dr. Kennedy told me that I should come to the base conference room with Aimi. He said we would join a tea service and meet other base officers. At noon on Friday, Aimi and I strolled in, hand in hand.

The room became hushed. Everyone turned to look at us. I felt as if a spotlight shone on my face. I glanced over and Aimi looked mortified. She clenched my arm.

"Here is our guest of honor," the colonel said. "Come up front with your wife."

I tugged Aimi as she resisted. I approached him and he said, "Stand here. We have a medal to present."

With Aimi demurely at my side, head bowed and eyes to the ground, he read the citation.

"The President of the United States authorizes me to present this Airman's Medal on behalf of a grateful nation. To honor your heroic efforts to save the life of Major Hassan." The colonel pinned the medal on my uniform jacket, and everyone applauded. Aimi would not look up, her red cheeks signaled her discomfort.

There were tables set up with hors d'oeuvres, so we took a place and sat with the Kennedys and the colonel and his wife. Aimi sat next to me without touching the food or saying a word, she seemed to feel so out of place. "We're extremely proud of you my boy. I will be giving you more opportunities to shine in the near future," the colonel said.

"He's quite the young man," Dr. Kennedy grinned. "This medal will certainly help him in his next promotion."

"Yes, and I have a chance for him to shine on an important exercise we have in Korea next month. I was going to send someone else, but young Lawrence is the right man," the colonel said, winking at Dr. Kennedy.

After an hour, Aimi was ready to go home. We said our good-byes, and I drove. "What does he mean, exercise in Korea next month?" Aimi frowned. "You go away?"

"I will find out and let you know. Hopefully it will not be a long assignment."

"Long assignment?"

"Yes, sometimes we have to go on temporary duty, and they can last as long as one month but are usually much less."

"You must go?"

"We will see, maybe not."

That put a tiny smile on her mouth. I leaned over and kissed her. She smiled and kept me in the bedroom for another half hour before she let me return to work.

As I departed, she held me at the door. "You must not leave me here alone. Tell them I am pregnant and need you. You cannot leave me." Her eyes reflected anxiety and fear.

"Don't worry. We will figure it out."

The next day, when I walked in the office door, Kennedy was beaming. "That was a real feather in your cap. It will sure look good when you are up for promotion."

"Thanks," I smiled. "but, I have a big concern. Is there any way I can get out of Korea? We just got married and she's pregnant, and I don't think this is a good time to leave her. She seems to be very attached to me right now."

"Lawrence." He looked serious. "You can't miss this chance to get your name in front of the big boys. Aimi is only a few months pregnant, and you will be gone less than one month. Mrs. Kennedy and I will check on her every day. We would love her to come and stay with us if she would like to."

When I strode in the door of our love nest, Aimi had the biggest smile. She ran up, jumped in my arms and hugged me. I hugged hard, then pulled my head back, looked in her eyes, and kissed her. My heart was full.

After another bout of bedroom gymnastics, we were lying there, quietly immersed in each other. I kissed her. "I have to go for a short time, to Korea."

Her face turned angry. "*No!* You must not go." She stormed out of the room. At the door, she turned to me. "My father warned me you would leave." She fled down the hall.

Astonished by her vehemence, I ran after her. She wouldn't let me touch her. I slept in the guest bedroom and left before she rose in the morning. I worried all morning with a sick feeling in my stomach.

At noon, Dr. Kim called, "We're going to my homeland. Now, I will truly show you the pearls of the Orient, and why our women have such a sexy reputation."

"No deal. I'm just there to do the work, and don't say anything even slightly off color, or Aimi will kill me. She is infinitely pissed that I am going. Don't even make any jokes."

Arriving home that evening, I had no idea what to expect. I was very surprised when Grandmother-sobo answered the door and gave me a quick and friendly bow.

"What a wonderful surprise," I said and kissed her cheek. Her English was limited but getting better, and I still did not speak much Japanese.

She led me upstairs, to where Aimi was in our bed. I rushed in. "Hi, how's the baby?"

She turned away. "Grandmother-sobo loves me and will stay with us."

I smiled. "That's good news."

"Grandmother says no touch Korean women. American men get disease from Korean whores."

"I would never cheat on you."

Her face smiled a tiny smile, and she seemed okay. "You swear, Lawrence-san, you never touch another woman?"

"I swear to you and Grandmother, I will never touch another woman."

CHAPTER 32

REUNION WITH CHRISTINA

I slogged through the rain to the C-130 Hercules transport with the sound of high-powered turbojets spinning in my ears. I hurried up the ramp behind Dr. Kim, shook off my raincoat, wiped my shirtsleeve across my brow, and sat in the red cloth seat along the side of the fuselage. The ramp was down, and I had to scream over the engine noise.

"Now we're in the real Air Force," I mock-saluted Dr. Kim.

"These airplanes make a noise that is the sound of freedom." He waved his hand around to take in the entire flight line of fifteen airplanes parked in two lines. "I never feel safe in these military contraptions." Dr. Kim frowned. "Give me a 747 with a couple pretty stewardesses and a martini any day."

Then he smiled. "Wait till we get to Korea. I'll show you some of the finest examples of female anatomy God ever created." He winked.

"I'm married. I have a baby on the way. Besides that, there are incurable diseases out here we never learned about in medical school." I wagged my finger in Kim's face. "No, thank you, I'm here to cure the locals, not screw them."

"Lighten up," Kim laughed. "Those are unfounded rumors started by the Christian missionaries who wanted to keep all the kimchi for themselves."

"Well, I'm keeping it zipped, Don Juan."

The airplane accelerated to life and was airborne in five minutes, racing across the Sea of Japan, southwest to Korea. We landed three hours later and were met by the hospital commander. He had a staff car and several enlisted men to carry our duffle bags.

Kim and I quickly unpacked in the visiting officers' quarters, where we had adjoining rooms. After showering and shaving, we went to the O' Club to meet our host and the people we would work with for the next month.

When we entered, the aroma of juicy steak set my mouth to watering. My feet moved to the beat of *Stayin' Alive.* The club was full of laughing and drinking officers. Three colonels were eating dinner. There were red Budweiser and blue Coor's signs over the bar, the light above the pool table was a Tiffany stained glass advertisement for something called Hite-Jinro Beer. There was only one woman in the place, and she was serving plates of steaming vegetables to the colonels.

The hospital commander, a Humpty Dumpty shaped colonel named Farmer, waved us over. He stood as we approached. Both Kim and I shook his hand.

"Jolly good, gentlemen!" Colonel Farmer lifted his glass in a toast. "We're delighted to have you assist our community outreach program. America gets a wealth of good publicity from our efforts." Colonel Farmer's artificial English accent matched his larger-than-life persona and his loud laugh.

"Thanks, sir." Kim said. "It's good to see you again."

"Take a seat, lads. Welcome to our humble abode." His imitated British accent gained steam. He signaled his arms toward the open chairs on either side of him.

I was famished. I had heard about the delicious steaks that made the Osan Officer's Club famous. I ordered a medium T-Bone and looked around as six flying crew members entered through the wide French doors. The first two wore green flying suits, obviously pilots. Four women wearing the Air Force blue coveralls with white nurse's hats followed them. The four females were the center of attention for the lieutenants and captains, as it was rare to see a round-eye woman in the club. There was a definite murmur of excitement among the guys.

The lighting was dim, and the crew members were across the room, but I could make out a gorgeous, long-haired, tanned girl. She looked familiar. Perhaps I had met her in training at Wright Pat. I knew I had seen her before, but I couldn't see her well enough to make out who she was. Col. Farmer said, "Our flight nurses are quite the rave with the boys. They fly over the entire Pacific Theater."

"They fly and pick up patients?" I asked.

"Indeed, Captain. Some isolated bases in the Pacific have no medical facilities at all. Islands like Saipan, Tinian, and Palau have runways but no physicians. Our aero medical evacuation crew members fly the C-9 Nightingale from base to base. They retrieve injured servicemen and fly them to the large regional hospital, where they are treated."

Dinner arrived, and I cut the tender steak. I had never tasted such juicy, flavorful meat in my life. "That was so good," I said, finishing the last piece on my plate, not wanting the feast to end.

Then I excused myself to go to the men's room.

As I passed the table with the medevac crew, I heard, "Lawrence, hola!"

I turned and looked into the brown eyes of the sultry, tanned woman in the nurse's uniform. "Christina!" I couldn't believe it.

She jumped up and ran to me. "Lawrence!" she shouted. I held my arms wide and she launched into me. "I wondered if I would ever see you again."

I hugged her with all my strength. Bull immediately came to my mind. I had to tell her the great news. "Christina…I missed you—How are you?"

She kissed me on the cheek, stepped back, and asked, "How are you, Lawrence? Where have you been? How did you get to Korea?" She eyed me up and down.

"Wow, you look wonderful," I said. "Even more beautiful than the last time I saw you."

"Look at you," she said with a wide smile. She pushed me back to better focus on me. She scanned me up and down. "Ooh, la, la, you're even more handsome."

My pulse raced as I stood next to her. After five or ten minutes, I saw Kim waving at me. "Let me excuse myself from my dinner companions. Can we talk?"

"I'll wait right here."

I rushed back to my table. "Excuse me, gentlemen. I met an old friend I haven't seen in a long time. We have to catch up."

"Surely, m'boy. Stop by the office tomorrow at nine for a proper arrival briefing. Cheerio."

Kim was miming intercourse with his hands, so that only I could see. He stuck his right index finger through a circle he made with his left thumb and index. I tried not to look at him.

I smiled back at Christina and enveloped both her hands in mine. She grinned at me and introduced me to all her crew. Honestly, I couldn't remember a single name. I was lost in her eyes. After a few minutes, we said good-bye to her crew and grabbed a table in the corner.

"I thought about you so many times."

"Oh, Lawrence, I see the wedding ring. Did you get that Japanese girl? Tell me everything. How do you like the Air Force? Have you been back to God's Home? Are you stationed here?"

"Wait a minute, not so fast." I smiled. "Remember when I called you and asked your advice about Aimi? We are happily married and expecting a baby. I love the Air Force because it gave me a chance to have a family with the love of my life. Yes, I have been back to God's Home a couple of times to visit."

"That's great. I'm contento for you." She touched her own bare ring finger and shook her head. "Still looking."

Bouncing in my seat, I was bursting. I couldn't hold in my news. "I have some interesting information about another kid from God's Home." I checked the area to the left of me, then to the right, like a secret agent would.

She turned her head to the side. "What kid? Who do you mean?"

"Not a kid so much. But someone you'll want to hear about."

"Bull?"

"Yes."

She pulled her hand away from me, glared into my eyes, and turned white. "That fucking monster, I don't want to hear about him." Her face looked hard.

"You'll want to hear this," I hinted.

She shook her head.

"Bull had an unfortunate accident and died right in my office. He's gone."

She looked dumbfounded. "What?" she mouthed. "Are you kidding?"

"I will have to fill you in when we can talk in private." I really grinned. Slid my eyeballs to the corner of my eyes in a very mysterious way.

"He's dead. Really, what?" Her face registered shock.

"Poor guy choked to death, right in my office." I snickered like a kid. "The best news is that they gave me an award for trying to save his life."

"You did it?" Her eyes were wide. "You said you would, you promised you would."

"An unfortunate accident," I repeated.

She leaned in close and whispered, "You did this? You got him for me?"

I stared at her. I tried to stare the vision of his death into her brain but couldn't.

Her smile broke out and lit up the room. She understood, no details, just understanding. She beamed from temple to temple and laughed aloud.

"Tell me everything later, promise."

"Yes, but not here."

"Let's have a toast," she said. "To you and your promises."

"To you and me, we've been a team from the first day I saw you." Looking down, I said, "No wedding ring. I can't believe that all the Air Force guys let you slip through."

"No one yet. I just broke up with my last boyfriend. He was cheating on me. I can't believe you took care of Bull." She grabbed my hands and held them warmly. "I have had so many sleepless nights and horrible nightmares about that filthy bastard."

"I wanted to call you and tell you, but I lost track of where you were." I felt proud and triumphant, the warrior coming home. I had kept my promise to her and avenged my cowardice.

In the pride of the moment, time disappeared. We sat by ourselves and discussed all the things that had happened together in our youth. She was beaming at me as if I had made the world a better place. The jukebox played some soft music, and we danced a slow dance. We had a couple more drinks, the conversation never paused. We danced again and Christina snuggled into my arms as if she belonged there. She stretched up on her tiptoes and kissed me. I forgot to feel guilty.

I didn't notice when Dr. Kim and Colonel Farmer departed. Even more, I didn't realize as the room slowly emptied until we were the only two remaining.

I moved my chair around to sit next to her. She snuggled over, held my hands, and whispered. My heart swelled, my hands sweated, and I was filled with warmth.

At midnight, the bartender turned the lights on, startling me. "Time, sir. The club is closed."

I stared at Christina, feeling like I was losing my old friend. "We have to go?"

"We can't stop now. I have a bottle of wine in my room, and I have to hear everything." She grabbed my hand. "Let's finish our reminiscing there."

We walked out of the club, arm in arm. She beamed like it was a new day in paradise.

CHAPTER 33

FRANTIC MESSAGES

When I finally got back into my room at 4:00 AM, the flashing red light on the telephone caught my attention, but I was too tired to listen to the messages. When I woke at 8:00 AM, I pushed the button to check the messages. There were fourteen. The first was from Aimi, telling me she missed me. In the second, Aimi was more emphatic. In the third message, she asked, "Where has my husband gone?" The following message, she was crying and pleading with me to call her.

The next few messages were indecipherable. She was babbling in Japanese. The tenth message was from Dr. Kim, calling me a whoremonger and a cheater. Being Dr. Kim, though, the message ended with laughter and a request for an introduction to the flight nurses that Christina knew.

The messages were stressing me out and giving me a headache. Message eleven was from Grandmother-sobo and I could barely understand it, but I heard Aimi screaming in the background. Twelve and thirteen were from Aimi, falling apart and unable to put together a coherent sentence. My heart raced, scared for my wife but annoyed that she was in such a state, and I had only been gone one day.

The last message was from Dr. Kennedy, castigating me for not calling Aimi. "You are torturing your wife. She thinks you have died in an airplane crash or have left her. Please call her immediately. I am going to give her a sedative to calm her down. I fear for the health of your unborn child. Call me immediately."

I dialed home. My voice came on the answering machine and asked me to leave a message. "Aimi, I am so sorry. I love you. The phone in my room was broken and I didn't know I had messages. Please call me at once. I love only you."

I dialed Dr. Kennedy's number. After four rings, Mrs. Kennedy answered.

"Lawrence, thank God it's you. Aimi has been frantic. We have tried to keep her calm, but she has worked herself into a mess."

"I am sorry, I had no idea she was so upset. Where's Dr. Kennedy?"

"—distraught so he took her to the hospital. That was six hours ago, and he has not returned home. Call him."

"I will. Thank you for taking care of Aimi."

Pacing, I dialed the number to the base command center, and had the duty officer connect me with the hospital back at Yokota. The operator connected me to Aimi's room.

I bounced my foot up and down, I had terrible misgivings, all the things I regretted doing and regretted not doing. It was an acute attack of the 'I should have' and the 'I shouldn't haves'. My head pounded.

I recognized Dr. Kennedy's voice immediately. "She's sleeping comfortably. We tried to get a hold of you."

"I didn't know I had messages. The ringer was off, I didn't know I had missed calls."

"Lawrence, I am sorry to tell you, but Aimi has a deep dependency on you. It is probably a short-term symptom of her pregnancy. But I must insist that you not go on any more TDY's until the baby is born."

"Dr. Kennedy, you're the one that encouraged me to go. Remember the feather in my cap speech? Anyway, when will she come out of it so I can talk to her?"

"Lawrence, I don't think you understand the seriousness of the situation. She is overwrought, and I fear for your child. Get on the next airplane home and come to see her immediately."

"I can't leave now. We haven't even started."

"Doctor Leo," he sounded serious. "This is a critical medical matter. As your supervisor and attending physician, I order you to return at once."

That got my attention. I ran over the options in my mind. *I have to explain it to Colonel Farmer. Man, what a screw up.*

I walked to the hospital in the cold rain, deep in thought. *She depended on me and I failed.*

When I hurried into Colonel Farmer's office, his secretary said, "We have already been called by Dr. Kennedy, and we understand that you have to go home. I hope your wife and baby are fine."

CHAPTER 34

POETRY AND FLOWERS THAT HEAL

Prior to departing Korea, I called our clinic and ordered the corpsman to drive the ambulance to the flight line to pick me up. My stomach churned on the entire flight back to Japan, and I had an excruciating headache. When we landed, the corpsman turned on the lights and siren as we raced to the base hospital. I darted up the steps with my legs pumping like pistons. I slammed open the door, tapped my fingers on the stainless-steel elevator call buttons, rode to the fifth floor and raced to Room 544.

My heart stopped. I thought about the mess I had caused. I rammed open the door and fell into a room of people. Dr. Herito, Hideki, Grandmother and Dr. and Mrs. Kennedy were all huddled around the bed. I was physically shaking when I pushed between Dr. Herito and Hideki to get to Aimi.

I studied her ashen face. Bending down, I kissed her. Her skin was cool. Her breath felt good on my cheek. Her thin lips were pale and bloodless, and her eyes were closed. I cradled my arms around her head and caressed her hair. Silent, pained tears streamed from my eyes. I had mixed feelings of guilt, and of joy that she was breathing and alive. I embraced her head and it was as if we were alone, the voices in the room became an inaudible murmur. *What if she had died? What if the baby died? I will be a better husband. I am not like my father.*

Dr. Kennedy nudged my head. I finally looked at him. "She is going to make it," he said.

I couldn't speak through my tears. I nodded and held Aimi for all I was worth.

Dr. Herito got right in my ear. "What were you thinking? How could you abandon my daughter in her delicate condition? What kind of husband are you?"

I stood and was stammering for words when Grandmother-sobo said something in a scolding tone to Dr. Herito. She stepped between us, clenched my hand and draped it over Aimi's stomach. She lovingly pushed me tighter to Aimi.

Sensing my touch, Aimi opened her eyes and looked directly into mine. I knew she could see the pain in my heart. She had such a loving demeanor that she felt sorry for how sad I was feeling. She reached out an arm to hug me.

"Lawrence-san, I was so worried. Something bad happened to you. You came back. I will be a better wife," she cried.

"You, you, you—are perfect. I'm sorry."

We hugged and kissed like we were alone. Our passion embarrassed everyone except Grandmother-sobo.

Dr. Kennedy broke the silence. "My patient requires a great deal of rest," he coughed. "May I say that she has undergone quite an ordeal? Let's leave them alone." He pointed to the door. "I'll be back to check on you after a while."

As the others left, I sat by Aimi's side, rubbing her hand. The room became quiet. I slipped back her blanket and kissed her naked belly resting my ear on her stomach to listen to my baby. Aimi kissed the top of my head. We pressed together for an hour, entwined in each other's arms, sharing heartbeats and breaths. She dozed off.

I hustled down to the cafeteria, then raced back with two cups of steaming hot tea. She woke up twenty minutes later, and we lay on her bed together, sipping our tea and rekindling the endless love and hope we had for our baby. She whispered, like a lover revealing her private secrets. I brought my mouth close to her ear and whispered to my love, feeling a deep sensual connection with her. It grew late and dark outside while I lay across her thumping chest, luxuriating in the warmth and sweetness that came off our bodies.

The nurse entered to check on Aimi, so I left and went down to the hospital flower shop. I spotted a book for sale, picked it up and read the love poems. One struck me as the most endearing. I took twelve gift tags to pen a line on each one. I bought a dozen red roses and wrote a part of the poem out on each tag and hung one tag on each flower.

"The flowers are beautiful," she beamed.

"I want to read you a poem by Elizabeth Barrett Browning. It expresses my feelings for you. Here is the first line." Pulling the flower from the vase, I read, "*How do I love thee? Let me count the ways.*"

"What?" she asked.

"It means I love you many ways, all ways." I grinned and picked off the second card. "*I love thee to the depth and breadth and height.*"

"This is the whole size of my soul in all ways from the top to the bottom. *My soul can reach, when feeling out of sight.*"

"This is lovely." She smiled.

"*For the ends of being and ideal grace.*"

"*I love thee to the level of everydays.*"

"*Most quiet need by candle and by sunlight.*"

"This means that I love you every day and all night every night." She blushed, absorbing my words.

"*I love thee freely, as men strive for right.*"

I lowered my eyes. "I love you so much." I read the next stanza. "*I love thee purely as they turn from praise.*"

"That says I am not looking to be praised for the poem, but loving you for yourself and just because you are you."

"*I love with the passion put to use.*"

"*In my old griefs and with my childhood's faith.*"

"*I love thee with a love I seem to lose.*"

"*With my lost saints, I love thee with the breath.*"

"Lost saints?" she asked.

"It means that I have a childish love that believes in the good and purity of man. I love you with the unquestioning love only children possess."

I kissed her deeply. "I believe that the saints were perfect. Now, the important line. *Smiles, tears of all my life! And if God choose.*"

"*I shall but love with the passion better after death.*" I put down my last card, lay down and hugged her.

She pushed away. "Why is that the most important line?" She had a quizzical look that brought back the color to her face.

"*I shall but love thee better after death*. That whatever happens in life, you can count on my love, even after I die."

She cupped her hands over her face. "I cry to think of your death. I must die first. I not live after you die. I will do like women of India." She choked up, "When my husband die, I have suti throw myself to burn on funeral pyre." Tears streaked down her cheeks. I kissed the salty tears away, found a napkin and wiped them.

"Don't cry, honey. I will be with you forever. I will never leave you. My job may require that I go on trips or even fight in wars, but I will always be with you. And until the baby is born, Bob said I do not have to go on any more trips."

She wiped her reddened eyes and looked deeply into mine. "No, Lawrence, I will love you after death."

CHAPTER 35

AIMI RETURNS HOME

The next morning, Dr. K called me to his office. It was a nicely appointed space with homey curtains and carpets on the floor. An upgrade from the standard government office. He had a model C-130 airplane on his desk and an old wooden propeller over his door. I knocked, and he told me to come in.

I smiled at him and looked around, surprised to see Dr. Herito and another American in a medical coat sitting on the easy chairs. I wondered what the occasion was.

"Lawrence, come in. Make yourself comfortable." Dr. K rose and pointed to an overstuffed leather chair. "I would like to introduce my colleague, Dr. Williams." I must have looked dumbfounded. I offered my hand and Dr. Williams shook it.

Dr. K walked over and placed his hand on my shoulder. "Son, you and Aimi are like my own children. I have been worried about my patient, your wife, and asked my learned friends for advice. I hope you won't be offended by my search for help."

"I'm not offended."

"I am worried about Aimi's health. I think her condition is perilous. She came exceedingly close to losing the baby. I fear for her mental health and anxiety," Dr. K explained.

Dr. Herito's face turned red, and he jumped up. "What do you mean mental health? There is nothing wrong with mental health of my daughter. Her husband must stay and be support for her. Like any good husband."

Now he pissed me off. "I had to go. I didn't volunteer."

He came over and got right in my face. "Your wife needs you. Husband duty to protect wife, not run all over world."

"Gentlemen, gentlemen," Dr. K said. "Stop this arguing. Please sit down. We must be logical. We all love Aimi, and we need to resolve her medical condition. Sit down, Lawrence."

I sat. It felt like Dr. Herito was blaming me for everything.

"I asked Dr. Williams to help out. He is a renowned psychiatrist who has a worldwide reputation. He read my patient's records and even had a short interview with her. Can we at least hear him out? I assure you both, you will be amazed by his insight."

Dr. Williams rose. "As physicians yourselves, you understand the frailties experienced during pregnancy. The hormonal component alone is enough to cause many women to feel extreme stress, emotional instability, which can lead to the loss of the child. After examining Mrs. Leo, I find her to be an intelligent, kind and emotionally dependent introvert who needs the support of—"

Dr. Herito sprang up. "What do you mean emotionally dependent and introvert? She perfect woman, just need husband."

"I was getting to that. Please sit. In her hormonal and delicate condition, she needs the support of her entire family. Her husband must remain at this base and not travel for the duration of the pregnancy. I recommend that the rest of her family remain extremely close to her. In fact, I met her Grandmother and think it would be advisable if she were to stay with Mrs. Leo for the duration of the pregnancy. And I would like to make sure that she gets plenty of rest until the successful birth of the child." He was very pointed.

"Thank you for your candid assessment. I can make sure Lawrence does not travel for work, at least until the birth of the baby."

Dr. Herito spoke. "I am sure my mother will love to be with Aimi. They have been close for her entire life." He glared at me. I felt the need to speak.

"I will do everything my wife needs."

I drove Aimi home from the hospital and carried her across the threshold despite her protestations.

Christina had been a close call. No more temporary duties or drinks with old friends. I swore to be with her when not at work. The baby should be here in less than six months.

Grandmother-sobo was in the kitchen preparing tea and snacks. I put my wife down in the easy rocker we bought for her to nurse the baby.

Grandmother looked at Aimi. "You rest," she said. Grandmother-sobo hugged Aimi and held her hand.

I pulled my chair next to Aimi and sipped my tea. "Your doctor ordered lots of rest until you go back for your next check-up."

"My husband." *I loved it when she called me that in her sing-song voice.* "My husband, I will not stay in bed while you and Grandmother do all the work."

Grandmother's face turned stern. "Follow doctor order." She wagged her finger. "No get out bed, I wash in bed, you. I have pan. Everything…" She pointed her finger at Aimi.

"I will be good patient, but I must get up to take care of myself. Grandmother not going to bathe me." Aimi laughed.

I knew when to shut up.

"Finish tea. Then bed." Grandmother pointed at Aimi.

I scooped up Aimi and carried her to the bedroom. I couldn't wait to see the face of my child.

CHAPTER 36

DELIVERY 101, 2002

The months raced by at the speed of light. Soon it would be time for the baby to come into our home. Every day the baby grew larger in Aimi's body and lodged more securely in my heart.

"It will be only a few weeks before we meet our new Leo," I said excitedly.

"I came across the little love poem cards. It made me think of baby."

"How so, Aimi?"

"To me, love is like saying hello to the new baby. Love is like opening your heart to the new baby. When I welcomed you into my heart, my husband, I unlocked my sensitivity to a future with more love than I ever experienced."

"I didn't think of love that way. To me, love is a deep feeling of expansion."

She smiled at me and said wistfully, "Love is saying hello, never saying good-bye. When you say hello, you receive new love into your heart. When you say good-bye, it is like when a good friend moves away."

Grandmother-sobo said, "Beautiful. Welcome love hello. Bye and send love away," she grinned. "Never to go, Lawrence-san. Never to say good-bye."

I heard Aimi shout, and it woke me up. "Okay, okay is it time to go?" I stammered.

"The baby wakes up inside me and wants to meet her father," Aimi said.

I jumped out of bed. "The baby is coming?"

"Yes, my husband. I felt the baby all night kicking."

"Get ready, I'll get the bag, Grandmother, it's time!" I shouted running around the room looking for my keys, wallet and shoes.

"Oh, it hurts, the cramps are getting worse." Aimi doubled over in pain.

Grandmother-sobo ran into the room wearing her old housecoat and one slipper. Her hair was frizzled and her face red. "Baby come," she said. "I get." She ran to the closet and retrieved the overnighter. Then she led Aimi into the bathroom, helped gather her things, and rushed her out the front door.

I ran to the car and started it. I jumped out, went around and opened the door for my wife. I carefully pulled out the seat belt and snapped it into place. I grabbed the bag from Grandmother, threw it sideways into the back seat, and raced off, throwing driveway gravel all over Grandmother. "I'll call Dr. K to bring you to the hospital."

I raced down the street, and Aimi saw three children standing at the corner waiting for the school bus. "Slow down, my husband, you will kill children who are already born," she laughed. Then another cramp hit her, and she doubled over.

I was frightened. I have never delivered a baby.

I raced like mad. I turned the next corner, and the force pushed Aimi up and back into the seat. She held tight to the handle and then she screamed and tried to stand.

"Lawrence, I am bleeding."

I looked over and my training kicked in. "Honey, your water broke. Don't worry about it. I'll have you in the hospital, four minutes—tops." I stomped on the gas and we sped up.

Then Aimi bent over as if she had been punched in the stomach and shouted, "Lawrence, baby comes."

I smashed on the brakes and slid the car into a vacant lot beside the road. I ran around, jerked off her seat belt and gently laid her back across both seats. Then I slipped off her underwear and pulled out the most beautiful little girl in the world.

My daughter was covered in blood and amniotic fluid. I lifted her up in both hands, flipped her over, gave her a little whack, and she let out a scream so loud, it scared me that I had hurt her.

"Whaaw, whaaaw!" she screamed. My heart filled with joy at her first sounds.

I wrapped my Mariko in a towel and placed her in my wife's arms. Aimi cuddled her with a sigh of relief. I finished driving to the hospital more carefully than I had begun. They were immediately admitted. Aimi passed out from exhaustion.

I called home to Pop and Momma.

"I can't wait to meet my grandbaby. When you come home?" Charmaine cried. "Thank God for the baby health. We going to celebrate with jerk chicken pot pie. Buddy eat it, too."

My mouth watered for the pie and their closeness. I couldn't wait to bring the baby to meet them.

I called Aimi's father and he asked, "Does she look American or Japanese?"

I laughed. He was so obvious. "She looks just like her mother."

"Good." He couldn't contain his pride.

I thought my family was complete, but I was wrong.

CHAPTER 37

Mariko Hope Leo

I held my baby daughter in the crook of my left arm and swayed from side to side. "Hush, little baby, don't you cry. Daddy's going to teach you how to fly."

She wrapped her hand around my right thumb, and I examined her tiny perfect fingers. The little nails were delicate and beautiful, and her grip was powerful. I stared into her gentle face, and I saw the image of Aimi. She was gorgeous, innocent and full of hope.

Hope would be the perfect name for her. She represented hopes, dreams and promises of a family bigger and better than I had ever known. Hope would be a great American name. But Aimi named her Mariko for truth. Mariko Hope Leo was perfect.

When my heart sang, its song was Mariko Hope, the sweetest sound ever to touch my ears. I felt unconditional love for this tiny, helpless creature who would be mine forever. Her eyes clenched closed, and I tickled her under her chin. She opened them slightly, the color of a perfect baby blue. They captivated me and drew me in. Actually, I was hers forever. *This is love at first sight. Only the second time in my life.* I danced around the kitchen with her when Grandmother-sobo entered.

She smiled a full and complete smile. Without Grandmother, we would not be a complete family and she knew it. She gave us wisdom, humility and grace.

Grandmother stole Mariko from me. She reached in and snatched her. Grandmother could not contain her happiness. "First great-granddaughter!"

I was the happiest I could ever remember. The joy of a stable family life and the closeness of my women gave me a security and serenity I had never known. I loved our home life. Friends called me to go to squadron parties, and I told them no. When Animal called to go to Tokyo with the boys, I made excuses and stayed home to play with my baby and family.

We had a fine life of closeness and togetherness. We spent weekends in the park, zoo, ancient buildings, or just at home. In the spring, Aimi brought her to the garden to hear the birds, and she giggled back at them. In the summer, I put a little hat on her and wheeled her in the pram around the neighborhood and showed her to the neighbors. When the leaves fell off the cherry trees and the wind howled, we lit a fire and huddled around the fireplace and played on the rug, as she crawled around and pinched my nose. I lay on my back on the floor and balanced her on my hands with her standing straight up.

Aimi shouted, "Stop. You will drop her." I stood up and let my girl touch the ceiling.

In the winter, she said, "Dada" first and three days later, "Mama" and brought a great smile to Aimi.

We took her to a large pet store in Tokyo, and her eyes lit up when she saw all the puppies and kittens. She loved the baby rabbits and little birds, while the pygmy hamsters from China made her squeal. She learned to walk almost like she learned to breathe. She just walked away from the table and grabbed my hand.

"She walked over to you, Lawrence-san," Aimi said.

"No, did she?" I placed her standing at the low table. I knelt five-feet away and held out my arms, and she walked over to me as if she had done it hundreds of times before. I wrapped her up in my arms and twirled around, singing.

"I'm walking to New Orleans, I'm walking to New Orleans," and spun around with Mariko in my arms. We danced away and made Aimi laugh with our silly bunny hop dance. Mariko giggled and laughed so hard, drool escaped from her mouth and she let out a loud fart, followed by a dirty diaper bomb.

CHAPTER 38

ENGLAND, 2004

Two years later in the fall, October 30th, to be exact, I was startled to receive a rejection to my tour extension request. I was assigned to England. I had known this time would come but I was expecting to be able to stay for another three years.

"We must leave Japan and go to our next assignment."

"We cannot leave," Aimi frowned. "Mariko not ready to travel."

"Honey, my assignment is over. The Air Force decides how long we stay and where we go. We stayed three years longer than usual, and they rejected my last request. In a few years, we can try to come back. And every year, you can come back home for vacation to see your family."

"Lawrence-san, I love you. I never say good-bye to you, but can you tell them we stay longer?"

"No, honey, I cannot. But the good news is, we are going to England, and Grandmother-sobo can come with us."

There was much fuss over the next three months as we prepared for what felt like relocating a family to the moon. There were going-away parties we had to attend. On top of that, before we could leave, we had to make visits to every living relative to show off the baby. There were social visits the family required with people Aimi did not even know. There was crying, sobbing, begging and pleading; that was just Dr. Herito. He could not part with his daughter, granddaughter and mother. I think he despised me for taking them away. He even directed me to desert the Air Force.

After all the nonsense and fuss, we packed up our belongings. Aimi made sure she bought all the Japanese noodles and oriental tea she would need for a year. Finally, she secured sixteen bottles of her favorite soy sauce, along with furniture and clothes to keep her and Grandmother comfortable for the future.

The morning the silver bird arrived at Yokota to take us away, Aimi's father, mother, brothers and thirty-five other relatives and friends came to see us off. Seeing everyone clamor for a last touch of the baby and Aimi almost made me cry. When we walked out of the passenger lounge onto the jetway into the aircraft, I looked back. They were all crying for Aimi. They liked me, but it was different for them and I understood.

CHAPTER 39

NEW FRIENDS

Mariko took to flying, as my Japanese relatives said, like a cat takes to swimming.

An hour into the flight, Mariko was crying and pulling at her ears. I sat on the aisle seat, Aimi next to me, attempting to comfort Mariko. Grandmother was next to the window. I looked up to see Christina walking down the aisle toward me. My stomach dropped. *How would Aimi react to meeting Christina?*

"Oh, Dios Mio, Lawrence. Is this your family?"

"Hi, Christina." I rose from my seat and gave her a tentative hug. Pulling away, I motioned toward Aimi, Mariko and Grandmother.

"This is my beautiful wife, Aimi, our little girl, Mariko, and our Grandmother."

"Oh, my gosh, you had the baby. When I saw Lawrence in Korea, he told me you were pregnant." I glared at Christina out of the corner of my eye. She got the hint, but it was too late.

"You were in Korea?" Aimi interrogated.

Grandmother gently placed her hand on Aimi's forearm.

"Um, yes. I was flying medevac missions out of Osan. We happened to run into each other at the Officers' Club."

Aimi shot a look at me, obviously pissed that I had not mentioned seeing Christina. As Aimi was about to speak, Mariko let out a huge helping of projectile vomit all over Aimi. Baby goo ran down her neck and into her shirt.

"Oh no! Let me get some paper towels." Christina took off toward the restrooms at the back.

"Give me baby," Grandmother said. Aimi handed Mariko over and headed to the bathroom at the back of the plane. Mariko spewed out another round of projectile vomit, covering half of Grandmother.

I took Mariko from Grandmother, and she grabbed her carry-on bag and she hurried to the bathroom.

Christina came back with an armload of paper towels, wet cloths and a stewardess in tow. There was only a little collateral damage to clean up as Aimi and Grandmother had both taken direct hits.

We cleaned up Mariko, and she lay asleep cuddled across Christina's chest. Aimi returned, wearing the same clothes with wet splotches all over them.

Staring at Christina, Aimi tersely instructed, "Hand me Mariko."

I could tell it annoyed Aimi that the baby was asleep in Christina's arms.

"Everything OK? I have a clean shirt in my carry-on bag. Lawrence, please hold the baby, and I will get it for her," Christina said.

"No, I am fine. Hand me my baby."

"It's no problem." Christina stood, handing Mariko to Aimi and walked toward the front of the plane.

Aimi glared at me. Time stood still. I still felt the need to speak.

"Honey, I can tell you are mad, but she is just a friend."

"Is that why you not answer phone in Korea?"

"No, the ringer was off, and I was asleep in my room." I gently took her hand. "I only love you, forever."

"How often do you talk to her?"

"I never talk to her unless I happen to run into her for work, and that has only been a couple of times. I will make sure to tell you about them in the future."

"Tell me when did you see her?"

Before I could answer, Christina was back. She handed Aimi a clean shirt.

"Thank you." Aimi turned curtly and marched to the bathroom.

Christina and I chatted for a few minutes, catching up with each other. Before Aimi returned I said, "Be careful what you say. I have only told her a little about you."

"What do you mean?"

Before I could answer, Aimi was back. She took the baby from me, and I scooted down to the middle seat. Aimi was in the aisle seat with Christina next to the window.

"Where are you going?" Aimi asked.

"I have been reassigned to RAF Lakenheath and I will be on the medical staff there. Lawrence and I will get to work together occasionally."

I turned my head toward Christina, clenched my teeth and mouthed *shut up*. I could feel Aimi's eyes burning a hole in the back of my head.

"Well, I won't see Lawrence that often because I have to travel a lot." Her explanation sounded forced.

Grandmother came down the aisle and stood at our row. Christina rose and edged her way out past us to let Grandmother have her seat.

"It was nice to meet all of you. Your baby is beautiful."

Aimi nodded at Christina, her mouth a firm line.

Christina returned to her seat. "Was she your girlfriend?" Aimi asked.

"No, we have always just been friends. You are the only one for me. You are the most beautiful woman in the world, you are smart, kind, and a good mother."

She looked into my eyes and smiled. *She knows I love her, but she needs constant reassurance.*

Grandmother interjected, "You no worry, Lawrence love you. I see love."

Aimi was quiet and pensive for the rest of the flight.

CHAPTER 40

WHAT ELSE CAN GO WRONG?

Dr. Perry, my new boss, met us at the airport with my new receptionist, Mrs. Breens. She had a soft and sweet British voice.

When introduced, she gave me a small curtsy and said "Elloooo, sirrr." She was so kind that Mariko went to her immediately. Mrs. Breens seemed to not notice the smell emanating from her diaper.

We departed Heathrow in an Air Force van and drove on the left side of the road, like in Japan. I was amazed by the lush green fields and beautiful centuries old buildings.

I leaned over and nuzzled Aimi's ear. "Home is where you are." She smiled back and gave an agreeing nod.

We arrived in the town of Mildenhall, where Dr. Perry had arranged for us to have a three-room suite at the Bird-in-Hand Public House. We had reservations until our household furniture arrived, and we were ready to move into our permanent house. I thought it was unusual for a family to stay in a pub, but my assistant said it was quite normal in Britain, and that the pub was more comfortable than the base hotel. When we checked in, there were American and British children on the playground.

Aimi and I went to our room and left Grandmother and Mariko playing.

"I believe that Christina only your friend." Aimi brought up the touchy subject.

"Thank you. I want you to believe me."

"Lawrence, I never be without you. I hate thought of you leaving, even for day."

"I know, but you understand that I am going to need to take some work trips."

"I cannot put the thought in my mind."

"Honey, I haven't taken a work trip since you were pregnant with Mariko. You may have postpartum depression, and that may be what is causing your anxiety. This will go away soon and my trips will not bother you."

"I not think so, my husband. I am pregnant."

I jumped up, let out a laugh, grabbing her belly, and kissing her on the lips. "I love you and we will get through anything together."

"I hope he looks just like you," as if she already knew it would be a boy.

I held Aimi's hand as we walked down the stairs and into the garden to find Grandmother and Mariko. Mariko was chasing small yellow butterflies from flower to flower and Grandmother was telling her, "Yasashi, gentle, yasashi."

After a long day of travel I was exhausted but wanted an English beer. Mariko was asleep by 6:00 PM, and Grandmother offered to stay and watch her so we could go out and celebrate alone. We happily accepted.

Aimi dressed in her finest silver and black kimono. Grandmother ordered fish and chips from room service. Grandmother was watching Benny Hill on the television, eating and laughing when we left.

We went to the small dining room that had only four tables. The sign over the door said, "The Snuggery," and this became our favorite room. It had a soft atmosphere with candles that dimly lit the walls. The smell of old English leather and 700 years of use enveloped us. Kings, knights, and horses were etched into brass panels hung on the dark and richly paneled walls. Soft music wafted through the air, and a bright warm fire blazed in the large stone fireplace. I looked across the linen tablecloth, held my wife's hands and gazed into her eyes. "So you think you will love England?"

"Yes, it is beautiful."

I had the roast beef and Yorkshire pudding, while Aimi had fish and chips. A handsome couple walked in and the lady looked Japanese. They took the table farthest from us. I heard the unmistakable sounds of a Japanese accent. I signaled with my eyes, glancing sideways at the table, and Aimi looked at me with a question on her face. "Japanese?"

I whispered toward Aimi, "Yes."

My wife's face lit up like a neon sign.

I caught the man's eye and waved to him. He had a military haircut and wore American clothes.

"Hi. My wife and I are new here. We just came to England from Yokota."

"Hi. We came here from Tegu, two years ago. We noticed your wife was Japanese when we walked in but didn't want to disturb you."

I extended my hand. "I'm Lawrence, and this is my wife, Aimi."

"I'm Joe Browning, and this is my wife, Aiko."

"Good to meet you, Joe. Would you like to join us? We would love to learn about England and meet other Japanese couples."

They came to our table, and Aimi greeted them in English. Then she addressed Aiko in Japanese. Aiko was wearing a modern mini-skirt above her knee. She also wore a figure-hugging white blouse that showed her bra, considered risqué in Japan.

"I love your kimono," Aiko said.

Aimi nodded. "Thank you. It is a family heirloom." I was taken aback by her formality.

"The Japanese girls stationed over here don't wear those old-fashioned clothes. We dress in London girl clothes. I saw in a magazine that trendy girls in Tokyo dress like us," Aiko said.

"My grandmother-sobo lives with us. She would not like me to dress so."

"This is the new world, darling," she said as if everyone else had already accepted it. "When in Rome, do like the Londoners." She had a wide grin. Aimi softened her smile and lowered her guard. They talked in half-Japanese and half-English. After thirty minutes of chatting, they got up and went to the restroom together.

When they came back, Joe and I watched as they babbled like teenagers for another hour. Aimi leaned in close to Aiko, and they whispered and laughed. I enjoyed my wife's appreciation of her new Japanese friend. Then Aiko suggested we go to the big room, called the Public Room, where there was a music group for dancing.

We took a small table, and I had a pint of Whatney's Red Barrel beer. "Bring me a G and T," Aiko called out.

"On the way," the bartender answered.

"Make it two, Aimi needs a drink."

"A small white wine," Aimi said.

"Come on, sister. Have a drink. We're going to have a great time together."

"Just a white wine for me, please," Aimi insisted.

Aiko told us that people around Mildenhall were countrified, which made Aimi giggle. She pointed out that the formal-looking British men were dressed in tweed jackets with ties, and that the older British women were dressed in long dresses. In London, that dress was old-fashioned.

"We are modern," Aiko said.

We danced until about 11:30 PM. The bartender called out, "Last call." We finished up our drinks and walked to the door.

"I will show you the town tomorrow," Aiko said to Aimi. "Can I pick you up at tea time? I'm being cheeky," she smiled. "How about 2:00 PM? We will go for lunch at the Officer's Club, and I'll introduce you to all the Japanese wives."

The next day, I awoke with a splitting headache. *Wow, I was not used to drinking so much English beer.* Aimi was ready early, and we watched Aiko drive up in her Jaguar.

"British racing green, of course, darling," she said. "It's fast."

I hitched a ride with them to the Officers' Club. Aiko was one hell of a driver; she raced around the tight curves and knocked me from side to side. The road was narrow, and I closed my eyes when we passed a truck going the opposite direction. I yelled, scared we would crash. Aiko laughed, stepped on the gas, and sped faster. "I have never ridden with a Japanese woman driver," I told her.

"Aimi simply must drive over here." She smiled as she put on a fancy British accent. "I will teach her on the way back to the Bird-In-Hand."

"I don't know—" Aimi was uncertain.

"Of course, darling. You're young and sophisticated and simply must drive."

We entered a brightly lit American Officer's Club. The dining room was a huge, high-ceilinged room, and Aiko waved at a table full of Japanese women.

They were all wearing miniskirts. Aimi was the only one in a kimono. They squealed when they saw Aiko. She ran over to the table. Aimi followed her at a more sedate pace. The girls huddled around Aiko like schoolgirls and jabbered. Their speech was half-English and half-Japanese. My mind was swimming trying to keep up. The girls sucked Aimi into their circle. I had only seen her relax like that with her friends in Tokyo. I smiled.

I knew two docs from Japan. We had lunch. Then I hitched a ride to the in-processing office to get my paperwork in order.

After two hours, I took a cab back to the Officers' Club to meet up with Aiko and Aimi.

"I don't think I'm ready—" Aimi said. Aiko was pressuring Aimi to drive us back to the pub. She had never driven before. Aimi was entirely reliant on public transportation, me and everyone else to drive her. But Aiko was confident and had the situation under control.

"You can do anything you want to do," Aiko said. "This is the modern world. I'll show you."

But at the last minute, Aimi put her foot down. "No, thank you. I am not ready to drive in foreign country on small road in race car. Not for first time."

Our furniture arrived in four weeks, and we were ready to move into our house in Isleham. A quaint little town of 2,000 with 500-year old pubs and a 900-year-old church was the setting for our next three years.

CHAPTER 41

A DIFFICULT DECISION, 2005

"Daddy, Mommy home?" Mariko asked.

"Very soon, baby," I lied. During her pregnancy, a routine test indicated Aimi had weakened renal function. Five months into the pregnancy, a test revealed that her kidneys were only operating at fifty percent. She was hospitalized at that point. Now, two months later, Mariko, Grandmother and I missed her sweet sound and gentle hand at home, but she needed hospital rest.

I held Mariko's tiny hand as she skipped up the sidewalk to the hospital entrance. Grandmother-sobo followed, carrying the birthday cake for a surprise party for Aimi. Jim Perry met us at the door, and Mrs. Breens was with him. They were all smiles, and each had a *Happy Birthday* balloon. Mrs. Breens picked up Mariko and tickled her under the chin.

"You are so beautiful, my darling girl," she said.

Mariko had started speaking a lot over the last three months and she answered, "Thank you."

"This is a special day, beautiful child. They measure how well Mommy and the baby are doing," she said.

I felt a pounding in my head, like a migraine. The tension was as thick as London fog. Jim put his arm over my shoulder and shepherded me to the elevator. It was only three stories high, this American Hospital at Lakenheath, but it was modern, with every resource needed to take excellent care of Aimi.

"Aimi has been doing okay. Her kidneys are deteriorating, but this could be temporary. I expect her to be able to carry the baby to term, we have only two months left, but there are risks of permanent damage, which Dr. Hertzog will go over with you. The good news is the baby is healthy and growing just fine." Jim smiled. "The baby's signs are all positive, and indications are that his development is normal."

There were competing medical opinions at work. Aimi's renal physician, an older specialist named Hertzog, had a different perspective. His primary concern was for Aimi, and he was consequently less concerned with the health of our baby.

After our birthday party for Aimi, a nurse came in and said that Dr. Hertzog had requested a meeting with us. Aimi whispered to me, "I do not trust that Dr. Hertzog. He does not like our baby."

"Sweetheart, he is concerned for you. You are his patient and he wants your health above everything else, even the baby."

She looked back with the blazing eyes of an angry protective mother.

Hertzog stood as we entered the office, gave me a short quick handshake, and got to business immediately. "When Aimi entered the hospital two months ago, her kidney function was at fifty percent. Since that time, her kidney function has continued to deteriorate, and the most recent test shows they are down to ten percent. We are days from the body automatically aborting the fetus. We are risking permanent and possibly fatal damage to her kidneys. As sad as it is to say, I recommend that we abort the fetus before we risk any further permanent damage to Mom." He spoke to me, avoiding eye contact with Aimi.

Aimi half-rose. I placed my hand on her shoulder. "Never. I feel his kicks. I hear his heart. I never kill my baby boy!" Aimi insisted.

"Mrs. Leo," Dr. Hertzog put his hands together. "I know how hard this is for you and your husband, but you have a daughter at home, and you are risking your life." He squeezed his teeth together and noisily sucked in air. "What good does it do for you to take a chance with your health? The daughter you have, could grow up without a mother."

"This is the unemotional and medically correct decision." He sounded cold and distant.

I felt dazed and dizzy. Aimi sat back, looking stunned and out of arguments. Hertzog went over some more test data to reinforce his point, but I was inside my head, thinking of the loss of our son. After ten minutes, Dr. Hertzog apologized for the bad news and excused himself.

My first concern was for Aimi. I was in danger of losing her. What would Mariko, Grandmother and I do without her? Life would be meaningless. My family destroyed.

On the other hand, to complete our family, both Aimi and I sincerely wanted this baby. I looked in my wife's eyes and saw determination, deeper and more assured than ever before. I knew I had to step in and take charge, maybe it was fear on my part, I had to be the man and make the hard, but safe, decision. Aimi was incapable of abandoning this baby, but I felt for the good of the family, there was only one answer. I steeled my will. *Be the man.*

Back in her room, I helped Aimi move over, so I could get on the bed. I lay on my side facing her, pulled her tight to me, turned my chin down, so she couldn't see the pain in my face and tears in my eyes. I felt heartbroken.

"Honey, what would we do without you?" Tears streamed down from my eyes. "I want this baby more than life, but we cannot take a chance on losing you. I could not do this without you. Without you, we are not a family. I am someone else, a lesser man."

Aimi shuddered in my arms, her face wet. "I love this baby. I cannot kill this baby. I feel his heart." She had imploring eyes. "My baby will live." She sniffed.

"Honey, if we wait too long, we could destroy the whole family. I can't make it without you. I need you, Mariko needs you."

"My husband, this is our baby." She had her pleading face on. "We love this baby. It will make our family whole. You must protect this baby. Never abor…"

"Not if it kills you. Aimi, we can't take a chance." I broke down and openly cried.

She wept a heart-wrenching cry. She could never make this decision. I had to find the strength to take the burden of a terrible decision off her. "I have decided. I am the husband. We abort the fetus tomorrow. We will have another baby when it is safe."

She looked at me, heartbroken. She sniffled. She hung her head. I stood up, leaned over her and held her close. "We must do this for Mariko."

She silently nodded. I saw the hurt all over her face.

I sat on the chair beside her bed for fifteen minutes. I held her hand. I felt cold, dirty and crushed. *I must do this for the family.* I fluffed her pillows, kissed her cheek, cuddled her, and reassured her as best as I could. "This is our only choice. If it was my life, we could risk it, but we cannot risk your life."

At home, I hugged Mariko and held her on my lap until bedtime. I had a special feeling for my little girl. I had gained an overwhelming respect for life. I was awash with an understanding of the fragility of a child, the wispiness of life. I held her close for the longest time. I couldn't let her go.

"She must be to bed," Grandmother softly pointed toward Mariko.

I couldn't say the words that hid in my aching heart. "Just let me hold her for a minute more, Grandmother." I hugged Mariko. She wriggled in my lap to get off. I held on.

Later, I passed Mariko's door and opened it. I stood beside her big girl bed, placed my hand on her forehead and cried. *If there were kidney problems the first time, we would not have this precious girl.* I could not imagine my life without her.

In bed, I lay awake all night. I tried every reason I could to justify aborting the baby. Tears filled my heart again, and I turned over. Sometime after midnight, I heard the soft sound of the door opening. I winked my eye open, and Mariko came over and crawled in bed beside me. She held on to my arm, grasped her teddy bear tightly, put her thumb in her mouth, and fell asleep, snuggled into me. I loved her, but my heart felt hollow.

At 4:00 AM, I went downstairs and made a cup of tea. I needed the caffeine. I stood at the open front door and watched as fog rolled over our lawn and a coldness dripped into me. I felt alone and miserable.

The memory of Mariko climbing into bed with me brought a smile to my face. Something clicked. I whispered, "I can't ask Aimi to abort the baby. I must trust that she knows what is best." My heart skipped. I felt right for the first time in fifteen hours.

I dressed without shaving and raced back to the base. It was just past 5:00 AM when I rolled through the gate and up to the hospital. I ran up the stairs and opened Aimi's door, expecting her to be asleep. She sat in her chair with the lights out. I went over to her and saw she was crying. I turned on the lamp, closed the door, fell to my knees in front of her, and held her hands. She leaned forward, hugged me and shuddered.

"I can't do it, Aimi."

She looked at me with her bloodshot eyes, and a smile crossed her face. "I cannot do it, Lawrence. I must have this baby." We stood and hugged. I held my wife with all my love. She held on to me just as tightly. We would go through whatever we had to as a family.

The constant battle between Dr. Hertzog and Dr. Jim Perry continued. Dr. Hertzog argued to abort the baby and save Aimi, while Perry argued to keep the baby until the last possible moment and save both. They monitored Aimi's kidney function and simultaneously evaluated the baby's lung development. The situation became critical when Aimi looked ashen, and her kidneys were down to five percent, yet the baby had not adequate lung development to survive. They infused the uterus with cortisone to quicken the baby's development.

Early that Saturday morning, Perry called. "Lawrence, we are at the point where the baby can survive. We have to take him now."

I raced to the base and arrived in Aimi's room as Jim was wheeling her on the gurney to the operating room theater. She looked weak, tired, and spent. I was scared.

"We get our boy today, my husband," she whispered. She closed her eyes. Jim hustled down the hall, pushing the gurney with all haste. I grabbed the other corner to help and held my breath.

I passed Hertzog in the hall. "I am praying for you all," he smiled. "Everyone is rooting for you."

"Thank you!" I said. He had no bad intentions, his position was medically correct, both Aimi and the baby were in dire danger.

At 8:30 AM, my son was born. His cry was weak, but he was alive. Jim handed the swaddled child to me. "Congratulations, Daddy."

I grinned. "How's Aimi?"

"She's resting. All signs are positive," he grinned back and my body sang.

"We couldn't have done this without your encouragement."

I held my little boy in my arms for the first time. I looked at his face. I was lost in love and guilt for what I had almost done. He opened his eyes, they were pale blue, and they captivated me immediately. My pulse raced. *My son. I have a son.* I was mesmerized, captivated. My heart beat so fast, I could hear it in my ears.

Jim knocked me out of my trance. "The nurse will take the baby. I will come get you when your wife is ready," he said. I handed John to the nurse, and hugged Jim. I loved that man.

We went to the canteen and had cups of tea. Mariko had hot chocolate. I read a British children's book to her until she fell asleep. Grandmother read a Japanese magazine and knitted a baby sweater to keep busy. After two hours, a nurse came and told us to come up.

I sped down the hall and into Aimi's room, leaving Grandmother to handle Mariko. "Lawrence-san," she had a great smile and bright eyes, but still looked grey and tired, "Lawrence-san, I miss you. Where is Mariko?"

I had a lump in my throat, so I just reached down and hugged her. She tried to look at me and ask questions, but I needed to feel her. I sucked in some bravery from her to buck up my nerves.

Grandmother-sobo came in carrying Mariko.

I took my girl from Grandmother and laid her on Aimi's bed. My wife cradled her head and kissed her cheek. She looked up. "Mommy, will you read to me?"

I laughed. Aimi coughed, took a drink of water, and kissed Mariko and hugged her. "Yes, baby."

"I'm not baby," she said.

Grandmother-sobo came over and kissed Aimi, then sobbed so loud, she shuddered with deep breaths, and tears streamed down her cheeks. In Japanese, she thanked the Gods for delivering her beautiful child back from the brink of death.

I can say this was the happiest day of my life. I had a healthy wife, new life, a fine son and a full family.

CHAPTER 42

TEMPORARY DUTY, 2006

Boomer bounded into my small office, grabbed my chair and spun me around.

"What the hell are you doing?" I laughed.

"Great news, my friend. I pulled temporary duty in Dubai."

"So? What's up with Dubai?"

He pinched my cheek. "An all-expense paid, thirty-day trip to a tropical paradise, and I can't wait to pack. The playground of the Middle East— beaches, ski slopes, luxury shopping. Dubai has it all. By the way, the prettiest girls in the world shop there." He pinched my cheek again and danced out my door. I heard him laughing as he walked away.

Because of the premature birth of our son, I was able to avoid TDY assignments, but this created tension within the office as it meant that someone had to go in my place. I knew that this would not last forever and my boss had made it clear that I would need to get into the rotation sooner than later.

During one of the office meetings, the list of TDY assignments was read out loud—and as had become the norm, my name was not on the list. Some of the doctors assumed I was shirking my responsibility. They were resentful of my special treatment.

One major said to me, "I have a son playing T-ball. I hate missing his games because I have to pull an extra trip away, since you won't pull your share of the load." He glared at me, then shouted, "Is that right, Captain? I have to miss his games because of you."

"Sir, my wife is seriously ill and has been going through a very rough time. I have two small children at home and my wife is suffering from postpartum depression. What am I supposed to do?" I asked the major.

"Nobody wants to go to Kuwait, Captain. My wife had a baby fifteen years ago, and she has never recovered," my commander snarked.

That following week, I came home to find Aimi and Grandmother both upset on the couch in our living room. As soon as I walked in the door, Aimi started in on me, "Why do you tell people I am sick?"

"Who came by the house?'

"Boomer's wife brought lasagna, and she was surprised to see me up. She think I am sick."

Thank goodness, it was Boomer's wife, because I could count on him to understand and not say anything. "I had to tell my boss that you have been feeling really ill, so that he would not make me go TDY. I have been taking a lot of heat."

"You cannot go, we have two small children."

"Everyone else goes, and lots of them have young kids. They all take their turns. If I don't go, they must send someone else to do my job."

"I call your boss and explain that I cannot sleep when you leave."

"Don't call my boss, it'll just make it worse for me. He'll think you are crazy, and he'll probably demote me for lying."

Later, I called Boomer and apologized. "I had to say that Aimi was sick because she freaks out every time I mention going on TDY."

He assured me that neither he nor his wife would say anything. "It's time you pulled your weight, my friend. There are some crappy assignments coming up and it's your turn."

I was sitting in a leather chair in the Hospital Commander's large office. He had a wall of pictures showing him with various generals shaking hands and smiling. I was not smiling.

"Lawrence, I won't beat around the bush. It's no secret that you are not pulling your share of the temporary duty." He stood and faced me. "It's affecting the morale of the flight surgeon's office."

I knew all the comments. I hung my head. "Sir, I, um, I don't know what to say. My wife is ill, and I have young kids. I'm not shirking…"

"Lawrence, you have to find a way to take trips. The pressure is strong. There is even talk of stopping your promotion to Major."

The threat of a passed-over promotion chilled me. I visualized being drummed out of the Air Force. I only knew of one passed-over doctor. He spent a year with his head hung down and embarrassed. I felt scared, lightheaded.

"Sir, I didn't realize it was that serious. I thought you would bear with me until my wife was better. When she's fully recovered, I'll pull my share of the TDY. I never considered that my promotion might be jeopardized."

"Captain, this has been going on for too long." He stood. "Now take care of your family, get your house in order and prepare to take some trips."

"Yes, sir."

Driving home, I struggled with the scene that was about to unfold. My ever-present headache was pounding. I had to tell Aimi that I needed to go TDY as soon as possible.

My pulse raced. *I must tell her I have a trip.* An idea caught me.

While Aimi had been in the hospital, Grandmother and I had been walking around the village, pushing Mariko in her stroller. Today, after dinner, Aimi cleaned up and I asked Grandmother to take a walk with me. I had thinking to do, and I needed her alliance.

A block away from the house, I turned to her. "Grandmother-sobo, I need your help with something."

She stopped, looked up at me and smiled. "My son, how I help?"

I spilled my guts. "My commander said if I don't go on a trip, they will not promote me. I would be a complete failure. The other doctors are complaining that I am getting special treatment and not pulling my fair share of trips. They are mad at me and my job is in jeopardy."

She frowned, and her eyebrows came together. "This bad news for Aimi."

"I know. What if you said something to her?"

"She need be without you. Her whole life, she very attach. As small girl of eight, she got goldfish for birthday. Goldfish live three week, then die. Aimi so upset, we thought something wrong with her. She not eat for week, or come out of room other than to bathroom. At last she get over fish but we know never buy pet. Loss too great for heart. She make her love so strong and true," Grandmother said.

"I don't know what to do."

"You must go?"

"Yes, I have to go."

"Then you go. Others go and you not go. It your turn."

"Yes, others have gone on multiple trips. I must go soon. There is a major's promotion board in six months. If I go on this trip, I have a chance to get promoted and keep my job."

"I break news slowly to Aimi."

I leaned in and kissed her wise face. "Thank you. I love you."

The next morning, I had a cup of coffee with Boomer in the hospital cafeteria. "I am going on TDY. Where did you say those next assignments were?"

"There's a health trip scheduled for Somalia and another for Ethiopia. Two ugly ones, no Dubai for you. I wondered who drew the short straw, at least the trip is only a week long."

Armed with my newfound drive, I went to our orderly room and retrieved my travel orders from the chief clerk. "The CO's sticking it to you because all the old bastards complained that you never had to take a trip."

I put all my travel documents in my briefcase and finished my day.

Three days later, Grandmother called me at work. "Lawrence-san, I tell Aimi today. We have fun day, time is right."

"Great, I will be home at 6 P.M. Good luck, and I love you."

Driving up to our house after work, I was startled by the sight of our front door wide open, every light on, and clothes strewn all over the yard. I heard a commotion upstairs. Two at a time, I jumped up the stairs. All the lights were on, and Aimi was shouting. I looked inside our bedroom, and Aimi was sitting on the floor, crying loudly with her hair flying in every direction, tears streaming down her face. There were torn and ripped papers and clothes everywhere.

She had my uniform in her left hand and a pair of scissors in her right. She cut through the breast pocket and ripped the two halves apart. "No!" she screamed. "No!"

I knelt beside her and grabbed her hand. "Stop!" I shouted. "Are you losing your mind?"

She looked at me with frantic eyes. "You liar." She seethed with anger.

She pushed me, holding the scissors in her hand, and gouged my shoulder. The pain was excruciating, blood ran out. She dropped the scissors and pounded on my chest with both fists. "You lie, Lawrence, you lie. You leave me. My father was right, you leave for other woman."

I grabbed her hand. She hit me in the shoulder with her other. I fell back, my shoulder bled profusely.

She saw the blood and turned white. Eyes big as Frisbees, she put one hand over her mouth and the other to my shoulder.

Grandmother came in and screamed in Japanese at Aimi. I tried to rise but the pain was terrific. I lay there for a minute, watching my life and career flash before my eyes. I felt lightheaded.

My neighbor, a British guy named Trevor, heard the commotion and walked right into our bedroom, saw the blood leaking from my shoulder, pulled off my jacket, ripped open my shirt, and looked at my wound. He compressed the shirt on my wound with a dumbfounded look on his face.

Aimi sprawled out face down, banging her fist on the bed. "You never leave me. You promise you never leave me or the family." She kicked out with her foot and caught Trevor in the back.

She mumbled, "You are such a liar. You leave me and cheat."

Grandmother knelt and tried to help Aimi, but she fought back. "You help the liar. You help him cheat."

Grandmother put both hands around Aimi's face and spoke calmly to her in Japanese. I had never seen Aimi act like this.

I tried to sit up, but my head pounded, and I fell back. Everything blurred—I heard an ambulance.

CHAPTER 43

AIRPLANE ACCIDENT

Dazed, I crawled on the bed, grabbed the phone off its cradle and rang Boomer.

"Boomer, can you come over? I've had a small accident."

"I've been expecting your call. Grandmother dropped the kids off at our house earlier today; she needed some time with Aimi."

He came over immediately and took charge of the chaos, sending away the neighbor and the ambulance. He gave Aimi a sedative to calm her, and me a painkiller for my shoulder. Boomer had Grandmother put Aimi to bed. He cleaned and wrapped my shoulder.

"What happened tonight, buddy?" Boomer asked.

"Aimi was freaking out and just stabbed me, it was an accident."

"How are you going to explain the wound at work?"

"I don't know. I am going to bed and will figure it out tomorrow."

My wife needed help. There had been indications of her intense fear of abandonment all along, but I didn't take them seriously. When she said, "Without you, there is no me," did she intend suicide? When I went to Korea, was that all psychosomatic? Was she bipolar or paranoid schizoid? I had to deal with her to get our lives on track.

The angel on one shoulder said, "*She is the woman of your dreams. You cannot go on TDY. You must tell the Air Force that you can never go away from your family. If they kick you out, go into private practice.*"

The devil on the shoulder spoke, *"That's utterly ridiculous. You are leaving for one week. Every Air Force family has to deal with this. Any career in medicine requires occasional trips to seminars and classes. The military is no different."*

I climbed into bed beside her. I spooned with her, afraid of what she might say or do when she woke up. Which Aimi would she be? She nestled into me. Her soft mewls, in her drug-induced sleep, reassured my heart. I knew our family would be stronger and more focused when we overcame Aimi's abandonment issues.

I fell asleep, exhausted and weary.

My shoulder woke me in the morning, reminding me that last night was not a bad dream. We had to face the results of last night. I started on a positive note. I pulled her close to me and whispered.

"I will always love you. No matter how badly we fight."

She stirred, still groggy from the night before. "You must not go, something might happen to you."

"Nothing is going to happen to me. I will be gone for only one week."

"I wish you to leave the Air Force. Like my father, you can work in a hospital and come home every night to your family."

"Honey, I have a contract. I have two years left on my contract and you know I cannot leave before that."

"They ask too much." She sat up and swept her hair out of her face.

I sat up. "This is my profession. I must go on some trips." I emphasized again, "My duty."

"I will go, too," she grimaced. "Grandmother can take care of the children, and I will fly to where you are sent."

She looked at the bandage on my shoulder. "Oh! Did I do that? Does it hurt? I am so sorry, my husband."

"Honey, the shoulder will be fine. But to come on official trips is impossible." I looked away. "They're in places where there are no hotels. You would not be allowed to go there."

She stood and put on her robe. "I can go, they will not know it is me."

I stood and firmly took her hands. "Aimi, you must accept that I am going. There is nothing either of us can do about that."

Her eyes grew moist, and she drew in her lips as if to weep. She turned and fled from our bedroom.

I readied and left. It was still dark. I walked the three blocks to Boomer's house.

As soon as I entered his house, Boomer said, "We don't make a big deal about last night." I carried my cup of coffee over to a corner table.

"You had an accident, slipped carrying a pair of scissors. I was at your house, playing chess with you, and I bandaged it. What do you think?"

"You're a true friend."

"Screw you, Doctor. I'll need an excuse when my wife is out of town, and I expect to use you." He winked at me.

The phone rang.

He held it to his ear and turned white. His face became serious. "We'll get there ASAP," he said as he slammed down the handset.

"Lawrence, a medical evacuation airplane has gone missing over Germany."

He raced to his car and I followed. Careening around the winding road, he threw me from side to side. I banged my right shoulder, and the pain throbbed, "Slow down, Boomer. There's no need to wreck your car."

He spoke rapidly. "With twelve members on the crew and the passengers described as patients, it had to be a medevac C-9 with our staff and patients aboard. Last night, one of our planes had to take patients to the regional hospital at Wiesbaden, Germany. Those are our friends. We have to get there to help."

He jammed on the gas, and I couldn't hear above the engine growl. In ten minutes, he skidded around the corner to the base entrance. The entire front gate area was spotlighted. There were armed security personnel around the gate. Boomer slid the car to a stop. The guard looked at the base sticker with the physician sticker next to it, saluted, and waved us on.

At the hospital entrance, the sun was just coming up, and I was surprised to see all the bright lights on the front of the hospital, like a major NATO combat exercise, with many people running around in fatigues.

Four huge men, carrying rifles and wearing face camouflage and battle dress uniforms, stood guard at the front door. Nurses came out of the hospital wheeling medicine chests, followed by technicians pushing instruments, and finally, three corpsmen carried boxes of medical supplies. Three portable light units flooded ten large aircraft pallets on four by four dunnage in the parking lot. The pallets were partially loaded and had cargo nets and camouflage sheets draped over the cargo stacks. Boomer parked, and we ran to the front of the building.

Captain Nett, the mobility officer, had a clipboard in his hands and checked off cargo as the others brought it. "Put the medicines on pallet seven. Hey, Buddy, the extra emergency equipment goes on pallet four."

Someone ran up with a handful of saline drips, and he pointed, "Pallet ten," he shouted.

"What's going on, Captain?" I asked.

"We're deploying the fly-away medical facility."

Boomer came up to me and walked me into the hospital entrance. "Lawrence, this is a real emergency. We have to go." He was dead serious.

"What, now?"

"They have not yet determined what brought down the plane. There is fear that a bomb was planted on the plane by terrorists, so all bases in Europe are on high alert. We are deploying the fly-away hospital." He wiped his forehead. "We're going to take this portable hospital to the crash site. The colonel issued travel orders, and your name is first on the list." He was sweating. He thrust a fist full of papers my way. "Take these."

I grabbed the orders. *How could I leave? What would happen to Aimi?*

"Let's go, buddy." He grabbed my shirt.

I pulled back, "Boomer, I can't just pick up and…"

"Doctor Leo, unless you want to be court-martialed, I suggest you get on the plane."

I knew he was right.

He turned away and hustled to the plane.

Boomer yelled back to me. "Isn't your friend, Christina Rodriquez, the flight nurse?"

"Yes, why?"

"She was on the missing plane."

CHAPTER 44

Finding Christina, 2006

On the flight, the Hospital Commander yelled over the engines to fill us all in.

"Here's the situation, folks. A base C-9 Nightingale medevac aircraft crashed in a remote German forest. We do not know the cause of the crash. There could have been a bomb or a mechanical failure. We will be landing at Ramstein AB in about an hour. It will take us three hours to drive to the temporary hospital site. The engineers are there now preparing the site for our arrival."

After landing, we loaded onto buses. These were long and slow blue school buses. I twiddled my thumbs for the next three hours. We pulled into the arrival site and huddled around our colonel.

"Six miles into this forest is the crash site. The only access is by foot. We do not have a count on the fatalities, but we do know that most of the patients survived, and the two pilots died. You cannot go to the crash site. Set up all your equipment in these tents. The generators will be on in a minute." I heard an engine cough to life.

"Good," he smiled, "it's going. As I was saying, set up your equipment here. First tent, triage. Second tent ER. Third tent OR. First and second tents will be manned by most of you docs, techs, and nurses and run by Dr. Ryan." Boomer raised his hand. "Third tent staffed by the surgical team, and I'll manage that. Now, go to it, the rescue people are five minutes away with the first four patients."

I raised my hand as he turned away. "Colonel," I shouted.

He turned back around with a scowl on his face. "What is it, Captain?"

"What about the staff on the plane, our colleagues?" I asked. The others murmured beside me. "Do we know who survived?"

"I don't know." He pressed his lips together. "I'll be sure to fill everyone in the instant I learn anything." He turned away and marched off.

I hustled to the first tent and opened the flap to see technicians and nurses surrounding Boomer. "Get the equipment from the trucks and set up in here." He pointed. "By the door is a reception station for triage. Next is a series of cots where the docs and nurses can examine each patient. When you find a critical patient, have the corpsmen carry them to the surgical tent. Okay, folks, get to it. First stretchers are on their way," Boomer said.

In the second tent, I cared for the first three patients, examining, evaluating, and bandaging for all I was worth. Four more patients came in a couple of hours later, and I spent a long time caring for each one individually. I staggered outside to stretch and was surprised that it was pitch dark. I hiked over to Boomer's tent and helped him for a few minutes.

Boomer said, "At midnight, there will be a relief shift. There is a bunk set up for you. Get as much rest as you can. There's a ton more patients coming at daybreak."

I finished my patients, bandaged one person, and put a temporary cast on the last fellow's arm. I stayed awake hoping for news on Christina, then stumbled my bones over to the sleeping tent. A night lantern dimly glowed as I crashed on a bunk at the back, falling asleep immediately.

That night my dreams were stressful, filled with images of Aimi confined to a mental institution.

CHAPTER 45

FLORENCE OF THE NIGHTINGALE SQUADRON

I woke at 4:00 AM, jerked on my jacket, and paced. I shivered, pulling my coat tight around my neck. I went over to the tent flap and peered outside, needing light. I grabbed my flashlight and stared around the corner before going outside to look for the cook tent. The ground was wet and muddy, and I splashed through the muck until I spied the lights of the cook tent. The sign above the door proclaimed, "Home of the Big Docs."

Inside, it was warm and bright, and a food line was set up. The reconstituted scrambled eggs and fake bacon in heated trays did not appeal to me that morning. I grabbed a cup of coffee and sat on a picnic bench.

Boomer came in and plopped down at my table. He had on the same wrinkled, stained scrubs from yesterday, his hair was matted and greasy, and his eyes were red.

"How are you? You look like crap," I said.

"Lawrence, you don't know the half. But no time to rest. They're bringing in a big bunch in an hour. On top of that, they're clearing trees for a landing pad, so the helicopter evacuations can begin."

"Boomer, you're doing one hell of a job."

"Grab a to-go cup and let's get ready for the arriving patients."

I returned to my injury tent and put new catheters on the trays, arranged the saline bottles, and straightened up. I heard a shout, pulled back the flap, surprised to see it was daylight. Four sets of stretchers emerged from the woods and headed to Boomer's tent. I followed and examined the first patient. He had a broken arm and various contusions. I instructed the litter bearers to bring him to my tent. The nurse and I attended to his injuries as quickly as possible, while the stretcher-bearers returned to the crash site for other injured.

I heard a ruckus outside.

"Please finish bandaging him, Nurse Rebecca," I said, rushing out.

As another stretcher came into view, my heart thumped. Walking behind the stretcher, holding a saline drip, was Christina. "Christina!" I ran up to her, took the bottle from her hand. Her flight suit was covered in mud, blotches of blood on the arm, left knee ripped, and a torn piece showing a raw gaping hole over her left thigh.

"Thanks," she said, and sank to her knees in the mud.

"Stop," I told the stretcher-bearers. I handed the drip bottle to the nearest person to hold aloft, while I knelt beside Christina. I held her head to my shoulder.

"Christina, you're okay."

She looked dazed. I was not sure she recognized me.

She sobbed and shuddered. I held on, and the stretchers continued to Boomer's triage tent. "Christina, it's me, Lawrence."

She stared into my eyes, smiled and melted into my arms. I held her silently. The chief nurse saw us and came over. "Thanks, Doc. I'll take over and get Nurse Rodriguez care and rest." She helped Christina up. Christina leaned on her, and they hobbled to the triage tent. Full of relief, anticipation, and excitement, I returned to my tent to see to my next patients.

In four hours, I returned to Boomer's triage tent to look in on Christina. She was up and comforting one of the patients. I waved to her, and she came over and hugged me. "Lawrence, I'm so happy to see you." She felt natural in my arms.

Boomer interrupted, "She was taking care of all the people at the crash site. The patients are calling her Florence of the Nightingale Squadron." He laughed at his joke.

Christina shook her head.

"Seriously, she did a great job stabilizing all the injured. She was terrific."

Christina smiled at him and then turned to me. "Let's get some chow. I'm famished, and I definitely need a cup of coffee." She turned to Boomer. "Doctor, do you mind if I take a break?"

"You deserve it. Bring me back a cup of coffee, black with two sugars," he shouted as we went out the door.

We strolled into bright sunshine and hiked on over to the mess hall. "I'm so glad you're safe, you must be so tired." I looked her up and down. "It sounds like you went through hell." I beamed at my old lover. "Florence of the Nightingale Squadron?" I chuckled.

"I'm fine. It's good to see you." She leaned in, wrapped her arms around my waist, and flowed into my body. Her eyes were warm and loving.

We devoured a pile of cold, undercooked bacon and reconstituted eggs.

"Let's take a walk," Christina said. She started down the trail where I had seen the stretchers emerge. Once out of earshot, she said, "Lawrence, I missed you." She reached over and embraced me. She turned her face up to me, closed her eyes, expecting a kiss.

I hugged her tight but kissed her cheek. "Christina, I'm a married man."

"Lawrence, I almost died in a plane crash. Life is too short. There are too many perils to delay love." She put her hand on the back of my head and pulled me down. "You have always been the one for me. When I thought I was dying, you were the one I thought about. I should have married you."

"Christina, I'm not just married. I have kids."

"It's not the same for old lovers. It's really not cheating."

"It is to my wife. You know I love you and always will, but I don't want to make any more mistakes in my marriage."

I heard a twig break behind us. I spun around. "Let's get back to the tent." I grabbed her hand, and we ran back down the path. It felt good to run like Jack and Jill, as we had those many years ago as children. When we were close, I let go of her hand.

We dashed into the clearing in front of the triage tent, and Boomer came out and saw us. "Listen boys and girls, time to frolic later. The last helicopter is on its way to pick up the final patients. Lawrence, you can get on the last helicopter as the attending physician." He glanced over at Christina before adding, "I'm giving you a chance to call your wife before we gather everything together." Then he said it again, for emphasis, "Call your wife." He looked into my eyes. "Tomorrow, we redeploy back to Lakenheath."

CHAPTER 46

A CALL HOME

"Grandmother, it's Lawrence." I shouted into the phone. It was difficult to hear over the combined American Military WATS Lines, connected to the German system, and across the English Channel to British Telecom— lots of loud static. "I am sorry that I have not been able to call, but I have been in the woods at a crash site without any access to a phone. I am sure Mrs. Breens called you."

A woman in scrubs looked up from her tray and glared at me and put her finger over her lips. I was in the cafeteria of the military hospital on a pay phone, trying to make a personal call home to update Aimi of my location and circumstances. Really, I was worried for her after the tumultuous confrontation of three days before. "Can I speak to Aimi?"

"She in bed and not get up. I take care Mariko and John-John."

"I will be home late tonight or tomorrow. Tell her that. If you need anything, call Boomer's wife, she will help. Tell Aimi that I am safe and fine. I love all of you."

Boomer walked through the door as I hung up. We grabbed a tray of food and sat at a table by the door. I looked at him. "I'm worried about Aimi."

"I know. She was paranoid the other night. What is she up to now? Is she mad about this trip?"

"I didn't get to talk to her. Grandmother said she was in bed."

"Sounds just like post-partum depression. After the birth of our son, Susan had post-partum depression off and on for over a year."

"I hope you are right, but it seems like there is more going on."

The loudspeaker called for me to go to the nurses' lounge.

"I'll see you in a bit, Boomer."

I went to the nurses' lounge as requested. I was surprised to see Christina waiting, wearing civilian clothes.

"Lawrence, we're not flying back until tomorrow morning. Let's spend the day exploring Germany. I have a rental car." She smiled warmly.

Christina drove the black Beamer convertible like she was part of the car, swaying around the corners and up the hills. She found a highway that followed the Rhine River, and the sun reflecting off the water gave me a peaceful feeling. At noon, she stopped at a Gasthaus that had a lush green lawn and a garden with red and yellow flowers. We ate schnitzel and walked among the flowers. She took my hand again, and I didn't stop her. The feeling of warmth, comfort and friendship washed over me. I imagined what it would be like to feel her wrapped in my arms again, smelling her perfume, and tasting her lips. I visualized kissing her, loving her, making love to her again. Nevertheless, the last thing I needed was to ruin my family.

"Christina, this is not right. You deserve better."

"Better than what? Being happy? You are what I need, even if it's only now and then."

"This will not work for me. We cannot see each other like this again. My wife is sick with worry, and I am running around Germany with you."

Her eyes moistened, and she ran to the car.

She opened the door and fell into the driver's seat, starting the car immediately. I put my hand on the door to open it and get in.

She shifted gears, backed out of the spot, spun the wheels forward, and threw gravel over three of four cars. I turned my face away as gravel hurled toward me.

I stood there for a minute, wondering what had just happened. I was pissed. She was unreasonable. Was it the scorned woman syndrome?

I went inside the Gasthaus, and the bartender called a cab for me. I returned to the hospital and called home.

"We need you," Grandmother said. "Aimi throwing up. She bad."

Anxiety flooded me. "I'll be home early tomorrow morning. How are Mariko and John-John?"

"They miss you and they miss Mommy."

"Hold it together until tomorrow," I said. "Good-bye. I love you, and give my love to Aimi and the kids."

I helped Boomer for a couple of hours and didn't see Christina. In the morning, we boarded a C-5 Galaxy for the flight home.

CHAPTER 47

A SPECIAL INVITATION, JULY 2006-DEC. 2007

"You left and didn't even tell us you were going!" Aimi screamed.

"There was an emergency, a plane crash. I didn't know I was going until I got to the base."

"You should not go. Something could happen to you. I was worried sick."

Mariko and John-John were upset and crying. Grandmother gathered the children and took them out the door.

"Come, we go outside and play." Grandmother looked at Aimi and said, "Shhhhush."

"I was gone for four days. I had no choice."

"We must have you every night. The children need their father. Mariko cannot sleep if you are not in the house. John-John will not eat his dinner until Daddy is home. Please, do not go again."

"The only reason the children are upset is because you will not get out of bed when I am gone. If you acted normally, they would, too."

We argued for hours. Finally, around 3:00 AM, she passed out. This was hell. I did not know how to handle another TDY. I feared for her sanity.

I asked for an appointment with my commander. A physician himself, he was receptive to my diagnosis of Aimi as postpartum depressed, and he promised to minimize the length of my trips. "I can send you on short trips so you are away from the home for less time, but that means you are going to get a lot of the crappy assignments." Three weeks later, I was in Somalia, a week long mosquito-filled malaria infested trip to Africa. I couldn't even call home to check on the family. When I returned, Grandmother looked five years older.

In November, Mrs. Breens opened my office door. "Dr. Leo, there is a call from America for you from Bob Kennedy. Shall I take a message or…"

"I'll take it, thank you."

"Hi, Bob. What a great surprise. How's Mrs. K?"

We talked for ten minutes and caught up on life. Then he hit his main point. "Lawrence, this is a business call. I have a rare opportunity for you, my boy."

"What opportunity? Tell me more."

"I have been selected to be the Medical Inspector General for the Air Force."

"Great, Bob. I'm not surprised. You're dedicated and hardworking. They couldn't have given such an important position to anyone more deserving."

"Yeah, yeah," he chuckled. "The important part is that I get to select my inspection team members. I can choose who I want, and I want you to work with me in the Pentagon."

"That would be a great honor. Wow, Bob, I'm flattered you want me. I couldn't be more delighted." With the thought of a possible promotion pass-over in my current assignment—selection to the IG team would be a great boost to my record. "Let me talk it over with Aimi. Can you call me tonight at home?"

The opportunity to be with the Kennedys again would delight Aimi. On top of that, going to DC would be great for my career. It would be a wonderful experience for the kids. This assignment could be a dream come true, but it sounded like a lot of travel.

I called home and told Grandmother that I had a surprise for everyone. When I walked through the door that evening, the aroma of stir-fried shrimp welcomed me and made my mouth water. The kids ran up and hugged my legs for me to pick them up. John-John held up his arms, and I hefted him and kissed his milky mouth. Mariko was full of excitement, showing me a crayon drawing of our family. I kissed Grandmother, carried John-John into the dining room, and put him in his high chair.

Aimi glided over, put her arms around me, and kissed me full on the lips.

I kissed her back. I smelled shrimp on her breath. I could taste it and smiled at her. "You're eating the shrimp before us," I kidded her. "I want some."

"Sit, eat," Grandmother said, pulling out my chair. "Food will get cold, we work hard to make it for you."

We sat and Mariko said a little prayer she learned in school. I reflected that this house was the scene of many of life's greatest pleasures. We enjoyed the formation of our family and the maturing of our love. We also had the birth of our son, and the development of a loving family. I was nostalgic and choked up at the thought of leaving this place, but the opportunity to go to an exciting place like Washington, DC and be closer to Pop and Charmain were the icing on the cake of my career.

The phone rang, and Aimi looked at me. I stood and answered it. "Lawrence, it's Mrs. K." Looking in the mirror, my face lit up like Christmas morning.

"Hold on, hold on. I want you to speak to Aimi."

Aimi had a quizzical look on her face. She rose slowly, came over and took the receiver from my hand. "Hello, this is Aimi." She listened for a second, a grin began on her lips and moved across her mouth and finally engulfed her entire face. With the widest beam, she shouted, "Mrs. Kennedy, so good to hear you. We miss you, Mariko is so big and you have to see John-John."

She listened for a couple of minutes. "It is exciting. I will be most happy to come to Washington and be with you again. It will be the best time for my family."

The Japanese have a saying, "The Gods make you happiest just before they torment you."

CHAPTER 48

GOING HOME JANUARY 2008

The sun rose through the windows of our gleaming Boeing 747 and flashed spotlight like circles across the cabin. They were basketball-sized bright halos playing across the rows of passengers. The touch of sunlight made my arm feel warm and my heartbeat faster. Sunlight made me smile—the entire world felt brighter.

My family was seated four abreast in the center seat row. I picked up my boy and sat him in my lap. "Miami is an incredible place, John-John. We are going to spend a whole month with Pop and Momma Slim, on their farm in Homestead."

He shielded his eyes from a spotlight of intense sunbeams that swept across his face. "First thing, I will get you some sunglasses. Remember that sunlight is happiness." I hummed, "Sunshine on my shoulder makes me happy." He grinned, and I grinned too.

Aimi and Mariko were still sleeping in the seats beside me. I put my hand on Aimi's forehead and caressed her. She stirred, and I leaned down and kissed her cheek. "Sweetheart, they are serving breakfast."

Mariko stirred and came awake like a flash. She rubbed her eyes, looked around, folded her blanket, put down her seat tray, looked to me and grinned. "I'm hungry, Daddy. I don't want tomatoes or mushrooms."

"I don't think you will have to worry about that sweetheart." I smiled and patted her knee.

Grandmother, seated directly behind her, leaned over, "Remember manners. Be humble and thankful for nice British food. Tomatoes and mushrooms, good for you grow." Grandmother's grasp of the English language was increasing daily.

Mariko quietly sang, "God save our Queen," with a wide grin. She had an authentic accent and loved to say, "Ello family, jolly good."

We laughed as the cabin servers passed breakfast trays to us. Seeing the seacoast through the window, I pointed and told them about the beaches. "Remember Brighton Beach with the pebbles and cold water? You are about to experience something totally different, soft white sand, almost like powder and warm water."

Mariko spoke up, "I can't wait to see Poppa and Momma Slim. I miss them."

"Miss them, you have never met them silly girl." I laughed, nudging her with my forearm.

"I know, but I have talked to them a million times and I love them."

"You wait till you taste Momma's chicken and meet Buddy Too."

We ate, and the cabin staff cleared the trays. The seat belt light came on and we made our descent into Miami International. We taxied for fifteen minutes and loved craning our necks, straining to see out the small windows at all the airplanes. Finally, we parked at the terminal. When they opened the cabin door, a wave of hundred-degree heat washed over me.

"It 'tis certainly bloody warm 'ere," Mariko laughed.

"Watch your language, young lady," Aimi said.

"Mother, it's not a curse word in America."

I spoke up, "Cool your jets girl."

We gathered our belongings and made our way to baggage claim. It was a long walk but felt good to stretch my legs. Heading down the escalator, I spotted Slim and Mama. "There they are."

The kids ran down the escalator with Mariko shouting, "POPPA," and sprinted to him. I feared she would knock him down; she ran with such force. We all soon joined in a group hug.

"It's good to see you." Pop smiled from ear to ear. The white mark of vitiligo around his eye had grown larger over time and now covered half of his nose.

"We been so excited for you coming." Momma couldn't contain her happiness. "Aimi, you even more beautiful than your pictures. We so glad you staying with us."

"Oh, we got lots of work for you," Slim looked at John-John and grabbed his bicep. "You look strong, how much can you lift?"

"Feel this, Poppa." John-John hit a double bicep pose with a serious face.

"Oh boy, those are big. We gonna put you through the test. Your daddy is real hard worker, we see if you keep up." Slim grinned at him.

I turned to give Momma a hug but she was embracing Grandmother-sobo who looked like she was swallowed in Momma's dress. I could tell Grandmother-sobo was a little taken back with the easy affection given to her.

I saw a break in the action and took my chance to grab Momma. I hugged her with all my might. Amazing, she still smelled like jerk chicken—smelled like home to me. Smelled like love and forever. Smelled like real family. Stepping back to survey the scene, my heart swelled. I choked up and could not speak. I covered my face and made a dash to the men's room.

After I rinsed my face, we gathered our luggage and struggled outside. On our once in a lifetime visit home, I especially wanted to spend family time with Slim, Momma Slim, and Buddy Too. When we arrived at Slim's farm, my true home, in Homestead, I had a headache. Really made me dizzy—headaches were becoming more frequent, I was starting to get concerned. I went to my old bedroom, closed the shades and lay on the bed to rest. I woke about three hours later and felt rejuvenated and full of energy. I jumped up and did twenty-five pushups, marched to the kitchen and made coffee for me and tea for the ladies. Mariko came in a few minutes later and hugged around my waist. I gave her a cup of tea and we sat on the porch listening to the Whippoorwills sing love songs to each other.

"What are those white birds, Daddy?"

"They are called Ibis—sometimes cow birds."

She said, "What do you mean cow birds Daddy? And can we go to the beach?"

"On the ranches you often see them riding on cattle eating the ticks and bugs. And as for the beach, sure thing, darling."

I grabbed Pop and asked him what needed to be done first.

"You relax today, we start the work tomorrow. Today we eat and visit."

"Alright, you're the boss." I was happy to have the day off to relax and visit.

Later that first day, the scent of chicken wafting through the air brought everyone to the kitchen. We ate jerk chicken, biscuits, fried potatoes and fresh fruit. After lunch, we piled into the minivan and drove northeast to South Beach. It was warm and lovely—a soft breeze blew my hair and made Aimi hold onto her hat. I waded into the soft surf with John-John making motorboat sounds. We jumped into the waves and built sand castles on the shoreline. The pelicans and sandpipers fascinated the children. Mariko tried to lure them in with pieces of half-eaten sandwiches—they "Caw-Cawed" at us, smiled and flew away. They were too smart for us. When the sun lowered, we cruised home stopping for ice cream to cool us down. That evening ended early, with everyone exhausted from the day's journey.

Mariko was lounging in Momma's rocking chair with Buddy Tres lying across her lap. She ran her hand over his head and he rolled his eyes back, mesmerized. "He is falling asleep," she giggled. Then she looked more seriously at me, "Daddy, can you operate and fix Buddy's ear?" She scratched his head.

"Sweetheart, that is Buddy's birthmark. It makes him special. His father and grandfather had ears bent over like that. It gives him character."

"Does it hurt him?"

"No, it does not hurt him at all. His ear is the marking of a brave and loyal blood line, he is very special. His great-grandfather was my puppy, and there were times when he could have run away, but he refused to leave me. He was the most loyal dog ever."

"Daddy, I want to take Buddy Tres home with us. I like his wrinkled ear."

"You have to ask Pop. Buddy is his dog."

Slim piped up, "Mon, your kids need a dog. Yo' take Buddy Tres, with you and make the kids happy. I know Buddy love you and will be yo' frien' forever." I picked up the little Buddy Tres, and he licked the side of my face.

That next day we voted to help Pop in his tomato fields. I took the kids and we trundled after him down the long rows of staked plants. Pop showed the kids how to pull out weeds so the roots would not regrow and steal the nutrients from his tomatoes. I pushed a wheelbarrow behind and the kids piled in the weeds. Following them with the sun on my shoulders made me feel warm and peaceful inside. It just felt right.

I heard the screen door slam from a hundred yards away. Buddy Tres came tumbling, running, yipping after us and ran right up to Mariko. She reached down and cradled him in her arms and then placed him in the wheelbarrow, on top of the weeds. He sat there watching us work away, like a boss.

The kids worked hard and actually helped Pop with his tomatoes. After a couple of hours, we were hungry for lunch. Momma Slim rang a triangle next to the door. It clanged-clanged-clanged for our attention. Mariko and John-John raced and skipped to the house with Buddy Tres nipping at their heels. I draped my arm over Pop's shoulder and we ambled home.

We ate ham sandwiches and potato chips and then we piled into the van and took Buddy Tres back to the beach. For the rest of the month we spent the first two to four hours of each day working on the farm and then after lunch we would do something fun. The kids did their best to help us and could usually be counted for about an hour of real help before they wandered off. The ladies had a great time talking, laughing, cooking and trading recipes. We were always surprised by the weird combinations of food they prepared. I was sure we were about to get jerk sushi. We ate our way through our month-long leave.

On our last day in town, we drove the thirty miles north to God's Home. I had to show my children where I grew up. Something in my heart always tugged me back, like gravity. I was drawn to return to a life I would have never known had we not gone out for my birthday all those years ago. We stopped at the office and met the new administrator; Mr. Zemanski.

"I am delighted to finally meet you, Dr. Leo," he rubbed his beard.

"Thank you. I wanted to show my family where I grew up. I would like to introduce you to my dad and mom, Slim and Charmain and my wife Aimi. Slim used to come and visit me about every weekend and Charmain used to work here in the kitchen and that is where they met."

"It's been so long since we been back." Slim shook his hand.

"Look the same as it did when I worked here." Charmain smiled at him.

"We are honored to give you all the grand tour. After all, you are one of our most consistent contributors." Mr. Zemanski stated while looking at me.

Aimi looked at me with a curved mouth, tilted her head to the side. "How do you mean that?" she asked.

"Your monthly donations have helped us enormously, Mrs. Leo." He grinned widely. "We are naming the playground pavilion the Aimi and Lawrence Leo Shelter." He pointed out the window across the field to the school. There was a wooden roof and half-finished brick walled building under construction.

"We have a small amount automatically deducted from my paycheck and sent to God's Home." I said. "I owe them for taking me in when I was scared and alone. The government has a matching program, so they get double what we give." Her look softened, and she wrapped her hands around my arm and snuggled in under my shoulder. She almost purred.

"Why didn't you tell me? I am so proud of you."

"Honey, I have been doing it since my first paycheck. I just never thought about it."

"You are the only graduate to finish medical school," Mr. Zemanski smiled at me. He walked past my kids to the door. They were shifting back and forth on their feet. John-John pulled Mariko's pony tail and she yelped. "Perhaps your children would be happier in our new playground, while I give you the tour of our facilities." Aimi grinned at me and nodded.

"Kids, let's go to the playground." They jumped and laughed.

After dropping off the children and Grandmother, the rest of us took a windshield tour of my old life. I saw my house, where Mrs. Altee had done her best to protect me. Mr. Zemanski stopped in front, and we climbed down. A young woman with the same stocky German features came up, opened the door, and greeted us. "I'm Miss Altee," she said.

I reached over and hugged her—she looked surprised. "I knew your mother," I said.

"You're the one." She beamed, "Mom told me so much about the smart young kid who came here scared and alone and grew up to become a doctor. I have to call her." She half turned.

"I'm sorry, there isn't time, Miss Altee," Zemanski said. "But we'll convince doctor and Mrs. Leo to return for the Christmas gala. We can renew old friendships then. Perhaps, doctor, you will be our guest speaker? The children would be well served to hear a child from our home tell them the advantages of a college education, and even becoming a doctor. You are a great role model," he beamed.

"That would be so good for the children." Miss. Altee took my hand, "Please, do it."

I glanced over at Aimi, and she grinned at me in pride.

Miss Altee led us through her house—my house, it was mine long before she came along. However, I never really felt like it was home. I never felt safe and there was a coolness, too officious, too sterile, too many rules. It was not home.

Miss Altee led us down the hallway to my childhood room. It was all freshly painted in powder blue, but it still had the same exact furniture. I looked at my old bunk bed and relived the first time I met Bull. Pins and needles washed over me. I walked over and touched the bed, *I wish I could go back and tell that scared boy that it would be okay and one day your revenge would be sweet.* I wondered if there was a new "Bull" at the Home. The room had nice new curtains on the windows, and I saw mature trees out in the yard. A picture of Woodstock flashed through my mind, and a cold chill grabbed me, I pictured Bull with the scissors. I finished the tour with mixed feelings, having forgotten how many times, I had felt lonely and scared.

We piled in the minivan, headed for the airport with Buddy Tres in Mariko's lap, Slim driving and me riding shotgun. The ladies squished in the row behind us with Momma in the middle and Grandmother-sobo to her left and Aimi to her right. We pulled in front of the departure zone and Aimi opened the door, Buddy took his cue and darted off Mariko's lap and out the door. I jumped out and yelled "Sit Buddy." He looked at me with the same devilish grin his father and grandfather had and darted into traffic, right in front of a taxi-cab. The cab slammed on its brakes, making a terrible screeching sound that scared Buddy so badly that he ran back and sat right between Slim's legs.

"You almost a speed bump." Slim said. "Lemme put the leash on you." Buddy didn't resist.

We unloaded the van and stood at the curb looking at each other. Momma broke the silence. "I hate to say goodbye but we much closer now and you will be able to come and visit us. Take care of Buddy."

John-John walked over and gave Momma a big hug. "Thank you for Buddy."

"Buddy is going to be so happy with us and you can come and visit him anytime you want," Mariko said as she joined in the hug to Momma.

I walked over and gave Pop a big hug. "Thank you for letting us stay with you."

"You help out so much on the farm. I am going to miss you all." Pop said.

I walked towards the American Airlines counter and handed the female agent our tickets. She looked over my shoulder at Pop and Momma Slim. Mariko yelled out, "Bye, Bye Poppa. We love you Momma."

The agent had a squint in her eye and said, "Is that your Grandpa and Grandma?" She had a strange grin on her face.

John-John spoke up, "Yes."

The ticket agent looked down her nose, "Are they now?"

I jumped in with a matter of fact tone, "They adopted me as their son when I lost my parents. They are as real to us as any grandparents in the world." I wanted to tell the snotty lady to do her job and mind her business, but I didn't.

She looked huffy.

"Oh, no, not here." The lady said while stepping away from the counter.

I looked down to find Buddy had wandered behind the counter and was peeing on the floor, right next to the lady's foot. "Buddy, no, no, no!" I raised my voice. I was secretly laughing inside.

"Mariko, you cannot let go of the leash."

Mariko giggled unrestrained. She glared at the ticket agent. For weeks after we laughed at Buddy for getting back at the ticket agent.

"Oh no, I get tissues, where is the bathroom?" Aimi asked.

The lady directed Aimi to the bathroom and she ran off. Aimi handed the lady some tissues to clean up the mess. With our bags checked in, it was time to put Buddy in his kennel for his flight under the plane.

"Bye, bye Buddy, we will see you soon." Mariko waved as he went through the hatch on the conveyor belt. "Don't pee on anyone," she shouted.

CHAPTER 49

NEW JOB, NEW TROUBLES, 2008

We landed in Washington D.C., Dr. and Mrs. K. were there to meet us. Dr. K. had gained a few more pounds and lost a little more hair. Mrs. K. looked slimmer and younger. We quickly fell back into our familiar comfort with them, and it was like we had never separated.

We were assigned a big white colonial house on Fort Myers. It was a small administrative base, half a mile south of the Pentagon that backed up to Arlington cemetery. All of our furniture had been shipped from our old house in England to our new home in DC. Behind our house were Arlington's grassy fields, unused and macabrely reserved for burial of future generations of heroes. In the field were six old majestic oak trees that gave the area a feeling of continuity and comfort. It felt eternal and welcoming. The children loved running through the fields of Arlington with Buddy. They threw a stick and a ball and chased Buddy. They rolled in the grass with him and played tug-o-war with an old rope. Buddy always won. It was a different story at night— Buddy spent every night climbing into bed and laying across me.

I settled into my new job working for Dr. Kennedy. I was the second in command of the office and eager to move into a training role as that would reduce the number of trips I would need to take. As a trainer, my job would be to teach those going on inspections what to look for.

"Bob, you know how Aimi has trouble with me leaving and not being home at night."

"Yes, I meant to ask you how that has been going. Has she improved over the years?"

"Sometimes it is less painful than others, but really it is about the same. Grandma has to basically take over all of the duties when I go out of town because Aimi has difficulty doing anything."

"Well, what can we do to make it easier for her?"

"I would like to become the head trainer and so reduce the number of inspections I need to make."

"You are certainly qualified for the job and I love the idea. You will still need to go on some trips to check on our staff and make sure they are performing properly, but yes, we can do this."

"Thank you, this is going to make Aimi happy, and it will really make Grandma happy."

"Happy to do it, but you still have the upcoming trip to Omaha that you cannot miss."

"I haven't told Aimi about that yet, but I will tonight."

"Aimi, you knew when I came here that I would have to go to Air Force bases and inspect their medical facilities."

"I know, and I am sorry, but I cannot help it. I worry when you leave." She was sobbing.

"Honey, we have been over this a hundred times." I felt so frustrated.

"Please, you cannot go," she cried.

"Dr. Kennedy has promoted me to lead trainer which means I will be traveling less than the rest of the inspection team. But, I will still need to travel occasionally. I already had the trip to Omaha booked and I cannot back out of it now."

"I do not feel well, I am going to lay down." Aimi went to our room.

I went over, hugged Grandmother-sobo, and pulled the kids closer to us. "Don't worry, I'm only going on a short inspection. I'll be home in less than a week."

I had my head down as I tiptoed to the bedroom and lay beside my crying wife. I was going to have to travel, and she was going to have to deal with it.

"Aimi, I love you, but I am going on this trip." I spoke firmly.

"You tear the heart out of me, you say goodbye and you promised. You go to see that woman." She kicked her feet and slammed her fists down.

"I swear there is no woman. I will be back before you know it. I love you."

Aimi stormed out of our bedroom and into Mariko's room.

I tossed and twisted all night long, getting the sheets tangled up, and waking repeatedly with fear and cold. I was distraught and beside myself, my head was killing me.

Rubbing my eyes, I went to check on Aimi at 5:30 AM that next morning. The door was locked. *Déjà vu.*

I showered, shaved, picked up my suitcase and went to the door. Dr. Kennedy was there in his Lincoln Continental to take us to the airport. I jumped in and looked at my mentor.

"Lawrence, you look like a zombie."

"I'm sorry. Aimi took it hard."

"You said she would. Well the needs of the country come before our wishes," he sighed.

"You know, she comes from an old-fashioned family, where the father is home every night."

"You have to do your job. She has to adapt, or you'll ruin your career."

"Do you remember the issue we had when she was pregnant with Mariko?"

"Yes, of course."

"Well, she has never adjusted to me traveling without her."

"So obviously, it is not postpartum depression."

"Not unless it is the longest case in medical history."

At the airport, I called home to say hello.

"Hello, sweetheart," I said. "I miss you already."

"When do you come home?"

"It's just five days from now, Friday night. Don't say good-bye, just say *until Friday* and call me on my cell phone whenever you need me."

"You lied. You are with that woman."

"No, it's Colonel Kennedy. He picked me up."

"The children are crying for you. Grandmother thinks you abandoned us."

"Grandmother does not think anything of the sort. I'll be home Friday."

"Then you never say good-bye ever again?" Her voice had a wistful appeal.

"Honey, I can't say that. I have to go on a trip every once in a while. They're calling my flight. I'll call you when we land in Omaha."

After landing, I called before picking up my bag. "Aimi, I love you."

"You don't love me. Why do you leave?"

"Call me on my cell, day or night. I will be here."

That evening, I called home and Grandmother answered. "How are you?" I asked.

"My son," her voice was shaky. "We are not well. Aimi in bed. She will not get up."

"This is giving me a headache. Let me speak to her, please."

"She will not take phone. Mrs. Kennedy called to go shopping. She refused. Lawrence, she need help. She get too upset."

"I'll be home in a few days, and we will figure it all out. I love you Grandmother-sobo, and tell Aimi and the kids I love them and miss them."

CHAPTER 50

HEADACHES, JAN. 2009

Over the following nine months I focused on being the best trainer possible. I spent my time training inspectors and their teams on the proper methods of inspecting and uncovering deficiencies at hospitals.

Time at home with my family was fun and easy. I was home every night for dinner and our weekends were spent visiting the various museums and sights around Washington. This was one of the longest periods of family harmony in our lives.

I had not been on an inspection since Omaha. However, there was an upcoming inspection taking place at Wright Patterson in Ohio that I needed to attend.

"Lawrence, I am going on the inspection to Wright Patterson and I want you to go with me. It will be a good opportunity for you to refresh yourself on what the team is doing in the field and look for ways to improve what we do."

"Bob, you can count me in. How long will we be gone?"

"Five days, we will leave next Monday and be home Friday evening. How is Amie going to take it?"

"Bob, you have been more than gracious to us. I don't want you to worry, she will be fine. Grandmother is a big help and can pick up the slack as necessary."

"You know Mrs. K is only a call away and she would love to help in any way possible."

"Thank you and I will let Aimi and Grandmother know."

Later that evening I mentioned my upcoming trip to Aimi, "I have an inspection that I need to go on with Bob. The inspection is in Ohio and is short, only five days. I will leave next Monday and be home Friday. Then I shouldn't have another trip for many months."

"But you are the trainer, why do you need to go?" Aimi asked.

"There are lots of reasons, but really it boils down to my boss wants me to go."

The week leading up to the trip was painful as always. Aimi pleading with me to make up excuses why I couldn't go and us arguing about how I needed to go. The stress of the situation caused me to have a continuous headache.

When Monday came, Bob picked me up at my house early to drive us to the airport. On the way, I consulted Dr. Kennedy. "Man, I have been having some rough headaches. They started after the car crash when I was a kid, but with all the stress at home, they have been getting worse."

"That is disconcerting, but it's probably related to your stress. While we're here, let's have them do a full work-up on you. We'll remove two warts with one laser, so to speak." He chuckled at his own humor.

"For the first three days, we need to inspect their paperwork. When that's done, we will have them perform a full work up."

Three days later, I marched into the hospital commander's office. "Sir, I have some tests for your lab."

"Right, we have a great technician. We're up to the test." He grinned at me.

"Let's have your folks perform a full work-up on a sample I'll give them. See if they can discover the hidden ailment that is undiagnosed."

After I gave them a blood sample I waited around working on paperwork. An hour later, the senior tech, working the blood analyzer, called the supervisor over to consult. They went in the other room as I wondered what they were discussing. I knew that personnel would hide problems and errors from the inspectors. I tiptoed around the corner to the partially open door where they were talking and eavesdropped on their conversation.

"Is it possible he substituted the sample without you seeing him?" the doctor asked.

"No, sir. I drew his blood myself."

"Call the hematologist. He is better at interpreting results than I am." There was a whispered conspiratorial revelation. "We have to do a good analysis or the whole hospital could fail the inspection."

Perplexed, I left the lab area and returned to the flight surgeon's office to continue my inspection. I spent the next four hours examining the files full of records. By early evening, my brain was fried and I needed a break.

"Lawrence, It is 6:00 PM. Let's go to the club. I could use a steak and a double martini."

"I'll be there in half an hour. I'm going to take a shower and call home. After that, I'll grab a steak with you."

I dialed home. It took ten minutes for Grandmother to get Aimi to talk to me. "Aimi, I am coming home tomorrow night."

"Lawrence-san, I miss you. Did you cheat on me?"

"Of course not. Stop it."

After ten minutes of loving and reassuring her, I hung up and walked to the Officer's Club. Dr. Kennedy was ordering dinner with the hospital commander. "Lawrence, come join us," Kennedy said.

I ordered the prime rib and a glass of red wine. The hospital commander broke the silence. "Lawrence, can you come to see me tomorrow? There was a problem with your test results." He looked pensive and thoughtful.

I was puzzled. "What problem?"

"I would rather discuss it with you in private," he smiled gently.

"Dr. Kennedy is like a father to me, and I would tell him anything you are going to tell me anyway."

The doctor continued. "We want to conduct some additional tests. The sample you gave us indicated some abnormalities."

"What kind of abnormalities?"

"Well, we just want to double check the results and do some additional tests."

"Ok, but what did you find."

"Markers for cancer."

I was stunned. "There must be some mistake."

"I wish there were, but we checked three times. There are cases of false positives, so we want you to have a brain scan."

"Brain scan?" Dr. Kennedy jumped in. "You believe it to be brain cancer?"

"Yes, unfortunately, that's what the markers show."

"I don't know what to say. How did I miss this? Please excuse me. I need to go back to my room and think about things." I got up to leave, upset and stunned.

"Do you want me to come with you?" Dr. Kennedy asked.

"No, thank you, my friend. Please don't tell Mrs. K yet."

Dr. Kennedy broke into tears, and he stood up and hugged me. I felt embarrassed for the public scene created, but he genuinely loved me.

It started to rain as I walked back to the temporary quarters from the parking lot. The rain wasn't drenching, but it was continuous enough to make me cold and miserable. Perfect ending for my day.

The wind blew my hat off, and I had to chase it down. It was wet and dirty. My mind kept going back to the conversation I had heard today—*God, I hoped there was some colossal mix-up in the test results.* I also thought back to all the headaches I had since I was eight years old. Was that a sign of the illness?

I felt lonely and decided to call Grandmother and speak to the kids. That always made me feel better. I returned to the room, dried off, changed and dialed my home number. It was busy.

I grabbed my raincoat and slushed to the hospital lab. I could conduct my own tests to verify the results. I decided to walk, even though the night was cold and miserable. I needed time to think.

The rain was icy going down my neck. The night streets were slippery, and I fell on my ass and got all wet under my raincoat. I walked slower and saw the blazing lights of the hospital like a beacon on the hill, welcoming me to its warmth.

The charge nurse called the duty tech. He came to the locked lab, rubbed his eyes, and yawned. He was the same sergeant from the tests earlier that morning.

"Pulling a lot of duty, aren't you?" I asked.

"Yes, sir. This inspection has us all on double shifts. You're leaving tomorrow, aren't you?" His face was hopeful.

"Yes, we are." He looked relieved. "I just want to reconfirm some test results from this morning."

"Go ahead, sir," he said as he opened the door and turned on the light. "I'll be on the cot in the tech's office if you need me."

"No problem, I'll be fine."

I drew blood from my arm, put it into the separator, and waited for it to stabilize. After fifteen minutes, I took out the marker dye and started the procedure. I felt kind of silly, but something inside made me hold my breath. Then I had a dizzy feeling. The dye marker came up positive.

Cancer. I looked in the mirror and beheld the tired face of a man with cancer. *Could it be a false positive?*

I said good-bye to the tech and trudged back in the rain. I kept my head down and reviewed all the information I had. I thought of my family. *What would happen to Aimi, the kids, Grandmother?* I felt sad, just deeply, deeply sad.

At 7:00 AM I went to the hospital and met the commander, the oncologist, and the radiologist. They scanned me and verified brain cancer.

Before I left Ohio, I called a friend, who was one of the best oncologists in the country. I set up an appointment to meet him the following Monday at his office in Washington.

The oncologist ran the same battery of tests, as well as some additional ones. Three days later, I got the heart-stopping news from Dr. Franken. "Stage four. When can you come in to see me? We need to start treatment immediately."

I was devastated. "I'll be in tomorrow morning."

Later that night, I arrived home to a nice family dinner. Aimi, the kids, and Buddy Tres were all over me, and Grandmother smiled. Mariko had painted a picture of our family together with Buddy. On the ground, she had painted a hundred hearts, it was like they all sensed what I needed without knowing. I cried when she gave me the picture.

"What's wrong, Daddy?" Mariko asked.

"Nothing, you just make me happy."

Buddy put his head in my lap and looked up with big gloomy eyes. Usually he followed the children around, but tonight, he was my shadow. Aimi took the children upstairs to prepare them for bed, and Grandmother and I were left alone in the family room. I had to tell her.

"Tired," she said. "Eyes red. You need rest. Stay home tomorrow."

"Grandmother, I have something bad to tell you, and I need your help with Aimi."

"I no hear bad. Only happy, be happy." She patted my hand.

"Grandmother, it is bad medical news."

"You sick. I make soup now." She started toward the kitchen.

"No, Grandmother. Soup can't help this. I have cancer."

She turned as white as the lotus blossoms I had once presented to her. "No, no cancer." She staggered.

I jumped up and hugged her. "Yes, Grandmother. I have bad cancer."

"My son will heal." She was shaking. She looked up into my eyes with tears in hers.

I loved Grandmother. She was more of a mother to me than anyone. She pleaded with me, "Lawrence, you no go, we need you."

"Grandmother, I will fight with all my power. But we must make plans."

She sobbed on my chest, and I felt strangely comforted by her grief. Her tears helped me realize I was wanted and important. Grandmother pleaded with me as if it were my choice. "Aimi, she not make it without you. The children not have father or mother. I cannot do this. I am old."

That Saturday, Grandmother asked our neighbor if the children could go over for a play date. She and I would gently tell Aimi.

That morning, Grandmother sat at the table sipping tea while Aimi walked the children over to the neighbor's. "OK," I said. "Here is how we'll do this. I will start out by asking Aimi to sit here next to you and me. Then I will just tell her right away that I have cancer and I am going to have more tests to see what stage it is in. We will see how she handles that and just take it from there. We will break her in slowly and over time to the reality of the situation."

Through the open back door, I head a gasp and a thunk.

CHAPTER 51

GRIM NEWS

Grandmother and I rushed over to Aimi crumpled in the doorway. Grandmother picked up Aimi's hand as I turned her head to the side to feel her pulse. Strong, but I timed it at 170. Grandmother snatched a damp cloth to revive Aimi.

I have so many things to prepare. How can I help Aimi deal with my loss? I have so much life left to experience with my family. I'm not ready to leave. Give me a few more years, God. I'll be worthier. I'll be perfect.

The cool cloth did the trick. Aimi stirred and murmured my name. I kissed her lips and held her to me. The ache in my stomach came back. I carried her back to bed and stayed with her all day. Later that night, we held each other and cried. She couldn't talk, she could only sleep, wake, and cry some more. Buddy left his dog bed beside Mariko and whimpered to get in with us. I let him up and he snuggled me all night. Aimi and I cried so much, the pillows were soaked with soulful tears.

Early Monday morning, Buddy was lying across me. I showered and left before Aimi woke up. I hoped she would get out of bed. I took my time driving to work. The end would come soon enough.

I called Christina, who had recently been stationed at Walter Reed Hospital, just outside of Washington, D.C. We talked and cried for an hour and planned to meet the next evening.

I went back to the specialists to go over the most current information available about handling my cancer. I took the Metro and arrived by 10:00 AM.

"Lawrence, did you not have excruciating headaches?"

"Yes, but I have had them on and off most of my life. They have been getting worse, but I thought it was the stress I had going on."

"I don't know how to tell you this, but I am surprised you can still operate at a high level, given the debilitating extent of the cancer."

"Are there any treatments that have promise?"

"I am sorry, but the level of the disease has reached the point where treating it would kill you more quickly than letting it run its course."

"Thanks for the good news. What's the bad news? Less than a year?"

"I wish, my friend, it's bad." He shook his head. I saw sorrow in his eyes. "Honestly three or four months at best." He hugged me like a dear friend.

The void in my heart grew, sucking in every emotion from my body. My entire life, events, relationships, everything was sucked in to the black hole of cancer. I grabbed the waste bin and puked out my guts. *Why hadn't I planned for Aimi and the kids? Air Force life insurance wasn't enough. $50,000 wouldn't get her far, and I had nothing else for my family. What would Aimi do? How will she survive without me? And what will happen to Grandmother?*

"Lawrence, I'll arrange everything. You'll have a medical retirement and a grateful government will make all the arrangements necessary. "What else can I do for you?" Dr. Franken gave me another hug.

"What about my children?"

"Lawrence, I have seen many miracles in my time. I know things look grim, but I don't want you to give up hope."

"I understand and appreciate that, but what will happen when—?" I asked.

"The government will provide death benefits for your wife and children. Go home now and be with them. Someone from scheduling will call you to set up the treatment schedule."

I struggled over to the Metro with my head full of grim thoughts. I stopped in Springfield and walked to the Holiday Inn for my clandestine meeting.

It was dark when I entered. I sensed a colorful flash running my way. Christina latched on to me. I couldn't see in the dark but felt two strong arms hugging me, and her familiar perfume wafting over me. Then I heard her angelic voice. "Oh, Lawrence, I'm so sorry. I'm broken-hearted," Christina cried. "There must be something we can do."

I turned my face to hers, and she kissed me on the lips. I could taste her salty tears. She shuddered, and I barely understood her words. "I'm shattered."

I pushed her back and looked into her molasses eyes. "I'm so glad you could meet me."

"Anything for you." She reached over and cupped my left hand in both of hers. "You mean everything to me, from God's Home to college, and from Korea to Germany. You have been there my whole life."

"You have been my rock, my longest and most true friend," I told her.

"Let's get drunk." She held up her hand for the bartender. "Two gin and tonics and keep them coming." She grinned at me and shouted, "Make them doubles." We drank too much, and at 8:00 PM, she invited me to her room. I needed her now more than ever.

CHAPTER 52

Unfinished Business

The night was freezing as I stepped out of my car at 11:00 PM. I pulled my collar around my throat and shuffled the fifty steps up the driveway. I quietly opened the door, the heat in the house instantly warmed me. Grandmother was standing there. She grabbed me around the head with both hands, bending me to her height, reminding me of her unconditional love.

"Where's Aimi?" I asked.

"Asleep in bed. You smell like drink." She frowned. "Kids in bed, too."

We sat at the kitchen table and she made us a cup of tea. I needed to tell Grandmother everything.

"I met my old friend from the orphanage, Christina." I told Grandmother about Christina and growing up together. The details about how she had protected me, and what life was like in the orphanage. I told her we had dated and that she was my first love. I told her that I had seen Christina throughout the years, and we had mutual feelings for each other. Christina was single and wanted more from me, but I would never allow it. I even told her the truth about the first trip I took to Korea, when Aimi had fallen sick. How my phone was not broken, but I was at Christina's all night. "Grandmother-sobo, I promise you that nothing sexual happened. I was tempted, but I never acted. I swear this to you."

"I know your eyes. I believe you."

I even told her everything about Bull, including how he died. She now knew all there was to know about me. I felt relieved. I embraced

Grandmother. I tried to undo my arms, but she held on for dear life, her chest quavering.

"Aimi not get up today. She broken."

Grandmother clasped tighter. My thoughts turned bitter, but I knew I couldn't allow myself to be swallowed by disappointment. There was not much time.

"I love my little family. I must go up to Aimi. She needs me." I arranged my face into a pained smile, as did Grandmother.

I creaked open the door to our bedroom. Very dark, there was no sound or movement. My eyes slowly adjusted to the dim lighting coming from the open door. I saw a lump in the middle of the bed, cocooned in a blanket. A mound of hurt, a pile of shattered dreams.

"Aimi," I whispered. Torn between wanting to be with my wife and fear of disturbing her, I reached down and pulled the blanket away. She moaned. She faced away from me in the fetal position, appearing to be detached from the world. I rubbed her back.

The following days were a haze. Grandmother tried to coax Aimi out of bed. The office secretaries brought me all the final paperwork I needed to clear up. They didn't know what to say to me. We were uncomfortable talking.

Within a week, my vision became blurred and the headaches worsened. I stayed home and surrounded myself with Grandmother and my children. I tried to make their lives as normal as possible while still preparing my final arrangements. Buddy would not leave my side, even to eat. At mealtime, I had to coax him to his bowl.

When I was a kid, time had an odd and strange feeling. I can remember daydreaming about summer, playing in the fields. Time stood still during those long spring days, waiting for the last school bell of the year. Then when summer came, time sped by like a Japanese bullet train.

When facing death, time took on a jewel-like quality for me. Time was like the Hope Diamond in my hand, eroding, disappearing more every day. When I went to bed at night, the thought always came that the diamond would be smaller tomorrow.

Each day, I played with the kids and Buddy. I wished I had spent vastly more time with them, and less time doing other things that didn't matter.

Every night, I would be in bed with Aimi and whisper my love in her ear. I reassured her that all would be fine. I begged her to become a mother again. The kids needed her. She barely responded.

Finally, the day arrived when the sickness overtook me, and I was hospitalized. Dr. Franken oversaw my treatment and assured me that he was doing everything to prolong my life. Aimi could not raise the strength to visit me in the hospital.

I had one piece of unfinished business before I could throw in the towel. My final swan song. Grandma and I had talked about it and the time had come. The butterfly had to be freed.

I called Christina and had her come over for a farewell visit. She flew into my hospital room, her hair going everywhere and her make-up running down her face. I could see fear in her eyes.

She fell on me hard and squeezed me tightly, crying uncontrollably for fifteen minutes.

"Shush, it will be all right, Shuuuuush," I said, holding on for dear life.

"I will never forget you. I will love you forever," she said.

"You were the only one I could trust in the orphanage. You helped me through the toughest time in my life. Things are very difficult for Aimi, and they are going to get worse. I am going to tell her that we have been having an affair and I need you to go along with it."

"Why? But we didn't, you wouldn't."

"She is totally emotionally dependent on me. She has been withdrawn and listless since I told her the diagnosis. I have to send her away from me, give her a reason to give up on me and go on with her life. Grandmother agrees that she thinks this is our only hope."

"But what about your kids, they are going to grow up thinking you were cheating on their mom?"

"When the time is right, Grandmother is going to fill them in and tell them the truth. I need you to make sure that Slim and Charmain know the truth about me but don't tell Aimi. I need them to play along. When the time is right, my name will be cleared."

She cried again and lay on my chest with her breath coming in spasms.

Later that day, I was released from the hospital and sent home. Hospice would be soon but not needed yet.

That night, Dr. Franken called, "How do you feel, Lawrence?"

"I'm weak and have indigestion and am having trouble getting out of bed to go to the bathroom. I'm confused and tired all the time."

"That is understandable. You are at the point where we can give you stronger drugs to alleviate the pain, but they will fog your mind and slur your speech."

"I won't take any more narcotics than I have to. I want to experience these last days as much as possible. Please don't give me anything that takes away my feelings."

"I wouldn't do that, but it is time for me to ask hospice to help you at home. Be comfortable and surround yourself with the people who love you."

"Thanks. I can't thank you enough."

"No thanks necessary. I wish I could do more."

CHAPTER 53

DIFFICULTIES OF LEAVING

Prayer was never a priority for me. At God's Home, we prayed before meals, but it felt forced and rehearsed. Prayer sounded counterfeit and self-serving. If what they said about God was true, God knew what I needed and what was best for me. But, I was desperate and as too often happens, I found religion when I needed it the most. The first night at home, I finally tried prayer. I wanted to make sure it wasn't phony, but a sincere appeal for my family after I was gone. I prayed for Grandma's strength, Aimi's mental health, and a long and wonderful life for my children.

An epiphany came over me, a need to come clean in my life. I called Dr. Kennedy and told him what really happened that night in the flight surgeon's office. "I didn't try to save Bull. As a matter of fact, I happily killed him. He deserved it, and I didn't feel guilty." I coughed a weak, wheezing cough. *Was the death of Bull my crowning achievement, ridding the world of one disgusting individual? No. My crowning achievement was my love for Aimi and my kids.*

"What's done is done." He let out a long sigh. "I'm coming to see you next week."

Mrs. Altee was on my guilty conscience, too, so I called her. I had stolen twenty dollars from her purse when Christina and I snuck out to see Tia Gloria, and I confessed my theft. She said she would pray for me. I addressed an envelope, put fifty bucks in it, and mailed it to her.

Next, I called Slim and Momma. I felt guilty for not calling them earlier. "You have been a father to me, and I love you as much as anyone loves their dad."

"You are my son, my only bwoy. My heart aches for you and your kids. Your family stay with me and Momma, we take care of them." He broke down. "I come to see you, but Momma just have foot surgery and she not get out of bed. I have to take care—" He could not finish his sentence.

"Pop, I know you would come if you could. I love you and I know you are here with me. Tell Momma that I love her and ask her to call me tomorrow. I need to go to sleep now."

"We love you, son."

I called out for Grandmother, and she shuffled in. I became aware of her extreme age and frailty. "Grandmother, today is the day I am going to tell Aimi."

"I be there. I help with Aimi."

When the nurse came at 8:00 PM I had her help me out of bed and up the stairs to Aimi. I asked for privacy and the nurse went back downstairs. I climbed into bed with Aimi, spooning her from behind. "You have to listen to me. I have to tell you some things that are very important."

"There is something I never told you. When we were kids at God's Home, the only friend I had was Christina. She helped me, she protected me, and she stood up for me. She was wonderful, and I will always have deep love for her because of that."

She turned toward me but did not say anything.

"Christina and I were lovers in college." I examined her eyes, expecting a reaction. She pursed her lips and turned her head to the side, not wanting to face me.

"Anyway, to make a bad story worse, I have seen Christina over the years, and I have been unfaithful to you." The lie stung my tongue.

She jumped up immediately as though she had been faking it the entire time and pointed a finger at me.

"You are the lover of Christina. No," she shouted. "No."

I lowered my head and cast my eyes to the floor. "I'm so sorry."

"That woman is your—how long? You go to that scum of a woman?"

"I'm sorry."

"When did you meet? How often? When was last time?"

I felt humiliated and distraught.

"You cheat on me? You are unfaithful? This is how you say good-bye to your wife?"

"Honey." Now I felt like I needed to backtrack. "I always love you."

"You throw me away to be with that tramp, you say good-bye to me."

"I never say good-bye."

She stood up with a frantic look in her eyes. "I say good-bye, you give me number to your tramp. I call her and tell her to keep you. Give it to me now! Right now! Where is it?" She was serious. I got out my phone and handed it to her.

She stormed out of the room and I heard her shout. "No, this not Lawrence. You are home-wrecker, this his wife with two children. You destroy my home. I hope it feel good." She hung up, kicked open the door, and flung the phone at me.

"I am leaving. I will never come back. Good-bye to unfaithful cheater," Aimi screamed in the other room. I heard doors slamming. I pulled the covers over my head and cried for the pain I was causing everyone.

"Granddaughter, do not leave. Let's talk, do not wake children."

"He lie. He cheat."

"All men cheat, he love you, even your grandfather cheat." I suspected that Grandmother was lying to make Aimi feel better.

"I not forgive him for this embarrassment. I want a divorce."

I heard Aimi wake the children up as Grandmother came into the room to gather a few things for Aimi.

"She go to hotel with children. I get her back tomorrow."

Ten minutes later, there was the sound of honking out front of the house. The front door slammed, and I heard a car drive off. Grandmother came into my room. She sat beside me on the bed, rubbed my head, and comforted me.

"You brave. One day, they know truth. I tell them. This only way."

I felt so alone, so sad, and ready to give up life. It was all so hard.

CHAPTER 54

GOOD-BYES

"Will she ever come back?" I was weak and raspy.

Grandmother said in her wise voice. "I think so. I talk to her. She do her duty. Someday she understand. Take medicine. Dr. Kennedy bring special pills." I took the pills and passed out.

I woke next morning, hungry for the first time in two weeks.

"You look better," Grandmother smiled and gave me a hand mirror. A bit of color had returned to my face.

She brought the extra phone, and I listened as she called Aimi. I knew enough Japanese to understand Aimi was fuming and wanted a divorce.

"Granddaughter, he is man. Do not poison children." Grandmother answered in English.

"Should have listened to my father. Never marry American."

"Do not hate. You Japanese wife. It happen many time. Japanese man take geisha every day."

"Stop!" Aimi shouted. "That why I marry Lawrence. He said his father cheated and he would never. I tied to him. I gave him my life forever, and he cheated."

"Maybe, but he sick now, even if he cheat, I old, I need help. You come back for me."

"No, he is a cheater," she screamed and hung up.

Grandmother called back. "I want to see children. I cannot leave him. Take taxi, I make lunch, we talk."

Then Grandmother smiled at me and mouthed, "Chekkumeito, check-mate." She voiced, "She bring children."

I heard Grandmother make a pot of miso-chicken soup to fill our house with the aroma we all loved. As the teakettle whistled, a taxi pulled into the driveway.

"Grandmother, Grandmother," Mariko shrieked in delight as she ran to her. I heard her from my bed in the living room.

Grandmother said, "Thank you. I miss you and children." I heard their chatter and smiled for the first time in a while.

"Where's Daddy?" Mariko asked.

"He in living room."

Mariko raced in and jumped on my bed. "Daddy, Daddy," she screamed and wrapped her arms around me.

She lay over me. "Daddy, you are grey. How do you feel?" She put her hand to my forehead, using her wrist exactly like I did when I felt her temperature.

"I'm a little sick," I said, mustering a smile. "Listen, I have an early birthday present for you. It is a silver crucifix given to me on my eighth birthday by my mom. She got it from her mom when she turned eight. It has been with me during some very tough times, and it will help you when you need it."

"Thank you, Daddy. I love it and will never take it off." She kissed me, examined the crucifix, and put it over her neck.

"You are beautiful, sweet and smart."

"Thank you. I am going to show Grandmother." She ran out of the room.

Aimi came into the room, her mouth crimped and her eyes cold. "I am so mad at you, but I must help you and Grandmother." Her eyes turned scared, and she felt my forehead. She swaddled the blankets around me, rose and poured me a glass of water from the pitcher on the nightstand. She handed it to me.

Very businesslike, she fluffed my pillows. Next, she opened the blinds to let in light.

I flashed a timid smile. "Aimi, thank you."

"It is not for you. I do this for Grandmother and the children. I move back tonight."

A backfire sounded in front of our house. I recognized Pop's old truck. I shouted, hoping he could hear me through the walls, and I felt delight for the first time in weeks. He crept into the room. Buddy was lying next to me and jumped down to greet Pop. Buddy's tail wagged like a windshield wiper in a hurricane, and his tongue licked like a squeegee on a dirty window. I laughed with tears in my eyes.

"I had to see you. I missed my bwoy."

"Thank you, I'm glad you're here."

Pop leaned in to me. "Christina called me. I know truth. You are not like your father," he whispered. "You never cheat, never." He wagged his finger. "I make sure the children know the truth."

"Don't say anything. Grandma knows, and she will tell Aimi and the kids when the time is right. You have been my father. I want you to have the wings from my grandfather."

He choked up, stared at the wings, "Son, I cherish them always. I will be buried with them." He wept.

Shortly, Aimi came in and sent Pop away so I could rest. Despite her coolness toward him, he visited me every day for the next week, often sitting and reading while I slept. Other times, we would laugh and reminisce about the old times and how he had changed my life. On the last day of his visit, I knew it would be the final time I laid eyes on my most trusted protector. "I have told you what you mean to me a thousand times. I will send you off with only this. I love you and it is my turn to watch over you now. When your time comes, I will be there to bring you home. Until then, I will be your angel."

Tears poured from his eyes. He embraced me, his only words, "I love you bwoy, I love you."

Aimi came into my room each day to check and bring me food, water, and medicine. I would still see her looking at me with disbelief in her eyes. I would sometimes wake up to find her staring at me with pursed bitter lips.

By the end of the third week, we settled into a regular routine. Aimi fed me three times a day and checked on me two other times, giving me medicine and the little food I could hold down. Grandmother spent time with me during the day. When I was awake, we watched soap operas or game shows. In the evenings, the kids sat with me and played games or watched TV.

I tried to stay awake as much as possible, but knew my end was near. Aimi was professional toward me, performing her duties as a good Japanese wife. It was killing me not to tell her the truth.

I took a turn for the worse. I won't describe the medical details, let it be said that death would come as a comfort. Cancer was a vengeful whore who invaded my body and sapped my energy, strength and will. I was ready to slip into the good night. As a last gift, I called for my beloved son John-John. He raced in.

"Jump up here on the bed with me, John-John." He clambered on the bed, snuggling up next to me. "I want to give you one of my most prized possessions." I opened my hand to reveal the Swiss army knife. John-John reached for it.

"Well, this is very sharp, and I need to show you how to use it." As I pulled open the large blade, I told him about my eighth birthday and how the knife had been with me since I was a kid. "This knife has all of the tools you will need to protect you from trouble. I will ask your mom to keep this for you and give it to you on your eighth birthday."

"Wow, can I see it?"

"Yes, here you go." I handed it to him after closing the blade. I showed him all of the various tools, and most importantly, how to hold a knife properly.

"Can I take it outside and show my friends?"

"No, it is a real knife, and it is too sharp to be played with."

"Can I show Grandma?"

"Yes you can, but don't open the blades, and bring it back to me when you are done."

He ran out of my room and I broke down.

Later, Aimi gave me my medicines and sat beside me. My mind was muddled, so I'm not sure I remember everything correctly, but she said, "You promised, Lawrence, not to be like your father. You promised."

"Your father was a cheater and you are a cheater," she cried and ran out of the room.

I said, "If you only knew how much I love you."

The next morning, I was awakened by the screams of Aimi, she came running into the room. "Grandmother is dead, she is gone. I just found her in her bed. This is your fault, her heart broke over what you did." Aimi sobbed and cried. My heart was on the floor. I passed out.

The next time I was awake, Dr. Herito was in my room, yelling at me. He had arrived from Japan to help Aimi prepare for the trip after I was gone.

"You ruined my family and you killed Grandmother." Dr. Herito was screaming mad and sobbing. "I glad when you die. I take children back to Japan and they never come visit your grave."

I felt like I had taken the whole charade too far, everything was wrong. I was panicked to set the record straight, but I knew they would not believe me.

"Aimi, please bring me the phone. I want to call Pop."

She entered the room without saying anything and brought the phone.

When she left the room, I called Christina, and her answering machine picked up. "Christina, everything is messed up. I need to fix it, don't call me back. I will try to call you again."

Aimi stormed in. "You liar, lie again! You called that woman after Grandmother died?" she stormed out.

I wish you could know the truth.

I wondered when my last lucid thought would come. I was in and out of consciousness.

I heard a voice, faint but resolute. "They all know truth one day, my Grandson. I here for you." *Was I hallucinating?* I felt a hand brush my hair as I listened to Grandmother's voice trail off.

THE END